Distant
   Palaces

Also by Abilio Estévez

Thine Is the Kingdom

Distant
Palaces

Abilio Estévez

Translated from the Spanish by David Frye

Arcade Publishing • New York

FIRST ENGLISH–LANGUAGE EDITION

First published in Spain by Tusquets Editores under the title *Los Palacios Distantes*

This is a work of fiction. Names, places, characters, and incidents are either the
product of the author's imagination or are used fictitiously.

Library of Congress Cataloging-in-Publication Data

    Estévez, Abilio, 1954–
      [Palacios distantes. English]
      Distant palaces / Abilio Estévez ; translated from the Spanish by David
    Frye.
      p. cm.
      ISBN 1-55970-700-3
        I. Frye, David L. II. Title.

    PQ7390.E844P3513 2004
    863'.64—dc22   2003061214

Published in the United States by Arcade Publishing, Inc., New York
Distributed by AOL Time Warner Book Group

Visit our Web site at www.arcadepub.com

10 9 8 7 6 5 4 3 2 1

Designed by API

EB

PRINTED IN THE UNITED STATES OF AMERICA

*To the memory of my grandfather Ramón
and of my cousin Carlos*

Contents

Note on the Translation

In the Spanish, *Distant Palaces* is built from long, undivided sections with minimal punctuation. Dialogue is indicated only by the tone of voice and the lack of any punctuation other than the comma, even when a character speaks for pages at a time. In the end I decided that the differences between English and Spanish, especially regarding punctuation conventions, are such that it would be pointless or worse to imitate the original in this regard. Instead, I have translated Estévez's very clear linguistic cues into English punctuation, adding quotation marks, dividing the paragraphs that are implicit in Estévez's sections, and breaking apart run-on sentences wherever I have felt the need. I have kept the original sections, indicating them with a space between the paragraphs: to imagine how the Spanish looks, try to pretend that the other paragraph divisions and quotation marks do not exist. My guiding principle has always been to communicate the sense and feeling of the original, without binding myself unthinkingly to its outward form.

I have generally kept the names of people and places in the original Spanish, except of course for Havana itself, which is *La Habana* in Spanish. *Calle* means street; *avenida* is avenue; *parque* is park. Most of the neighborhoods mentioned are in "marginal" (that is, poor and working-class) areas far from the touristic center of the city, and most can be located on a good map of Havana, with the notable exception of Victorio's fictional home neighborhood of Santa Felisa. Apart from Don Fuco's mythic Pequeño Liceo ("Small Theater") of Havana, the buildings, houses, department stores, museums, and so forth are also real places that can be viewed today (if they have not collapsed in the meantime) by anyone who has the fortune to visit that beautiful, haunting, and haunted city.

David Frye

Part One

1

The old Royal Palm Hotel on Calle Galiano and the aged palace of a noble family whose name no one now remembers are buildings united by the mutual fate of their support beams. A tangled web of struts and braces is strung between one structure and the other, appearing to offer some prospect of solidity. Blackened by the passage of so many days and nights, by the harshness of the sun and the squalls, by the ubiquity of salt sea spray, these boards aim to prevent a collapse that in any case seems imminent. The walls display the same earthy gray and black hues as any ancient wall in any devastated city, in a world that abounds in wars, earthquakes, and other less obvious catastrophes. At many points the stones are on naked display with their surprisingly ruddy tones. Gaping rifts in the walls nevertheless allow opulent green ferns to grow unexpectedly amid the ruins; blooming paradise shrubs, too, and zucchini vines heavy with large, bell-shaped yellow flowers.

The Royal Palm Hotel has lost its roof and many of its walls, so it is uninhabited, or at least that is the impression it gives: there are occasions, on dark and endless nights — too dark and too stifling — when you could swear that bright lights rise up inside as if bonfires were being lit, and you could declare, too, that you heard voices and even praise-songs, singing in tongues, even though you could never tell for sure whether the songs were what they call really-real, much less what they were trying to praise, or in what tongue they were singing.

The other building, the palace of an ancient lineage that no one remembers any longer, is still occupied. Two centuries ago, a single well-to-do family lived here: a married couple, two or three children, or perhaps four — boys in college, girls learning to embroider, to knit, to play piano, to get married; and also slaves, no doubt many more slaves than family members, twenty enslaved Mandingas, Yorubas, Lucumís. Today, of course, there are neither masters nor slaves, nor is the palace inhabited by a single peaceful and spacious clan, but by twenty, thirty, forty crowded families: the results of the lusts of masters and slaves in a land given to mixing, to letting off steam, and to lechery. The mansion has been divided into meager rooms, and therefore should no longer be called a palace, but rather an apartment building, a tenement, a row house, a warren, a slum.

To stand before this pair of buildings united by a scaffold of blackened planks and to call them "the palace" and "the hotel" would be cynical, even perverse.

For some time Victorio has lived in one of the countless rooms in the once magnificent mansion. He himself could not corroborate how long. You couldn't call him happy — or you could call him that, since happiness is apparently blurred and subjective, just like unhappiness, and sometimes it rests upon just a few things, or upon nothing.

"After all, a roof is a roof," he exclaims with some sarcasm, mocking his own phrase: you couldn't say that Victorio is a fool, either, or that he doesn't notice when he says something foolish. He would have liked to be the young student from the Seminary of San Carlos and San Ambrosio who lived here, as he imagines him, in pampered luxury, a hundred and fifty years ago or more. He will be satisfied, however, with the four walls, the roof, and the windows that he always keeps closed despite the heat. "It's easier to put up with the heat than with the humid brightness of the sun, or the bright humidity of the moon," he explains. Perhaps that is why Victorio's room exudes the shadowy dimness and the smell of a museum closed for repairs.

It is still night; dawn seems a long way off. Victorio opens his eyes and turns on the draftsman's lamp that allows him to read during his frequent nights of insomnia. Very early, at daybreak, his shaded room does not smell of a closed museum, but of coffee, of gas, of candles burning, of dreams not yet vanished.

Victorio gets up the same way he gets up every morning: with difficulty, as if he found his own body too much to manage, too heavy, too alien, or as if the act of getting out of bed were burdened with more responsibility than merely being awake and still alive. If he doesn't find the passage from wakefulness to sleep easy, sometimes the passage from sleep to wakefulness is even harder. He slips his feet into canvas sandals that have been broken in by long use, and puts on a long silk robe that must have been elegant in eras other than this one, and cities other than this one. In Havana, a man's house robe, whether made of silk or not, has always been the pretentious garment of the nouveau riche. Maybe he didn't sleep well. Sleep is not one of the blessings that God has bestowed on him. "And what are the blessings that God has bestowed on me?" he wonders, while shuffling toward the chamber pot to relieve his swollen bladder. Since all the apartments in the building have to share a single toilet, when he gets up he usually urinates in the porcelain chamber pot that once belonged to his grandmother — though for greater needs, of course, he is obliged to turn to the communal bathroom.

A clumsy rose is painted at the bottom of the chamber pot. He does not urinate right away; in fact, it takes him some time, because Victorio is not so old yet as to wake up with the humiliation of being flaccid. When his member has quieted down he urinates in abundance, listening to the joyous ringing of the jet against the porcelain and enjoying the foam that the liquid produces: his eyes redden with pleasure. He looks at himself in the mirror, and as always, he thinks he is younger than he really is. He smiles, screws up his face, winks, picks up the empty metal bucket, and leaves the room.

The hallways of the building are still empty, devoid of the clamor and commotion that will fill them shortly. The neighbors are sleeping, or perhaps just beginning to wake up, and Victorio has to hurry, ascend the spiral staircase that was built from costly timbers carved elegantly in the days when people had the patience to work. He reaches the rooftop terrace and as soon as he steps through the broken door, which turns like a weathercock to every passing breeze, he can see the spectacle of dawn, an event that despite its daily occurrence never ceases to bring some new surprise.

The rooftops of Havana: at the first flash of daylight. The terraces, inoffensive for now, don't assault you yet with glaring reflections, but allow your eyes to pass peacefully over them. They seem nothing like the terraces that they will become by noon, at the moment when the sun will cruelly mount the tiles, the metal roofs, the slate shingles, and hinder you from looking directly at them. The perpetual flame of the oil refinery. The Bacardí Building. The Capitol dome. The bell tower of the Church of Espíritu Santo. A bit to the left and in the distance, the other dome of the Lonja del Comercio, minus the statue of Mercury, who has been dashed to the ground and deprived of his errand-running mission by the indifferent ire of hurricanes. The sea cannot be seen, but its presence is felt. That is why a ship entering the bay at this very minute passes between buildings and monuments, looking like a cheap prop for a poor zarzuela production. Toward that invisible but present sea, in the same instant, a flock of doves, herons, or gulls fly, and you cannot tell whether they are white, gray, or black. And, since Havana has always been an astonishing city, a few roosters crow.

The city makes two impressions on Victorio at once: that of having been bombarded, of a city that is only waiting for the lightest thunderstorm, the slightest gust of wind, to tumble into a pile of stones; and that of a sumptuous and everlasting city, one that has just been built, erected as a concession to future immortality. Havana is never the same and is always the same. Dawn in Havana has infinite ways of seeming always identical, diverse and exact, with the blurred color of the sky, dubious tonalities wandering behind low white clouds that fly quickly and precisely; and the dawn breeze, always scant, but opening up regardless over the city like an enormous and beneficent bird.

The breeze seems to be escaping from an old leather suitcase that is held open by a boy on the terrace of what in another era was Flogar, one of the celebrated department stores from the vanished days of Havana's glamour. Victorio sees this rare image as if he were still caught up in an odd eddy of a dream. It's a young boy, or an adolescent, with red hair and colorful clothes. He has opened a suitcase and is looking at himself in a hand mirror and putting on makeup. And the boy, or the adolescent, stands up and opens an umbrella, flips it in the air, looks closely at it, tries out a few dance steps, and then, holding the suitcase in one hand and the umbrella in the other, leaps to another terrace and then another, until he is out of sight.

Victorio goes to one of the huge fiberglass tanks where they store the water trucked in from the aqueduct, fills his bucket, and goes back down, balancing on the staircase built with patience and precious timbers.

The light from the draftsman's lamp transforms the room into a deceptive scene. The bed is covered with untidy sheets that don't look white, even though that is what they must have been in some not-too-distant past. The bed is not a bed but a mattress, worn out by years of long use, set on the floor. The shadowy dimness cannot disguise the room's small size, its mildewed walls, the worm-eaten furniture; it cannot hide the dust-covered photos of idols who, thanks to the art of photography, have remained fixed in eternal beauty: Rudolph Valentino, Johnny Weissmuller, Freddie Mercury. Nor does it dull the scintillation of the only reproduction (and a good one, too) of a famous painting hanging on the wall, *The Embarkation for Cythera* by Antoine Watteau. Above all, you can see the photograph of El Moro waving good-bye from his tiny plane, next to the great, ornate iron key that El Moro claimed could open the doors to the palace.

Is there ever a morning when Victorio does not think about El Moro? He owes him so many things. Thanks to him, he became (and remains) certain that a proud palace exists somewhere, waiting for him. El Moro talked to him about the palace on the merciless afternoon that Victorio would never forget. The two of them were alone, resting in the footloose shade of a guanabana tree laden with small green guanabana fruit, close by the airplane in which El Moro had just finished his morning's work, fumigating banana trees over there around Güira de Melena. Through his unbuttoned shirt you could see his hairless chest, heaving and sweaty. Around him the sun transformed the solidity of the earth into a luminous sea. They were enfolded in the watery light, typical of that time of day and of the country in which fate had forced them to survive. El Moro was hugging the boy in his delicately rough way. The boy smelled El Moro's sweat, more intense than the smell of earth.

"Tell me, what do you see from the sky?"

Before smiling, the man spat on the ground and wiped his mouth clean with the back of his hand.

"There's no place like the sky, boy," he said, as if thinking out loud. Then he sat silent, pensive, for several seconds, before adding, "God created the Earth so that we could look at it from the sky. Climbing into the sky in a plane is like going into a mirror and looking at yourself from the other side."

"Have you gone really far in the plane?"

He made a gesture with his hand as if to say that he had been in lots and lots of places, and then he smiled maliciously and commented, "In this little junk bucket, I've gone around the world."

"Around the world?"

He nodded emphatically before exclaiming, "You heard it."

"And have you seen Paris and Bogotá and Seville?"

"And Nairobi and Rome and Bangkok, and let me tell you something, boy, when you're up in the sky you realize that all those places are just one place." Though he didn't glance at the boy, he must have understood his bewilderment. "Yes, listen, understand what I'm saying, one place is every place, don't you doubt it. You're up in the sky, you're flying over Venice, which is a city without streets, instead people get around in little boats on rivers of dirty water, and you realize that it's all the same, just the same. People have the same desires, identical dreams, the same hopes, the same sort of needs that they do in Bombay. The forms, the fashions, the wealth changes, but the rest, what you don't see, is all the same, boy. Their hunger, their grief, their loneliness, their disappointments, their struggles are all the same, don't forget it." With his eyes half closed, he seemed to be admiring the waves of light that all but drowned out the landscape there on the outskirts of Havana. "The important thing, Victorio, is to find your palace."

The boy moved away from his embrace, stood up, and under his tiny hand felt the strength of the aviator's strong biceps.

"What palace, Moro?"

The man smiled, leaned toward the boy as if he were about to reveal the greatest secret. "This is important, boy! Don't you know that each of us has a palace somewhere?" He squeezed his nose without ceasing to smile. "Yes, don't look at me with that face, like you don't have a clue what I'm talking about! Everybody's born with a palace assigned to them, so they can live there and do whatever they want or desire or aspire to do . . ."

"Every everybody?"

The man wiped his hand across his sweaty brow, spat once again, wiped his mouth clean again. He smiled, as if he were having a great time. "Right now I've got to get back to fumigating the banana trees in Güira de Melena," he said in a tone that implied the conversation was over.

"Where's my mamá's palace, and my papá's?" the boy insisted.

"They've got palaces, but that doesn't mean that they've found them. You have to search for your palace, search good and hard. Maybe lots of people never find theirs."

"Have you seen yours?"

"When my plane flies off toward the fields, I take a little spin first around my palace to make sure it's still there, see how it's doing."

"And what's it like?"

"Don't ask so many questions, Victorio, boy."

"Moro, where will I find mine?"

"Listen to you, all you ever do is ask. Don't ask so much. Shit, whoever said it takes so many questions to find something? Look for it, and you'll find it."

More than before, the afternoon had turned into bright light that annihilated the appearances of things, and the trees, the landscape, seemed immersed in water.

"Every day I take a spin around my palace. It isn't big, just a little house up on a hill, surrounded by mangos, sapodillas, mameys, lemon trees, orange trees, mamoncillos, and a cow and a horse — oh, and a well, and a pool with colored fish, and nearby there's a pond where the cattle and the wild ducks drink. The grass and the trees are green

10

green green, and the flowers are red as red, and there's also yellow, pink, mauve flowers, roses, lots of roses, sunflowers, piscualas, orchids, forget-me-nots, pansies. My palace is built of wood, redwood, red as the flowers, and white as the clouds. The kind of clouds that are white, I mean, not the other ones that mean a storm is brewing. Some days it does rain, of course, it rains on my palace, except the rain is never violent, it rains to make the green of the trees and grass even greener. To get to the house, the palace, you have to go down a long highway all lined with royal palms, and that's no problem, that's why there's a gypsy wagon pulled by Nero the burro."

To avoid having to climb constantly up and down from the terrace, Victorio has furnished himself with a metal water tank, which he has attempted to ennoble, on the visible side, with a phrase from Bergson: "But society does not simply want to live. It aspires to live well."

He washes up in a pail. Without drying his face, his mouth fresh with toothpaste, he begins the ritual of the window. It isn't a very complicated ritual: it consists of shutting his eyes, shutting them tight, no peeking, opening one of the shutters, and contemplating a certain figure that humidity has formed on the walls of the Royal Palm. Depending on what figure he discovers at that instant — a flower, a child, an elephant, a ballerina, a car, a devil, a palm tree, a cloud, a butterfly — he guesses what his life will be for the next few hours. He can't help being superstitious, ruled by obsessive habits, so he feels obliged to think and repeat the phrase *May God's grace enter,* just as La Pucha, Hortensia, his mother, taught him many years ago. He opens the window, and with his eyes still closed acknowledges the purity of the early morning breeze, which smells of sea salt, of sargasso, of garbage, of a city asleep, of a city that dreams and perishes by the sea. *May God's grace enter,* he repeats the spell, and when he opens his eyes he looks out toward the framework of trusses that holds up the old Royal Palm Hotel and conjoins it to the building of the ancient noble family, the building where he lives, at the corner of Calle Águila.

Today he sees something he has never seen before.

It isn't the figure on the wall.

There, way up there, almost at the level of the rooftops, an adolescent is balancing on the lumber. He realizes that it is the same person he had seen contemplating himself in a hand mirror on the Flogar terrace. And this time he notices immediately that it isn't an adolescent, that if he had paid better attention, as he is doing now, he would have been able to see that it isn't a boy at all but a tiny old man, practically a dwarf, covered in makeup: an old man who looks like a boy is balancing on the lumber. His hair is inconceivably red, topped by a stovepipe hat made of Scottish plaid, and he is dressed like a circus piano player, or to be precise, like an ideal piano player from an ideal circus, in a multicolored tailcoat spangled with blue stars, a mauve shirt, a green tie, and red-and-black-striped pants that spill over his white slippers. By his side dances a marionette that reproduces his figure with prodigious fidelity. A magnificent wooden marionette, moved by invisible strings, is an exact copy of the clown. The dexterity with which the clown dances and makes the marionette dance is surprising; much more so, the balance he manages to keep on the worn and blackened beams, along which he is strutting to the beat of music that doesn't exist, yet can still be heard. No one knows where the silence has come from on this Havana dawn, a total silence turned into music by the movements of a clown and his marionette. All Havana seems to have fallen quiet to let the clown and his puppet dance. He lifts one leg, lifts the other, and the marionette repeats his every movement, the two of them in perfect equilibrium; their red mouths, their great red mouths never lose the pair of smiles that not only make you want to laugh, but to kiss and hug and sing and dance on other beams to the beat of other silences, or what amounts to the same thing, to other music.

The old clown advances from the terrace of the old uninhabited hotel toward the former house of the noble family that is still inhabited. Victorio breaks the spell for a moment and stops looking at the old clown and his puppet, and he turns his grateful eyes down toward the street and sidewalk. A small crowd has gathered down there, stopped in their tracks by their astonishment. They don't move, don't applaud, don't laugh. The old man and his puppet reach the terrace of the aged palace and vanish along the pathways of the rooftops, pathways of filthy water tanks, junk, improvised housing, television antennas, and mysteries.

Silence continues its tenacious, and for the moment, victorious battle against the clamorous awakening of the city. All that can be seen of Havana is a scaffolding of blackened beams that, like the timbers of a grounded sailboat, suddenly lack any purpose, an inert street, and a bewitched crowd that refuses to be disenchanted.

He closes the window. He goes back to enjoying the shadowy dimness of his room. He stretches out on the bed. He doesn't care that it's getting late for going to work. He gazes once more at the photograph of El Moro, smiling from his plane, and gazes as well at the key to the palace that doesn't exist. In the photograph, El Moro is climbing happily into his plane, his chest bare: he's saying goodbye. He can still hear him: "Come on, boy, let's go fly," and he can see himself, a fearful and fascinated child who would have loved to climb into the plane and hug the pilot, a child who longs for the heights that El Moro knows how to reach better than anybody.

After seeing the dancing clown with the puppet, balancing on the beams, he has thought about El Moro. He doesn't know if it's logical, but who would dare to spell out the laws of such a logic.

He gets up, goes to his Crown record player, which in the sixties was the envy of the whole neighborhood of Santa Felisa, and puts down a worn-out acetate, Sindo Garay as interpreted by Ela Calvo. The music induces the opposite of the effect he had expected: it overwhelms him with an unwonted sensation of heaviness.

Ya yo no soy tan sensible
como lo era en otro tiempo,
la costumbre de las penas
me ha robado el sentimiento . . .

My feelings aren't so sensitive,
not the way they used to be.
Sorrow's a habit for me now,
it's stolen my feelings from me . . .

The song serves as background while he makes coffee. Since the coffee that they sell in the bodega comes mixed with a thousand other things and tends to clog up the espresso filter, he long ago decided to return to tradition, to the cloth filter, yielding a lighter coffee that tastes of dirty laundry, which, in spite of everything, saves Victorio from his ill humor and from the risk of having an accident. He takes a piece of day-old bread and sits down at the table, which also serves as the desk, which also is the nightstand, which also serves as the place where he keeps the electric hotplate and cooks; the table whose principal decoration is a cannonball, no telling whether iron or bronze, a little bigger than an orange, which he stole from one of the excavations in the castles that stand in the oldest sections of Havana. Someone assured him that the ball is harmless, containing no gunpowder, and Victorio has decided that, since life is an everyday war, it

14

should sit at the center of his house, that is, in the center of his table, as a paperweight: what better decoration, what better souvenir, he repeats over and over, than a symbol of the constant strife among men.

He dips the stale bread in the watery coffee that tastes of rags. His palate registers the sorry mix. He closes his eyes and reaches the same conclusion as always: there can't be anyone in the world more wretched. Not even the princess of Monaco, nor the Dalai Lama, despite the generous smile he offers at every appearance, nor Mother Teresa of Calcutta, recently deceased, the lucky woman, nor even the pope, nor the calamitous queen of England with her stern expression. Yes, it's true, it's so true: the coffee tastes like stale bread, with a touch of cardboard. He is thinking once more that no satisfaction will ever come from this room, nor from the street, nor even from Havana. He picks up and moves to a house in Majorca on the Mediterranean coast. Of course, Victorio has never been to Majorca. He has never left Cuban territory. So he can't explain the reason why he has come to see himself in a Majorcan house with a discreet iron gate and an enormous adobe fence surrounding pine trees that lead to a garden, a little cobblestone path that leads up to the front door. It's a mansion, a palace: broad, spacious, filled with light, decorated with such good taste that he pays no notice to how expensive the furniture is, for Jean Cocteau's mot juste had been purposely followed to the letter, to the effect that invisibility is the highest form of elegance. At the back of the main drawing room, a glass door gives access to a terrace that opens onto the Mediterranean. Victorio sees himself stepping up onto the terrace, where a table is set for him with an outstanding breakfast: fruit juices, blueberry jam, fresh-baked croissants, Jabugo ham, Colombian coffee, strong, black, not too much sugar. Aware of the superb breakfast that awaits, he delays the moment of pleasure; he looks out to sea; the morning shines above the Mediterranean. In the distance, a few yachts are floating palaces. Three old men are strolling along the beach. "They're philosophers," he exclaims, and then immediately corrects himself, "No, they're not philosophers, they're the three forms of God, the one true God." And just when he is about to turn himself into another God strolling on the Majorcan beach, a knock at the door returns him to Sindo Garay, to Ela Calvo, to the all-purpose table, to the coffee and bread that taste like old rags, to the windows of his room in a building that once upon a time was sumptuous.

And there, of course, stands Mema Turné, who else? It's her, the omniscient, omnipresent Havana image of God, sticking her nose in the door, her bald head, her thin mustache, her suction-cup eyes, despite the fact that Victorio, trying to avoid those eyes, head, and mustache, barely cracks open the door. After all, how could a more or less worm-eaten door stack up against the energy of higher powers? It has come to be said of Mema Turné that, among the vast number of things she has stolen, two of the most important, the two that she has put to greatest use, are the wisdom and the power of an unwary *babalawo* named Nolo. Others deny this, such as Yaya the Quadriplegic, the neighbor on the right, who maintains that the poor, bald old woman is merely a miserable megalomaniac who doesn't have the good sense to know that she's already dead.

Mema Turné doesn't say good morning. She never says hello. She contends that wishing someone a good morning is the most flagrant example of bourgeois hypocrisy. "I heard music and I thought it was odd," she declaims in her outrageous baritone martin voice, while displaying her blackened tongue, covered with white spots. Many people attribute Mema's evil, along with her domineering halitosis, to her blackened tongue and its white spots. Others, less benevolent, argue that these are malignant diseases. In any case, she seems to be proud of her tongue. She understands the value of pauses, when silence allows her to inspect the room's darkness while her diseased tongue flicks ceaselessly in and out. "You should be at work by now," she adds, sure of herself as always.

"What the fuck do you care, you old lesbian" (they also say that hiding behind Mema is a man disguised as a woman), "shameless hag, old bastard," Victorio would like to tell her, red with indignation; he quickly recalls that this woman, famed as a witch, is also the local deputy of the Committee for the Defense of the Revolution, and that her soul is as poisoned as her tongue, so he limits himself to whispering, "I'm sick."

Mema Turné turns her suction-cup eyes and fastens them, expertly, on Victorio's face, while her baritone voice rises to attack an aria with bravura: "We should never allow weakness to keep us from carrying out the duties imposed on us by the society in which we live," and she moves both arms to make her bracelets jingle. She has said the entire sentence without a pause. Mema can be a prodigy at times; you might say that, like the bronze busts of national heroes, she doesn't need to breathe.

Victorio searches unsuccessfully for a rejoinder. He sighs as if he wishes to make patent the truth of his illness, and it occurs to him that this might be the perfect occasion to look for a hatchet and split her head in two. Many nights Victorio relaxes with a fantasy in which, like a second Raskolnikov, he obliterates this harpy with hatchet blows, saving himself and saving humanity from that viperous tongue, that baneful model. He is certain that humanity — that is, the twenty or so families living in the building — would applaud him. Some people seem not to deserve to live. Besides, since Mema's room adjoins his own, Victorio would be in a good (legal) position to cut a doorway and enjoy two rooms just for himself.

Mema stares at him as if she could read his mind: evil beings have that gift. Despite her necklaces for Changó and Obbatalá, she is dressed all in black like a pious sister on Good Friday. He imagines it must be her constant spying that has irritated her eyes. And her lips, scarcely a scrawled line under the thin mustache, flecked with rancid saliva, disgustingly rancid, smile and with remarkable malice insist, "Ay, son, have I got bad news for you, listen up and get ready: next week, the demolition brigade is coming."

And she turns around and leaves without saying good-bye, because good-byes, comrade, are typical of wicked bourgeois hypocrisy.

So the demolition brigade is finally coming. Since he has been expecting it for more than a month, he has forgotten that the building can be razed at any moment. Defensive mechanisms of the mind. Now the destruction has a precise time. He doesn't notice that Ela Calvo stopped singing a while back. He doesn't remember that the crust of bread, the measured cup of coffee, and the antique cannon-ball are awaiting him on the all-purpose table. He sits in a corner of the room, his back leaning against the wall, and contemplates the hazy tiles that slope toward the center of the room in a menacing depression. A depression, he thinks, is a sad and unstable form to be associated with a floor: it is important for a man to know that he's standing on solid ground.

He may have gone back to sleep. It is easier than it would seem to go to sleep at difficult times. Maybe he wakes up hours later. Perhaps he leaves the hoary palace of the family whose patrician name no one now has any interest in recalling; perhaps he joins the commotion in the Fe del Valle park (where long ago stood El Encanto, the most chic store in the city), and finds a midafternoon sun that proclaims the definitive disappearance of Havana from the maps of the world.

2

At five in the afternoon, with exquisite exactitude — that is to say, at quitting time in his bureaucratic post at the Albear aqueduct in Palatino — Victorio feels a sudden desire to gaze at the enormous holding ponds. This attitude is surprising: the holding ponds were constructed in the 1880s, about a hundred and twenty years earlier; Victorio has been working at the aqueduct for a long time; so he has seen them, day after day, year after year, and from having them in front of his eyes for so long he must not even notice them any longer. Hence the oddity of his impulse. The strangest thing is what happens next: after shutting the windows, he opens them again, stares once more at the reservoirs, at the frogs carved in dark stone that crouch at each corner; he lingers to view the sumptuous gate built by the genius of the distinguished Havana engineer, Don Francisco de Albear y Lara, perfectly engineered, still functioning, without any need for energy other than what the force of gravity provides, because of which it was awarded a prize in the Paris Exposition of 1889.

He leaves the office without shutting the windows. The door, however, he shuts and locks, and checks to see that it is properly closed. A second impulse, no less capricious, makes him toss the key down a drain.

★

He does not walk up Palatino as he should, then taking the Calzada del Cerro and continuing along Monte until, after a few twists and turns, returning to Galiano, the street where he lives; he finds himself instead in Fomento Park, one of the loveliest and most tree-filled parks in the city, fortunately still undiscovered by the marauding troops of tourists. He is standing next to the Ciudad Deportiva. He has no idea what he is doing there. Nor does he care. A group of athletes is resting under the acacias, drinking coconut milk, laughing and making obscene jokes that, when they say them, do not sound obscene. He thinks that a group of athletes drinking coconut milk under the shade of acacia trees is as sublime as any fresco in the Sistine Chapel, perhaps more so, because the bodies before him now are alive, alive, alive, breathing, sweating, smelling, tensing, laughing, talking, shouting, and the coconut milk is spilling over the corners of their mouths, dripping, running down their necks to their naked chests, drenching their training shorts.

Could anything be more beautiful than the human body, when it is a beautiful body? On the other hand, a living body always evokes the nostalgia of the ephemeral, Victorio tells himself; isn't the glory of human beauty based in its fleeting nature?

In the center of the sports complex there are ten or twelve hot-air balloons: immense, graceful, with imitation wicker baskets and endless colors, brilliant colors and flags. This is the first time Victorio has ever seen hot-air balloons. He is overwhelmed by nostalgia for the years when he delighted in reading Jules Verne. He thinks it must be fascinating to climb into one of those baskets and rise up and up, through the sky, to the outermost limits, to get to see the elegant yellow of the Schönbrunn, the exotic palace of Dolmabache, the Porter's Lodge on the Lake of Love in Bruges, the Great Golden Palace of Bangkok.

An old man in suit and tie, his hair dyed an intense black and gleaming with brilliantine, who is selling newspapers on the corner of Calle Primelles, explains to Victorio, without waiting to be asked, that the balloons are there for a sports competition that will take place on the last night of the year 2000. "That'll be a tough event!" he reasons. "Don't you know, the winds on the Island are like the Island itself: variable, capricious, totally unfit for aerial competitions. It's crazy, just like everything else, truly crazy."

The woman who sweeps the street, dressed in a filth-green jumpsuit, has stopped to listen in on the conversation; she looks at the well-dressed newspaper hawker with inordinate outrage and refutes him categorically: "Don't talk if you don't know what you're talking about, comrade: that's why this country's in the shape it's in, because of people running their mouths off. They're filming a movie, a movie about the first Cuban who got lost among the stars, about Matías Pérez."

Night is falling with the sadness of all pointless and foredoomed events. The pointlessness and doom are aggravated, he feels, by the absence of streetlights. He has walked through El Vedado and along the Calle Cien to the library of Marianao, in whose window-lined reading rooms he once studied and conversed with his friend Marta, the young blind woman from the art department, the one who had died at the age of twenty-eight with too many aspirations. Near the library, during the forties, in the perfidious century just drawing to a close, they built a Romanesque castle. Havana can engender that kind of insanity. Frenzies of Greek temples, Roman amphitheaters, Florentine palaces, Gothic churches, rococo pavilions. Places for showing off. The capital of the Island even flaunts a Napoleonic Museum, where objects belonging to Joséphine de Beauharnais and the emperor of the French are on display; even a tooth, which, they say, was extracted from Napoleon during the campaign in Egypt, is displayed in a crystal urn that sits on a piece of crimson velvet.

Victorio wanders past the gloriously reconstructed government palaces as if he were walking in some other era, the time of Julián del Casal, the great decadent poet. He knows full well — no one has to tell him — that the poet's era was not exactly fascinating; quite the contrary, those were years of horror, of material and moral poverty; yet he gladly gives in to the whim of the imagination which treacherously and frivolously enough deems that "any time in the past was better."

He approaches the gardens, inhales the aroma of all that untended vegetation, hears the water falling into the fountains, which are now dry, and catches a glimpse of stone walls through distant gates. He thinks he can hear music from old dances, just as he can imagine sumptuous interiors. Night ennobles Havana. The shadows' spell hides its coarseness, corrects its imperfections, disguises its corrosion and squalor. Havana in the evening and at night (and night in Havana is crushingly absolute) has little or nothing in common with Havana in its harsh mornings, at its unbearable, damp, demanding middays.

Up ahead, here and there, are windows and lights. The anonymous windows of daytime have nothing in common with the omen-filled windows of night. How lucky to discover the certainty of a little light during Havana's definitive night. At night there are no houses, no collapsing buildings, no palaces; just light. Light, and all that it signifies: lights that exalt balconies and doorways, tall windows, early lights, yellow lights, cheerful, sad, insinuating, sullen lights, light escaping through lace curtains, through windowpanes, through stained-glass window sashes, through arched skylights . . . That's all it is, light; yet he has to admit that any light refers to other realities. A light always proposes something else, hides different messages, multiple suggestions, infinite meanings, and anyone who has ever been outside and exposed on any night will know how many messages can be deciphered in the glow of a light.

★

He has walked beyond Jaimanitas to the beach at Mayanima, the Marina Hemingway. This place holds a peculiar attraction for him: the houses (*bungalows,* their owners like to call them) overlooking the canal, contemplating the yachts as they sail in from all over the world, facing a sea breeze with its strong smell of salt, algae, dead fish, rotting wood, and shipwrecks. He walks along the gutters at a slow pace, staring at the wooden walls of the houses, their quality, their colors, admiring their pitched roofs of tiles blackened by sea and rain. He imagines what it would be like to sit in a comfortable corner on one of these terraces with their happy vistas, the line of the horizon stretching before him, the breeze, in a cool armchair with its footstool and its floor lamp.

He reaches a restaurant, the Laurel, named after an enormous tree that grows in front of it, decorated with colored lights as if it were Christmas. He doesn't have a single dollar in his pocket. He greets the waiter at the door and enters. All the tables are set in the tree-lined patio overlooking the sea. This would be an earthly paradise if it weren't for the tyrannical presence of music, the horrid mania of Cubans to crank up dance music full volume, as if they were living under a permanent obligation to appear cheerful: joy as decree, edict, ukase, the tyrannical duty to cheer up everyone else, as if joy could only be expressed in laughter, hullabaloo, and deafening guarachas.

A handsome young man (handsome? God, he's *beautiful!*) in Bermuda shorts and uncovered torso asks, "Would monsieur care to dine? Today's specials are excellent." Though he talks like a European who has just learned Spanish, the young man cannot hide, try as he might, his Cuban accent; no matter why and no matter how, he yearns to sound European, and because of that, he only ends up sounding even more Cuban. A certain gleam in his eyes singles him out as the most Cuban of Cubans. Perhaps it is the radiance of so many unsatisfied yearnings, so many frustrated embraces, so many vain insinuations.

Haughtily, Victorio marches toward the sea's edge; he has quickly and rather slyly noticed that the tables closest to the sea are all occupied. "Do you have any spots by the sea?" he asks in a capricious tone.

The handsome Cuban god puts on a graceful and false expression of disappointment and replies, "Not at this very moment, sir, if you would like to wait a few minutes." He no longer sounds like a European but rather like an Asian who has barely learned the rudiments of Spanish, but there it is, giving him away: the gleam in his eyes.

A brief, fabulous silence follows. The guaracha record has apparently reached the end, and Victorio takes advantage of these seconds of silence to feel the sea, to hear its rumbling, to watch how other people eat, drink, talk, laugh, apparently without a worry in the world, apparently happy, under the trees, at the edge of the sea, facing the Strait of Florida. Handsome and Cuban, the young god returns to the attack: he is in no mood to lose a client. "Shall I set you a table right here?"

Victorio realizes that he has run out of alternatives, that he quickly has to think up a lightning solution; he reflects for a second and remembers that private restaurants are forbidden to serve lobster. "I'll have the lobster," he says.

The Cuban pulls another grimace. "I'm sorry, sir."

Victorio sighs, feigns disappointment, turns his back, walks away, goes back to the street. He conceals from himself the humiliation of knowing that he doesn't have a dollar, not one single dollar, and that the waiter-youth-wiseman-Cuban-god was able to find him out. The worst part: his stroll among the tables at the restaurant has awakened his appetite. Not exactly hunger, but something much more refined. A hunger for flavor, for delicacies. A yearning, a need to appease his palate.

★

Furtively, hesitantly, he enters his room. He is almost ready to believe that he has opened the wrong door. He looks around as if he were an intruder. He examines each piece of furniture, each painting, twice, three times, four times, as if he has to make sure that he isn't walking in on someone else's privacy. There are the walls stained by humidity, the worm-eaten all-purpose table, the mattress on the floor, the porcelain chamber pot, the basin, the Crown record player, the reproduction of *The Embarkation for Cythera* by Antoine Watteau. His cautious gaze halts there. This painting, in any of its versions, has always held a special fascination for him. Watteau, like Fragonard, attracts him because of the joie de vivre that radiates from his paintings. Both were able to paint the joy of the *dolce far niente,* just as Mozart was able to turn happiness into sounds.

"No doubt about it," he exclaims out loud, talking with the travelers in the painting, "art has charms that reality has never heard of."

He opens the window. He picks up the metal basin, pours alcohol into it, and lights it. He meticulously yanks the photographs from the wall and rips them up one by one before letting them fall into the fire. The only photograph that is saved is the one of El Moro in his plane.

Then it's time for the books. There aren't many of them, fortunately. A minor outburst of sentimentality keeps him from looking at them, not that it matters whether he looks or not, because Victorio knows them so well, he can tell which book he is holding by the feel of it, which author, which epoch, which part of the world it is from; for books are like people, each with their own traits and dignities and elegance and foolishness and whims. Each book has a body and soul. Sometimes, on innumerable occasions, they have even more soul than the very authors who gave them life. And Victorio thinks he could cite multiple examples. Only an old and cherished volume from the memoirs of the duc de Saint-Simon, *The Princess of the Ursines,* is saved from the flames. Why this volume and no others?

He also smashes the records. Quickly, not to see what he is destroying, though this undoubtedly does not prevent him from being conscious how much Mozart, Bach, Tartini, Matamoros, Garay, Vivaldi, Marta Valdés is scattered in smithereens across the floor.

The mattress burns feebly, reluctantly, in fruitless licks of flame that rise up already half-extinguished, and that, half-extinguished, smother themselves, as is only proper for a mattress so far past its time, one that has given much more of itself than any similar mattress would have to give anywhere else on the planet.

In a primitive black bag he gathers his toothbrush, soap, a few clothes, and the copy of Saint-Simon. He keeps the photograph of El Moro. He ties the key to the palace on to a cord and wears it around his neck. Although he is not sure why, he also keeps a lovely beach towel, in vivid colors.

He lies down on the floor. He would have liked his sleep to bring a long dream, a happy dream, in which he would have seen beaches, palm trees, and picnics. He sees himself as a child in the sand on the Havana beach at Baracoa, under the seagrapes, at the edge of the greenish, grimy, sargasso-laced water. Nearby, his family, the comings and goings of his riotous family. They are preparing yuca, using lots of oil and garlic to make the *mojo* for it. The suckling pig was roasted the day before, which is how suckling pig ought to be eaten if you want it to taste the way it's supposed to. Grandmother dips the skimmer, glistening with pork grease, into the rice and beans, the *congrí.* They are improvising baseball games, domino games. They are talking with each other at the tops of their lungs, you'd almost say they are arguing, and drinking beer, listing to music (boleros sung by Ñico

Membiela, Orlando Contreras, Rolando Laserie, Olga Guillot).
Singing along.

Victorio, a child, sitting at the edge of the filthy sea on the Havana beach, in Baracoa. He has returned to that territory of childhood, of happy irresponsibility, in which there are no collapsing buildings, no diseases, no torture, no growing old, no death. He deduces that, in this blessed region, there is no room for evil. Victorio-as-a-child can see himself at the water's edge. He's about six or seven years old. No older. He moves away from the family hubbub. It seems his family has already eaten lunch, had a few drinks, and the inevitable lethargy is descending on them. Games, songs, dips in the sea have all been suspended for a time. A few uncles, a few cousins have stretched out under the seagrapes for a snooze. Married couples embrace. Sleeping bodies take on the look of sand statues. The afternoon has turned into an immense, transparent dome. The few clouds highlight the clean blue of the sky. The sun is reflected in the trees, in the sand, in the water, in the breeze, in the eyes of this boy at the edge of the sea whose name is Victorio.

He walks along the beach. The sea, the gentle lapping of the waves, an attractive sound that completes the afternoon's blissfulness. Victorio-as-a-child enters the water — just a few steps; he's been warned, "Don't you ever go swimming on a full stomach, boy, you'll get an obstruction . . ." And his mother has told him stories about children who have died from obstructions, because La Pucha, Hortensia, his mother, always has disastrous examples at hand whenever it is time to give an example. Victorio-as-a-child takes a few steps, just a few steps, so the sea can at least cover his feet, his ankles. He feels the breeze blow through him, that is, that his body isn't his body but something that joins with the breeze, that becomes breeze. Discovering the relation between the sky, the sea, the breeze, and himself. Or what amounts to the same thing, the certainty that no one else in this world, or any other, could occupy the marvelous place that he is occupying. "Me, a unique and singular being," Victorio-as-a-child says through his adult mouth. "I am the light, the sea, the afternoon, the landscape, and I am also the god who not only creates but who enjoys what he has created."

Victorio-as-an-adult remembers Victorio-as-a-child walking along the beach. The adult, who no longer lives this experience, can, however, explain it, while the child, who possesses the same certainty, is nonetheless unable to put it into words, into something clear, something explicable. And that is why, later that night, at home, after a hot shower has removed the salt from his body and left each muscle delightfully exhausted, he, the boy named Victorio, tries to explain to his mother, "Today I realized," except that sleep overcomes him, and he never, so far as he can recall, manages to finish the sentence.

Could it be that the sun is entering through the slits in the blinds and forming cheerful patterns on the worn old floor tiles? Is he really hearing sounds from neighboring rooms, shouts from the park, the neighbor women singing along with some salsa singer's hit:

> *La chica del son*
> *es una gata insaciable,*
> *la chica del son . . .*

> The girl who dances *son*
> is a cat who can't be satisfied
> the girl who dances *son . . .*

Victorio wants to look at himself in the mirror. There are no mirrors left in the house. He persists; he has to look at himself in some mirror, perhaps to be certain that he is really there — that's what mirrors were invented for, so that a man can believe he's woken up from his dreams, so that he can imagine compiling enough evidence, no matter how inverted and distorted, that he is himself, one certainty among all the certainties in the world.

There is nothing in the house: it doesn't even look like his house, or like anybody's house. It's more like a gloomy, empty, dark room, where footsteps echo and the songs that reach in from the park and from the street lose their levity, acquiring the tonalities of ancient chants. All that remains is the reproduction of *The Embarkation for Cythera*. He observes the characters in the painting: serene, tranquil, gallant, distinguished, happy, noble, ready (without making a fuss of it) for good fortune, genteelly blissful; he discerns the trees, the garden with the feel and color of all idyllic gardens, the pink sails on the boat, the playful cherubs, the marble Venus who supervises, sanctifies, and approves of them; and Victorio experiences the sudden, fierce sensation of someone who has been deceived. He doesn't know what corner of his resentment is exuding the wrath that now invades his body like a wave of corrupted blood. He picks up the primitive bag in which he has gathered all his belongings, and leaves the building that will be demolished. Like some Eugène de Rastignac, he walks out into the beloved and abhorred city. The difference is noteworthy: he isn't in nineteenth-century Paris, but in Havana on a common sort of day at the tail end of the twentieth century, yet that does not keep him from passionately shouting, "We'll soon see about this!" to which the city, as might have been expected, makes no reply. Or perhaps its reply comes in the voice of a mulatta in makeup, perfume, and a tight-fitting dress, who upon bumping into him replies, "Watch out, boy, what's up with you?"

3

They say that in other more contented times, Havana could be fairly liberal toward the homeless. Sometimes the wide covered entrance-ways, the broad, roofed sidewalks in the City of Columns, served as refuges for hundreds upon hundreds of bums. On stormy days and on days of unforgiving sun, on nights of humidity and of cold bearing no relationship to the supposed truth told by the thermometer, many indigents found refuge in the maternal nobility of Havana's many galleries. They say that not only did covered and columned passage-ways abound, but the fountains also flowed with fresh, healthy water, the gardens were filled with trees, there was fruit on the trees in the gardens, bread and soup were distributed in the church sacristies, and there were fish, lots of fish, in the sea. It is said that there was shade on the sidewalks and a permanent breeze under the colonnades.

Despite all this generosity, bit by bit Havana ceased to tolerate the beggars: it denied them the charity of covered entranceways, the blessing of breezes, and protections from the savage night dews. Some have gone so far as to claim (it is well-known how novelistic the popular imagination can be) that the change began to be noticed the day that Havana allowed one of its most famous vagrants, El Caballero de París, to be locked up in an asylum. On that unlucky day, night fell in Havana at four in the afternoon, and the early dusk astonished the people of the city. Since they know nothing of seasons, since they have never expected the season to change, the skeptical people of Havana have never believed the sun could come at the wrong time or that the moon might rise prematurely. It was, they say, a true catastrophe. Confused, tormented, the city came unhinged: it felt different, as if it were at a different latitude, as if Havana (in a manner of speaking) had thought it were Brussels, and the people of Havana, the poor inhabitants of the confused city, had no space in a world of such tremendous metamorphoses. True or false (more true than false), it is a proven fact: Havana turned its back on the needy.

Disoriented, not knowing what to do, Victorio thinks about the demolition of the old palace where he lives (or used to live), and he has an opportunity to feel in the flesh how Havana despises those who have no houses. Now he can learn the meaning of the destitution of the dark, desolate streets, the empty sidewalks, the dry fountains, the tree-less gardens, the fruitless trees, where the accumulation of grime seems to have grown from the depths of time. He enjoys classifying the pallid bushes and sickly ferns that chose to sprout on ruins. He imagines he can detect the unique color of filthy walls, the firm footsteps of the police, the no less firm steps of criminals, the distrustful, anguished clicking heels of whores, the unexpected open jackknife that someone hurls from a balcony, the sighs of relief or of pleasure, two people giving in to an embrace in which they each hope to recognize their own reality, to learn, perhaps, that they have not turned into ghosts. Victorio enjoys the sea breeze that blows the miasma up from the port, and the land wind that blows down from other rotting masses. He also deciphers the language of the beheaded statues, examines the feeble light of the streetlamps, watches the sewer water flowing down the broken sidewalks, learns to distinguish which screams arise from nightmares, learns that nothing explains the city so well as the desperate cries and songs that break the silence of the night, and feels certain that Havana loves to withdraw completely from the normal rhythms of the planet.

★

He wanders off toward the old church of San Francisco de Paula, that district of railroad tracks and train crossings, out past the Talla-piedra wharf where so many people were once killed in the explosion of a French ship. The reason why he has set out for this horrific part of the city is something he couldn't explain. For days, the sky has been growing obstinately red at night, and the salty sea breeze, no less stubborn, has stirred the red clouds, or better, reddish-gray. He hasn't thought of rain as any kind of threat, so he hasn't been frightened by the sight of scudding clouds, and he has observed that the sea breeze has stopped. He has also noticed the intense blackness of the blackened walls. When the walls of Havana become blacker than they should be, a thunderstorm is imminent. Victorio has observed that the doves, blackbirds, and sparrows have disappeared, and he has seen a desperate line of fire ants forming, just like rats fleeing a sinking ship.

He hasn't let himself be intimidated. Does he really not care about the rain, even though it is the most terrible form of helplessness that the homeless face? Or is it that his fear of police and men, and his sense of loneliness, are more powerful than the looming tempest? Nonetheless, on stormy nights, Victorio always comes to see how alone he is. Where are all his friends? They've died, left, or ceased to be friends. In any case, the result is, all three amount to the same thing.

"A city where you no longer have any friends is a city that excludes you, forgets you, and doesn't concern you," Victorio thinks; "a city isn't just made of buildings, banks, houses, parks, monuments, statues, covered walkways, bays. Without a house, without friends, a city becomes remote, alien, incomprehensible, and hostile." So says Victorio to the blackened walls that announce the coming storm.

And since this city is the way it is, the walls are not always the only things listening. A woman in her sixties, whose presence Victorio hasn't noticed, sweeps the sidewalk in front of her house and shouts in a rum-besotted voice, "Hey, kid, don't get worked up about it, there's another hundred years of this to go."

★

Gods do not send their messages in vain. The clocks have just struck nine, and the thunderstorm has started. Victorio hears the firing of the cannons in the fortress of La Cabaña. At first he mistakes the cannon fire for a thunderclap; then the reverse; and it begins to rain.

The deluge falls callously, as if it were no big deal. Victorio walks along the train tracks, balancing on the rails. Here and there the rain produces a beautiful effect when it passes through the spaces lit up by the flickering streetlamps, and he discovers two columns supporting a kind of half-demolished archway. Victorio sees the blurry figure of a woman.

"You're gonna get sick, you," she declares, smiling. He comes closer and she traces a quick gesture with her hand to indicate the archway, stating categorically, "It's not bad under here."

The girl is tall. Or looks it. She's dressed in red, in an old-fashioned, clumsily altered evening dress that reveals two underdeveloped breasts. She wears her hair long, dripping wet, and black, with light blond, nearly white, highlights on the tips. The rain has smeared her overdone mascara. Her pale white cheeks are stained. In one of her hands she displays a high-heeled shoe with a pointed toe and laces, hardly the latest fashion. She shows Victorio the sole of the shoe, which has come unglued in the rain.

"Just when you think you've got your life settled, boom! There comes life." She underscores the pause with a movement of her head.

"Yes, three steps forward and five or six back, and start all over again," Victorio notes.

She smiles and notes, "It's like my mother says: if you're born to make charcoal, heaven will shower you with firewood."

Victorio looks at her with curiosity, and concludes, "The myth of Sisyphus!"

She pulls a face as if to say she doesn't understand and couldn't care less. "Today I made a little money and thought I could take a couple days off, and lookie here, Cinderella's slipper went and broke, so what's a Cinderella to do if there aren't any more fairy god-mothers, or Prince Charmings, or fucking anything, huh?, tell me, you." And she looks at Victorio with a hint of anger, as if he knew the answer and was refusing to tell her.

He shrugs.

She mimics him. "Don't worry about it, you. You look pretty screwed up yourself."

They keep silent. Apparently they want to listen to the intensity of the rain. She closes her eyes and sighs. She looks tired, he thinks. She opens her eyes again and is gazing in some other direction. "I was hoping I could sleep in for a couple of nights, and look at this," and she raises the shoe toward the rain as if it were some kind of trophy, a cup of champagne, and hurls it far away, turning suddenly and in all innocence into a deteriorated image of Violetta Valéry. She does the same with the other shoe, which is not broken. "I don't know any one-legged woman I could give it to," she explains. Then she leaves a languid arm lying on Victorio's shoulder. "You like it when it rains?" And she puts her face in his, smiling, mellifluous. He perceives a faint breath of alcohol.

"I don't have a cent on me," he warns.

Her hand squeezes his shoulder, as if she needs to prop herself up while she laughs out loud. "Think I'm an idiot, you? You don't have a cent, and you don't like the ladies."

Both of them laugh happily, both of them, finding shelter from the rain under the ruins of the ancient city wall.

"You're going to love my boyfriend, what a man! A big mulatto from Sancti Spíritus, the models at La Maison only wish they could look like him," and she caresses Victorio's forehead, fixing a couple of dangling locks of wet hair. "He's cheap," she adds wickedly.

Victorio thinks he can see the Atarés fortress in the distance, through the curtain of rain; he can't be sure because the storm is so intense now, and as everybody knows, thunderstorms can falsify reality, cast doubt on it, turn it into a mirage. A dog walks down the center of the street, head and tail tucked in. "He's worse off than we are," Victorio observes.

"Don't believe it," she insists, while she hugs Victorio and leans her forehead on his chest; she's looking for warmth, the way a little girl looks for affection. After thinking it over (he has always been frightened of showing tenderness to any woman other than his mother), Victorio presses her head against his chest.

"Cold, isn't it?"

Victorio doesn't answer.

"Like it was snowing, not raining," she persists.

Victorio doesn't want to contradict her, point out to her that they're in Havana, and that the only season in Havana is summer, everlasting summer, interrupted only by the squalls that take it upon themselves to raise even more steam from the ground. If she feels cold, it must be true. "Yes, girl, look how it's snowing."

"And what's your name?"

"Victorio."

"Victorio?" She steps back to look at him, and sarcasm and surprise shine in her eyes. "Victorio? What, did your parents hate you?"

"No, they didn't hate me," he explains, "they loved the revolution. I was born in 1953, the year Fidel and his men assaulted the Moncada barracks." This sentence, repeated so many times over so many years, no longer holds any meaning for him.

She allows a dramatically ironic "ah! ah!" to escape her lips, and goes back to resting her forehead on the man's chest. She introduces herself: "My name is Salma." The rain begins to slow. The dog has stopped at the corner, as if it doesn't know which way to turn. Her voice becomes a whisper: "Well, my name isn't really Salma, it's Isabel, Isabelita, it's just that Salma is prettier, don't you think?"

"Besides, it's the name of an actress," he observes with a smile.

"Yeah, I know, Salma, Salma Hayek."

This time Victorio doesn't respond. He supposes it wouldn't make much sense to point out to her that Isabel is also a lovely name, and in any case it's more authentic, since she's Isabel, not Salma.

"Know what?" she suddenly reveals, squeezing even closer to him. "I'd love to be a rock singer, or an actress. A Hollywood actress, of course."

"What for?" he asks, almost mechanically, still stroking the girl's head.

She stares into distances foreign to the reality where they both find themselves. Her eyes have obviously gone away, somewhere else. Then she blinks repeatedly, as if trying to erase what she just saw. "I dunno, to sing, I guess, to stand on the stage in a crowded theater and wear clothes by some famous designer, like Miyake, maybe, and I'll have colored lights pointed at me, and my own band'll play *Likavirgin,* and I'll sing and sing, all glamorous, you know, and my voice all pretty, all sexy, and there I am moving from one side of the stage to the other and singing *Likavirgin* and the audience is screaming, they're amazed, they're applauding, what a thrill, you! Can't you hear the applause?"

"No, that's the rain."

She pays no attention. "Working in the movies! Fixed on film forever! I'll play the wicked Abigail, and Daniel Day-Lewis will be my supporting actor — he's a great actor and he's hot, too. Don't you think I'd make a great Abigail? And there I'd be at the Academy Awards, walking up to the stage, you bet, you, because I won one of them, and I'm so choked up I can't speak, I'm crying, opening my arms wide and holding up the little statue in the air, telling my adoring, applauding public, *Thankyuverimoch, iluvyoo, I dedicate this award to my mother and to Chichi, my brother.*"

Silence returns. It must have stopped raining, Victorio thinks. He says nothing. He doesn't want to interrupt her.

She explains that the concert and the Oscar ceremony have left her exhausted, so exhausted! "I'm dead, I'm so dead, I can't tell you how tired I am, Victorio! But the lucky thing is, Andy's waiting for me outside, Andy Garcia, my boyfriend, I hope you know my boyfriend Andy Garcia, Victorio, what an actor! He was born in Bejucal, I think, and now he's like a total star there in Beverly Hills."

"Yes," he agrees. "Who doesn't know Andy Garcia? And he's waiting for you with his bodyguard, and they've also had to set up a police barricade to let you through, and there's your limousine, your Porsche, or Mercedes-Benz, they've taken better care of it than they'd do for a head of state, because actors are always more charming than heads of state, aren't they? And you come out all happy, running, laughing, holding up the little statue, saying good-bye to your public, and you shout *iluvyoo* and get into your Porsche or your Mercedes-Benz, and you kiss your actor and he kisses you, full of passion because you're so in love with each other, and you kiss him and kiss him and tell him —"

Smiling, happy, she lifts her face from Victorio's chest and finishes his sentence with an exaggerated elegance in her voice and gestures: "Ay, my darling, I am very tired, can't we go faster to our mansion on the coast?"

They laugh. It's let up, yes, it has stopped raining. "It stopped raining a while ago," he points out.

Very serious for a brief instant, she says, "Dreaming doesn't cost anything, you. It's the only thing that doesn't cost anything and that nobody can catch you doing, it's the greatest thing you can have, don't you think?" And after a pause, "Listen, Triumpho, wouldn't you like a little soup?"

Victorio doesn't bother to point out that his name isn't Triumpho. The prospect of some soup makes moot any attempted rectification or any other plan. "Soup? Right now a bit of soup is worth a lot more than any Oscar, with or without Andy Garcia. And where is the soup?"

"At my house, I live close to here, real close, on Calle Apodaca near the train station. My mother knows how hard I work, and whenever I get home, at five or six in the morning, she has a little hot soup waiting for me that she makes from whatever she can find, anything, because even stone soup tastes good if you add a little salt, garlic, onion, and soy sauce — this job is hard, hard, it's so hard, you."

In what was once a photography studio, formerly called Van Dyck, Salma lives with her mother. The aging sign still hangs, faded from lack of use and too much sun and rain, and letters are etched in the window of the door: EMPUJE / PUSH. ENGLISH SPOKEN. It is a small and solitary space, strewn about with three unmade beds, doorless wardrobes, cardboard boxes piled on top of each other, and a primitive Singer sewing machine, and Victorio thinks, if the Singer company could see that museum piece, they'd feel so proud, so incredibly proud, and they'd give a prize to whoever could make it work. Victorio also discovers a kerosene stove and a lampshade held aloft by a porcelain Buddha, fat, festive, and contented, who smiles and touches his belly, and when he reflects the light off his forehead and stomach, he projects it over the rest of the room, creating gigantic shadows and blurring the outlines of things. On the walls, papered with luminous photographs, hang portraits of people decked out in outlandish scarves, nonsensical leather overcoats, capes, kerchiefs, hats with flowers and without, or with black hatbands in the case of men; people wearing the makeup, gazes, and smiles of the forties and fifties, and the false security with which people look and smile at the ephemeral interval that is concealed in the illusion of "forever."

There are also chinaberry branches on the walls. "To keep the mosquitoes away," Salma explains. The old photography studio, now converted into living quarters, is pervaded with the smell of onions, urine, chinaberry leaves, kerosene, and jasmine, which comes from a corner shelf that stands in as an altar dedicated to Obbatalá, the white, immaculate Virgin of Mercy.

Salma's mother looks more like her grandmother. She is wearing an old housecoat of some odd indefinable color, with equally imprecise decorations, and she is sitting on the edge of one of the beds, her eyes bleary, her gaze fixed, her hands clasped in her lap. She looks like a woman who, tired of marching, has decided to let herself fall down by the roadside. On her forehead she has plastered a cross of sage leaves, a very old-fashioned home remedy for insomnia and headache. She is going blind. "Cataracts," Salma explains to Victorio in an undertone.

"I've brought company, Mamá."

"I know."

Salma smiles and winks. "And Chichi? Not home yet?"

"Your brother's with some friends, off to Viñales."

"My brother lives the life . . . !"

"Your brother works hard, girl."

"I work hard, too, Mamá, what do you think? I work and work, and nobody ever invites me off to Varadero or Soroa or Viñales, not even to their own stinking house . . ."

"Not everybody is born with the same kind of luck."

"That's just what I mean, Mamá."

"Your brother is good-looking, Isabel."

"I'm not all that ugly myself."

"Your brother is more than good-looking, Isabel."

Salma turns to Victorio with an uncomprehending look on her face. "Don't you think beauty is one of the greatest injustices, you? Don't you? So, how can you demand equality from men, from governments, from North American imperialism, from the United Nations, from the European Community, if the first in injustice was God? No less than Him, God Almighty, yes, He's unjust, and after Him all the men started dreaming about building communism — ha! Communism! Everybody equal! Baloney, Triumpho, lies! Marx and

Engels were so ugly that they invented communism, and what can you tell me about that bald Russian named Vladimir Ilyich? Ugly, spiteful people, people who got enraged when they saw how beautiful other people were. You know why the Berlin Wall fell? Simple: because there were, and are, good-looking Germans and ugly Germans, and that's where you'll find all the differences you could want! The first in injustice is God."

"If He exists," adds Victorio, amused.

"Sweet Jesus save us!" Salma's mother screams in terror, raising her hands energetically; she keeps her gaze as fixed and severe as ever. "In this house we don't allow heresy, sir, whoever you might be. We believe in God and respect Him, we revere Him as He deserves, sir, keep that in mind: with God, everything; without God, nothing."

"And Country or Death, *Venceremos,*" Salma concludes gaily, and immediately adds, "He's a friend, Mamá, his name is Triumpho, and despite the stuff he says, he's very devout, so devout, Mamá, that he studied to be a priest, and he's one of my best friends — what am I saying? my very best friend, one of the people I love most in this world, after you, Mother Dear, and after my brother Chichi."

Victorio is amused and at the same time touched by her shameless way of lying.

"Well, then, you should know, Triumpho, especially if you had thought of becoming a priest, and if you are my daughter's best friend, that in this house God lurks in every corner and He is our consolation and our hope."

"Don't worry, ma'am, I also believe in God, and I know that He forgives me when I make jokes at His expense." Victorio knows that God doesn't abide by jokes: as if any god has ever had a sense of humor!

The old lady sighs. "If it weren't for God." She joins her hands and raises them, clasped. "If it weren't for God, do you think we could bear this horror?"

Victorio doesn't have to look at the unmade beds, the doorless wardrobes, and the luminous photographs on the walls. "I understand," he exclaims.

"And why didn't you finish your studies for the priesthood?"

"The seminary building collapsed," Victorio says without skipping a beat. "It was a very old seminary, it just collapsed."

The old lady lowers her head without unclasping her hands, without surrendering, and sighs: "God, Lord of the Universe . . ."

Salma, meanwhile, has gotten completely undressed as if it were no big deal, while singing in a sweet voice,

> *Rezando a Dios, se lanzaban al mar.*
> *Dejándonos, hacia ningún lugar . . .*

> With a prayer to God, they set out to sea.
> Leaving us here, their direction unknown . . .

She isn't wearing a bra, and Victorio can see her small, kneaded breasts, her underwear, as bright red as the dress and so small it seems like a child's panties, too little to fit her well-developed hips. Victorio realizes that the girl is younger and more charming than he had imagined. He notices her handsome eyes: large, dark, endowed with a look of intelligence and curiosity, not the sort to be intimidated. Since they are intelligent, you can also see a hint of sarcasm in them. Salma kisses one of her hands and brings it to her sex, her mons veneris, which has been carefully shaved. "This has been my pot of gold," she says. Then she caresses her stomach, her thighs, draws a finger across the lips. "All this is gold, you, pure gold, with rubies and diamonds and coral." And he notes the mockery and self-pity hidden in her words. Salma sings again,

> *Rezando a Dios, se lanzaban al mar . . .*

"Whose song is that?" he asks.

She looks at him as if the question incensed her. "Whose do

you think, you? Carlitos Varela, the finest composer in this little patch of land we call Cuba."

"I like Pablo Milanés, too."

She seems not to hear him. "I'm tired, Triumpho, very tired, *iamverrytired, Andy dearr . . .*"

"Go on, get to bed, sweet," he advises her.

She goes up to Victorio and removes his drenched shirt. There is no wickedness in her movements, but rather something maternal that keeps him from stepping back. She dries him with an old, foul-smelling towel, and gives him one of Chichi's shirts, which doesn't look too bad on him. "Triumpho, you must be about forty, right?"

"Forty-six. Remember, the assault on Moncada," he clarifies.

"I don't know a thing about those barracks, you, I don't have a memory, not at all, not at all. Say, you're not so bad, you, to tell the truth, you could still get by for a while, it's a pity that . . ." She looks at her mother, amused, and puts her finger to her lips. "Know what women say when they see a fag they like? *Girl, what a waste.*" She yawns. "Yes, I oughta sleep, true enough, but let's have that soup first and then we'll sleep, you can sleep in Chichi's bed if you want, he's off in Viñales, the lucky bastard." She begins serving the soup in a pair of bowls. "Oh, God, what a miracle, carrot soup with greens! Mamá, you've outdone yourself, it's like you had a premonition that Triumpho, our grand Triumpho, was on his way."

The mother smiles with satisfaction. "The carrots and the greens, my friend Dulce brought them for me, the one who cleans the chapel of La Dolorosa, in Calle Corrales, next to the fire station, do you know who Dulce is?"

The soup tastes good indeed, like something cooked in an old convent, Victorio thinks. Sitting on these beds, in this sweltering photography studio converted into living quarters, at this hour of the night, when wet clothes have left traces on his burning skin, this soup has become the most exquisite delicacy possible: it tastes heavenly.

43

"Did you see the balloons?" Salma suddenly asks. She is holding the bowl between her thighs, next to her shaved pubis. Victorio doesn't know what she is talking about. "Don't tell me you didn't see the balloons? Oh, they're beautiful, you, with thousands of colors and flags and baskets like they're made of wicker, and with 2001 painted on them, like, in phosphorescent colors, they're so lovely, you, those balloons are so lovely for traveling through the sky, I swear."

"What balloons are those?" asks the mother.

"They're in the field where people go to run, next to the Ciudad Deportiva . . ."

"Oh, you mean the hot-air balloons!" exclaims Victorio. "Yes, there's ten of them, exactly ten, ten hot-air balloons like the ones in Jules Verne."

"Big balloons, for traveling," Salma explains. "They say they're going to set them loose into the sky on the thirty-first of December, at twelve midnight, to celebrate the arrival of 2001."

"A nice idea," the mother approves, "balloons to go up on high and come closer to God, a nice idea, yes indeed, nice, very nice."

Salma has remained holding her empty spoon suspended in the air, and with a gesture in the other hand, as if she were taking time out to reflect, says, "Those balloons would be good to steal, to go up in the air in search of Andy Garcia, what do you think, Triumpho, get to Hollywood by balloon?"

"To New York!" the mother proposes excitedly.

Victorio looks at the mother in surprise. The soup is so good and its reality is so tangible that New York seems like a pipe dream to him.

"You know, Triumpho, because I told you, that New York is the city of my mother's dreams."

Victorio is on the verge of reminding her that they just met, under an arch in the ancient city wall; he looks at the mother in her enigmatic housecoat and inscrutable smile, and all he can do is agree: "Yeah, I know, New York, your dear mother's obsession, Fifth Avenue, Central Park, Lincoln Center . . . , right, but the thing is, New York is so far away."

The mother suddenly lifts her head and wipes the smile off her face, like someone who has heard a danger signal. Salma throws Victorio a look of desperation, reproach, incredulity, . . . hatred? "What are you saying? Idiot, imbecile, *Defeato!* How did you get it into your head to say that New York is far away?" He gets the impression that Salma is set to hurl the soup bowl at his head. "After Matanzas, the closest city to Havana is New York, my boy, and if you didn't know that, then listen and learn! Two or three hours in one of those balloons, tops!"

Silence overtakes the old photography studio. A tense, biting silence. Stubborn as a stone wall. The mother has clasped her hands again. This time she is squeezing them between her knees. Then she speaks in muted tones, in a soft, withered, tame, tired voice that seems to rise from the depths of a pit of disillusions. "As you doubtless know, Triumpho, sir, my husband, Bernardo, the father of Isabelita and Robertico, lives in New York, in a very good neighborhood, he says, at least that is what he has always told us, and you will have to forgive me if I don't tell you the name of the neighborhood, my memory is gone, I have no memory. My husband is a musician, as you know, a flautist who has played in Cuban bands since he was a very young man, beginning years ago with Tito Gómez and the Orquesta Riverside, right after Robertico was born; he went on tour to Bulgaria and he deserted there, caught a ride and didn't stop until he got to . . . , to where, Isabelita?"

"To Vienna, Mamá."

"Yes, until he got to Vienna, and then his friends from New York sent to find him, Vicentico Valdés and Tito Puente and La Lupe, the singer, she's a marvelous singer, a marvelous woman, you know? and we always called her Yi-yi-yi, because we knew her in Santiago de Cuba; she was studying in the normal school to be a teacher and she was singing and trying to sound like Olga Guillot and Imperio

Argentina. And as I was telling you, Triumpho, sir, that's where my husband ended up, and I had no idea what his plans were in Bulgaria. It didn't surprise me, to tell the truth, he hated this poverty; later he wrote and promised to bring us there, but the trip is expensive, so expensive, that much you know — it isn't far away, but it certainly is expensive. And he doesn't send letters, either: he says he forgot how to write in Christian, and why bother writing to us in English? Since all the English we know is *gudmornin* . . ."

Victorio quickly finishes his soup and makes as if to leave.

Salma attempts a conciliatory sign. "The fact is, there are ten lovely balloons in the Ciudad Deportiva," she says, standing up, and she places her empty bowl on top of the sewing machine.

Victorio observes that Salma's backside is more beautiful than the rest of her body, that its gentle skin calls out to be caressed.

"Mamá," Salma exclaims in the jubilant tone of someone who has been struck by a wonderful recollection: "Mamá, today I saw the clowniest clown I've ever seen."

"What clown is that, Isabelita?" the mother asks, as excited as a little girl.

"I was walking around the Parque Central and there I see a bunch of people looking up, I don't like to look in the same direction everybody else is looking because sometimes people do that just to mess with you, so I lifted my eyes like this, just a little bit, and I saw him, you, it was so great! At first I thought it was a little boy, and then an old man, and now I couldn't tell you if it was a boy or an old man; he was dressed like a sultan, in red, red, incandescent red, a red flame, with his tunic and his turban, and his suit had golden stripes, ay! How ridiculous! And the most ridiculous thing, you, was that he was walking — what do I mean, walking — dancing, dancing, dancing above the balustrades of the Hotel Inglaterra. If he had fallen he would have killed himself right there, you, because if he fell from up there he would have totally died, he would have splattered, but there

he is, would you believe it, Mamá, Triumpho, fearless, absolutely fearless, and he kept on dancing across the roof of the hotel, and the best
part: pulling doves from his turban. Every time he took off his turban, out came ten, twelve doves, and they'd fly off happy as could be.
It must be fab-u-lous for a dove that's been locked up inside a turban
to escape and fly up into the sky, which is infinite, isn't it? Yes, infinite, endless; let me tell you, there's nothing like freedom, for doves
or for anybody, freedom, flying and flying and flying. And I stood
there astounded, and everybody around me was just as astounded, all
silent, it didn't seem like Havana, not at all, the silence was intense:
like a Vienna or a Geneva silence, a civilized silence, I mean, everybody
standing still, quiet, fascinated, watching that man, who you couldn't
tell if he was a boy or an old guy, dressed like a sultan from the *Thousand and One Nights,* dancing and setting doves free."

The mother can't stop smiling and nodding her head, as if she
were seeing it through the reality of her blindness. Victorio remembers the clown he had seen dancing on the scaffold that holds up (or
held up) the building where he lived until very recently.

Salma begins to move in the middle of the hushed sluggishness
of the old Van Dyck photography studio. She is dancing with slow
movements, very slow, voluptuous movements, not without a certain
elegance, a certain refinement, as if she is discovering her body as she
dances. Suddenly she stops, eyes closed, lips embellished by a strange
joy. She approaches Victorio and kisses him on the lips. Naked as she
is, she accompanies him to the door of the old photography studio
and goes out with him to the sidewalk, where night is so deep, so
dark, that it seems final. Dawn will never come. Fortunately there
isn't a soul in the street, and if nobody's there and nobody can judge,
there's nothing immodest about Salma's nakedness.

"Dawn will never come," says Victorio, and he adjusts his coarse
bag on his shoulder.

She kisses him again on the lips. "Don't be a pessimist, and if you decide to steal one of the balloons, let me know, I'd love to take a balloon to Beverly Hills, that would be the greatest way to get Andy Garcia's attention, and even Brad Pitt's or Robert De Niro's, don't you think?"

"If we take a balloon to Beverly Hills, they'll ask us to do a remake of *Around the World in Eighty Days,* and I'll play Phileas Fogg, that is, David Niven, and you'll do Cantinflas."

"They'll sign the deal with us for sure," she exclaims, and claps her hands.

"One of these days I'll come back here," he promises, trying to empty his voice of emotion.

"I'll be waiting," she says, still dreaming of her Hollywood deal.

The sky is so clear and so full of stars that it seems it never rained, that the thunderstorm was a fantasy. To refute it, however, here are the streets and sidewalks, covered with puddles. Victorio looks at his watch and confirms that it has lost its crystal, that the hour hand has disappeared, that the minute hand is bent.

"If there's no watch," he tells himself, "there's no time, and if there's no time, eternity is come." And he liberates his wrist from the useless artifact. "Time is finished: I'm immortal."

And though the sky might be clear, there are the puddled streets, ground down by time, poverty, and lack of care. The minor lakes in the streets of Havana reproduce the facades of buildings more sharply than the timid light of the streetlamps can illuminate them. Victorio halts before a puddle and thinks he sees, reflected in its crystal water, the silhouette of a hot-air balloon. The balloon has sloughed off its colors and now has the same earth tone as the clouds and the facades of buildings. It slips through the clouds in the mirror of a puddle. Victorio looks up in search of the real balloon. All he can see is the patient, tidy, pious sky, animated by numberless stars.

4

To the exposed vulnerability of loneliness, Victorio adds the coldness of fear. If loneliness is like not having a house, fear is similar to the humid cold of Cuba. When a northern blows on this island, it is pointless to close doors and windows, wrap up warmly, try to hide. An inveterate traveler, Leonora Duse, used to say that in the North you could see the cold but not feel it, while in the South you feel it but can't see it. In Cuba it is always hot, and when it is cold, it is a stubborn cold, a ubiquitous cold, a cold that won't let you be.

"This has always been a country of diabolical extremes," Victorio explains, and perhaps he is talking to the night, "heat and cold here have no limits, neither of them. When it's hot, the heat's got you panting, suffocating; when it's cold, the cold gets under your skin, freezes you. The cold is like the heat here: humid, very humid, too humid; after all, the sea has the Island surrounded."

Like the cold, fear is unrelenting. It follows you everywhere like a spotlight in the theater. It doesn't do you any good trying to squeeze into your favorite disappearing spot, no, no good at all: the shaft of light, the cold, finds you and shines on you.

"What am I afraid of?" Victorio shrugs. He doesn't know. Fear: I'm afraid, he's afraid, that ought to be sufficient. When all is said and done, you suffer the same, so what's the point in knowing whether what induces your fear is authentic or not?

Victorio feels that he is being watched. He doesn't admit that he is being watched, but that he feels it — which could be worse. He believes he has noticed them observing his steps, recording his gestures, taking down his words. He has never seen anyone following him. But he must recognize, after all, that the most treacherous enemy is the invisible one, the one who is ever-hidden, the one who never shows his weapons or his face. Which do you prefer, he asks himself, the Beautiful Angel of Darkness or the Repulsive Monster of Light? Immateriality, he tries to explain, confers power on your enemy, inordinate power, and your enemy knows this and therefore does not let himself be seen, and you might say he doesn't exist. Fear knows all about mistrust, and, being as old as man, it is familiar with ancient, subtle, ever more refined wiles.

The eyes that observe Victorio without his ever knowing when, why, or where are always the vilest, the most dangerous ones. Victorio has stopped acting naturally, and his own eyes have taken up the task of controlling him. Here, he thinks, is where the Beautiful Angel of Darkness scores his greatest success: the moment when the angel no longer has any need of watching him, the moment when the watched becomes his own adversary, his self-censor, his own inquisitor. Victorio is the greatest adversary of Victorio, then, his greatest accuser.

And thus he reaches many conclusions. One of them is that self-vigilance means, and will always mean, the total victory of the Demon of Vigilance.

He doesn't wander around Havana, he doesn't stroll: he slips through the ruins, through the neighborhoods in the south, the west, the southeast, where people's lives are even worse. He supposes that, if the inhabitants of these suburbs have too much on their hands just trying to find a way to survive, they'll have less time to snoop. He finds himself in neighborhoods where he never would have ventured before: Jesús María, Pogolotti, La Lisa, Zamora, El Fanguito, La Jata.

There are days and nights when he dreams of having the blessed gift of invisibility, the pride and glory of the powerful enemy. He would give more than he owns for a philter that would turn him translucent and allow him to walk around the city without fear. Since magical philters don't exist, or have been lost with the lack of poetry in this savage era, Victorio tries to go unnoticed, which is the closest you can get to invisibility. He discovers an effective way of attaining this, consisting of two steps: first, speak only if spoken to, in monosyllables if at all possible; second, never look anyone in the eye. Mouth closed and eyes down.

He also takes pains not to look like what he is already becoming: a bum. True, he goes for days without bathing, and he knows that his looks must have deteriorated. To sweat as little as possible, however, he avoids walking during the day, endeavoring to avoid exposure to the sun as much as he can. He looks for the shade of a tree, of a ruin, of a covered entrance, and tries to sit there as long as possible.

The book of Saint-Simon also comes in very handy. Victorio knows that a man sitting under a tree enjoys an appearance of meekness; he knows, moreover, that a man sitting under a tree is never the same as a man with a book sitting under a tree. It is easy to see that the book endows the man with a more harmless look, a bold touch of innocence. He has no idea where he picked up this ridiculous and erroneous misconception. Victorio recognizes the danger of books perfectly well, and he knows that a man with a book is much, much more dangerous than a man without a book. The police lack the capacity or the subtlety they would need to understand such fine nuances. The police know nothing about books. So sitting ingenuously, simplemindedly under a tree with a book open on your lap is something that, for a policeman, doesn't count as a threat.

He can master his fear with strong doses of patience and

concentration. Long ago, Valéry taught men that everything can arise from endlessly waiting. Calm, humbleness, endurance: excellent weapons against the Hidden Enemy. His terror seems to disperse, thanks to *The Princess of the Ursines,* thanks to the poems and songs that he memorizes and repeats like obstinate prayers, and thanks to a slightly idiotic half-smile that he attempts to keep fixed on his lips.

Another good ruse is the false rhythm he forces on his body, a rhythm that is the opposite of the rhythm his body demands: utter slowness, a calculated slowness in his every gesture, since a fearful person can never be a calm person.

He also learns to run away from the police. In this case, the key is not to run away from them, but to face them. Victorio has discovered that a policeman's poor temperament is only prepared to pursue someone who is running away, never someone who stays and faces him. Therefore, whenever he sees a pair of policemen (and in the Havana of the year 2000 this happens every minute, every second, every fraction of a second), he goes straight up to them and asks them what time it is, or asks for some complicated directions, or greets them — simply, calmly, amiably, not smiling too broadly, because any kind of excess is suspicious.

He thus becomes the man–who–has–nothing–to–fear.

Havana is not only the city of columns, or the city of palaces: it is also the city of collapsing buildings. It offers multiple, varied ways for buildings to collapse, and not precisely along the lines of Rome. Its ruins aren't like the Coliseum, which announces man's march through History; quite the contrary, these are ruins that announce History's march over men.

Victorio would like to imagine that there is some essential difference between the ruins of the Thermae of Caracalla and the ruins of the Campoamor Theater, or the Hotel Trotcha, or the steam baths that existed, in Havana's distant and glorious era, at the intersection of Águila and Neptuno.

If there is too much of anything in the city, it is collapsing buildings.

On Calle Salud, behind the Church of La Caridad del Cobre, there is something extraordinary. Years ago, they say, this was the headquarters of a Chinese association. No one who walks down the sidewalk or drives by in the street could tell, since the municipal authorities have managed to hide it conveniently behind enormous posters that surround it and that declare, in huge and elaborate red and black lettering, that the party (the communist and therefore the only party) is immortal. Nonetheless, if you walk around to the side that faces Calle Campanario, you can find a narrow little door, which you have to crawl through on hands and knees. During the day, the collapsed building is full of people searching for plumbing items, toilets, sinks, doors, windows, old furniture, iron fittings, tiles from Seville, and bricks that might come in handy.

On the walls that are still standing, you can see Chinese characters and melancholy drawings of lakes with seagulls flying overhead, as well as images of the Great Wall, Buddha, Confucius, and impossible visions of Lao-Tzu and Chuang-Tzu. Victorio likes the rays of light, defined beautifully by the dust, that descend in every direction from the enormous holes in the ceiling, like in one of those affected, pretentious, "poetic" theater pieces that can still be seen in a few tiny theaters in Havana.

Despite the time that has passed since the ruin housed an

association of former coolies, you can still find books here (in
·Chinese, of course), red paper lanterns, and torn photographs of the
August Empress and the Forbidden City.

There's no place left to settle here. The only space that has
miraculously kept its ceiling intact is the property of Fung the Chinaman. Victorio guesses that Fung must be a centenarian: any Chinaman who's a little bit old looks like a centenarian. At night few
people venture into the destruction, and it is fairly easy to find the
Chinaman, due to the fact that he uses an oil lamp for lighting, and
it is the only light among those shadows. Fung is accustomed to reading old newspapers that disappeared long ago — ancient, yellowed papers that he later discusses with anyone who dares enter his hideaway.
"I think Thiers is the man that France needs," he declares in his awful, comically accented Spanish, full of L's and spoken in a tone sig-
nifying humbleness and self-satisfaction in equal measures, an odd
tone in this year 2000 of our era, the year of the one hundred
twenty-third anniversary of the death of Thiers. Then he smiles, perhaps apologetically, and exclaims, "Anna Pavlova will be in Havana
next month."

On some occasions, he sings the virtues of the cannon Big
Bertha; on others, he laments these same virtues. He complains about
how the August Empress has forgotten her people in Cuba, and he
expresses his sorrow over the death of Madero, "the good Mexican,"
he says, and the death of that poor woman, María Guerrero, *an excellent actress, yes, sir, an excellent actress, though I've never seen her acting.* He
is excited by the apparition of the Virgin of Fatima, insisting, *If the Virgin appears it is for a reason.* He raises a professorial finger and continues: "On one hand, a group of heretics, the devils known as
Bolsheviks, have taken power in a barbarous country; on the other,
and to counteract the devil's determined action, in a small city in
Portugal — a barbarous country, like all the countries of Europe, and

at the same time one of the most beautiful and saddest countries in the world — She appears, all goodness and love."

Evidently Fung the Chinaman is no longer a Confucian or a Taoist, but has converted to Catholicism.

Old newspapers are all you can see in Fung's room. The old man sleeps over them, cooks over them, becomes sad or desperate or calm over them, and pisses and craps over them. Newspapers, fragile and yellowed, that can fall to pieces if you look at them too hard. And crumble they will; but the strange odor of old paper, of sadness, of rancid soup, of dejection, of urine and shit, does not dissipate, nor will it ever dissipate, even if the building comes crashing down with the first passing hurricane, as very soon it no doubt shall.

The only door that leads to the rest of the ruined building is likewise lined with newspapers. There are no windows. There never were: the Chinese who mistakenly came to Cuba have always felt cold. Victorio looks into every corner and wonders how he can breathe in that cavern.

As if he could read his thoughts, Fung the Chinaman explains: "I'm so old that just a bit of oxygen is enough to keep me from dying completely; I'm so old that my sweat glands have dried up; I can't tell hot from cold; and besides, son, you should bear in mind that old age is called the winter of life, so if you are idiotic enough to live a hundred years, if you are capable of such pointlessness, you will understand what I mean: you will think you are walking through Siberia or some such place, exposed to wind and weather and snowstorms. Old age is the only winter that comes with no hope of spring." And, perhaps to give his words legitimacy, he wraps himself in blankets, pulls down his straw hat, rubs his hands and holds them to his cheeks, which are as old and yellowed as the newspapers, and much smoother.

There is something about Fung the Chinaman that attracts

Victorio, and that, perhaps for the same reason, frightens him. The Chinaman seems as crazy as he is wise. Victorio cannot deny it: nothing scares him more than the wisdom born from having lived too long, maybe because that kind of wisdom cannot be debated.

The Chinaman's voice rises sadly in the night and the ruins to prophesy: "There's going to be war, son, don't you doubt it, there's going to be war," and he displays a photograph of Archduke Franz Ferdinand and his wife surrounded by strict protocol, leaving the city hall of Sarajevo.

Word is out that one day recently an asylum for the mentally handicapped has fallen down on the street formerly called General Lee, today known as Calle 114, near the Military Hospital in Marianao. Victorio runs there as if by command. Fortunately there were no victims to mourn. Alerted to the dire state of the construction, the public health authorities had time to evacuate the patients. At the moment Victorio arrives, columns of dust are still rising. One of the most relevant traits of a building collapse (as anyone who has occasion can and should confirm) is the length of time that columns of dust continue to rise. The stones take seconds to hit ground; the rising dust lasts for weeks, months, years. Dust, which veils one's vision, blurs buildings and objects, and transforms reality with charming decadence, is something to be very thankful for in a city where the sun is a crude divinity.

Victorio thinks he has at last found a ruin where he can shelter himself. He has reached it ahead of the rest, he has the privilege of surveying it before the other bums, and he gets the advantage of seeing the architraves that have managed to hold up, the obstinate columns that no longer support anything, the cracked, stained walls painted in two tones, two shades of gray, as is appropriate in an asylum for the mentally ill. He finds chamber pots, sheets in earthy hues, first-aid tools, torn pajamas, soup pots, framed photographs of heroes who look grim (like all heroes), false teeth, coins, pillows, tools, chains, hammers, axes, and Cuban flags. One of the rest rooms has escaped the catastrophe. Nearby, he discovers a room, also intact, with the remains of an iron bed. Victorio comes to believe that this is his room, that the divinity (whoever that may be) has at last granted him a place to stay. At least he won't have to sleep in the open.

He would rather not use the iron bed, for he is revolted by the urine-stained mattress, the fiendish smell of so many things given off by the visible cotton batting. That is why he spreads out the brightly colored beach towel, the very one that his intuition made him grab on the day he set fire to all his possessions. He clasps the key that dangles around his neck. He is happy, utterly happy. He could swear to it.

For a few days and a few nights, he is the king of the rubble. His happiness wakes him up and gets him outside every day before sunrise.

He makes sure no one discovers that he is living in the collapsed building. He strolls far away from the Military Hospital, because he hates hospitals, hates doctors and nurses, as well as cotton balls and the smell of chloroform. He hates anything that reminds him of illness and death.

He walks towards the San Alejandro Art Academy. He lingers on the benches around the Finlay obelisk. He played here as a child. Near the place where the ninety-year-old Doña Juana caused a devastating fire on the thirty-first of December in 1958. This is the same spot where, days later, Papá Robespierre brought him to see the rebels entering the Columbia barracks. "I want you to see the beginning of

History," exclaimed Papá Robespierre, lifting him onto his shoulders, brimming with joy. "You, son, you're being called to be a protagonist in this new, immortal chapter of our country."

Victorio never saw the rebels. He saw nothing, no one. He remembers briefly, very briefly, seeing the water reservoir of the main barracks turned into flames by the light of the sun. The street was swarming. Crowds ran and shouted, and light, so much light, seemed to be escaping from the enormous water tank, forming luminous waves that erased reality. Gathered into the metal walls of the cistern, the sun dazzled him. He closed his eyes then, so that if you talk with Victorio about the first two or three days of January, the days when Comandante Camilo Cienfuegos entered the Columbia barracks, all he can recall is the kaleidoscope of light, the burst of fireworks that the sun creates in your eyes when it forces you to close your lids quickly.

He goes to watch the kids playing baseball on the playing fields of the Marianao institute; later, at lunchtime, he passes by the courtyard of a fat black woman, who is always smiling, always enjoying herself, and who goes by the name Alhelí, with whom he never exchanges a word. Alhelí usually leaves him a plate of food on the courtyard wall, and then disappears, while she discreetly sings,

> *Dicen que no es vida*
> *ésta que yo vivo . . .*
>
> They say this life I'm living
> ain't no life at all . . .

in an excellent, mannish, extremely subtle voice, like some Freddy escaped from the remote past, from some distant cemetery or the pages of a wonderful novel. On the plate, which Victorio's voracity licks clean, he leaves behind a slip of paper with the word "Thanks."

★

He strolls past the houses in the Buen Retiro neighborhood, where social climbers once lived and where you can still see Gothic castles and Venetian palaces in ludicrously small scales. Nevertheless, the truth be told, Victorio loves wandering through these streets and passing by the gardens of these architectonic monstrosities. This neighborhood has been sanctified by his childhood memories. As a little boy he thought that the house of Máxima the Doctor Lady — an awful reproduction of the palace of Sans Souci that Frederick II of Prussia had built for himself in Potsdam — was the very height of elegance. Victorio's innocence kept him from noticing the poor quality of the chinaware, the scant virtue of the imitation rooms. He did not realize what horrors were committed by the fatuous tapestries that covered the walls, and he was dazzled by the cheap imitations of palace furniture that were crammed into miniscule salons lined with fictitious marble.

He tries to justify himself to himself; he tells himself that everything in life is relative, that for someone who does not have the good fortune to walk by a legitimate Gothic castle, an ersatz grotesquerie may suffice. Holding on to the hand of his sister Victoria, who in turn held the hand of La Pucha, Hortensia, his mother, he used to walk through the Buen Retiro neighborhood on the way to the house of Máxima the Doctor Lady so that she could auscultate his lungs, which were inflamed by the dust, the humidity, and the perverse sea breezes of Havana. Victorio-as-a-child thought, ingenuously, that he was being given access to elegance. He passed through exclusive areas that were forbidden to him, that he was only allowed to glimpse, for a limited time, on mornings of asthma attacks, allergies, fevers, and illnesses.

The laughable palaces of Marianao possess a noble side for Victorio. The feeble columns, the ill-formed lions at the doors, the sad pointed arches, the deceitfully studded doors, the garages in which it is doubtful any car could fit: all this, as deceptive as it may have been, sends him back to unknown pleasures, to a way, to a quality of life that plunges him for several days into melancholy.

He hates hospitals, but he has discovered that the Military Hospital is another good place to get fed. Near the new apartment buildings that look out over the Zamora neighborhood, they have constructed a new emergency clinic. There you will also find the custodians' cafeteria, a large gray hall — gray because of the color it is painted, but also because of its squalor, its filth, its foul odors. It has long gray granite tables, rows of gray granite benches, and in the door, the rusty rim of a truck wheel, which is used as a bell to let the workers know lunch is served. Around noontime the wheel rim, or bell, is tolled, and the hospital sweepers form a line. Victorio has managed to blend in with them, and the woman at the door, a blond with ribbons in her hair who weighs in at four hundred pounds and makes up her face with a vengeance, fans herself and sweats, sweats and fans herself, talks about herself incessantly, and never notices (or prefers not to notice) that he doesn't have a lunch coupon.

Not that the food is any good; it is, rather, a horror: rice with small black pebbles, unseasoned porridge that hasn't been heated properly, boiled plantains served cold, and on holidays, greenish scrambled eggs.

"It's true," Victorio tells himself, "better bad than nothing; this is no time for daintiness; it's a matter of survival, of keeping myself on my feet as long as I can manage."

Around eleven in the morning Victorio is walking across the large park of this stony, unmerciful Mussolinian hospital, built by Fulgencio Batista (one of the incarnations of the Eternal Tyrant) during his term as commander-in-chief of the army after the coup of September 4, 1933. The edifices built by tyrants endeavor to be as solid and everlasting as their notions of themselves. Victorio cuts through bushes that have been given military haircuts, and suddenly he sees a man dressed in many colors, riding a bicycle with a single wheel, some kind of celeripede constructed of crude aluminum. Victorio remembers him immediately. It is the bizarre clown he saw dancing on the props that shored up and united the old Royal Palm Hotel and the building where he used to live, there on Calle Galiano. Here comes the clown again, balancing on a one-wheeled bicycle while singing in a tenorino voice.

The peace and quiet of his improvised room in the old mental asylum prove ephemeral, as is always the case with happiness. Victorio's problem is not with the days but the nights, and of all the mortal sins, lust is definitely the one that has put its mark on those nights. As soon as the sun's weak rays begin to retreat back toward the crevices through which they have managed to filter, the ruins start filling with the comings and goings of anxious shades. The collapsed building is peopled with blurred human figures — errant, desperate figures that search yearningly for one another, as if the body were the only possible cause for so great a disturbance. The voices do not matter, the gazes do not matter, it matters even less what is behind them: all that matter are the bodies.

The nightmarish nights in the collapsed building on the street formerly known as General Lee reveal to him how versatile human tastes and needs can be. He sees fragile lads possessed by grotesque truck drivers, as well as grotesque truck drivers possessed by fragile lads; underclass mulattos together with white policemen; black athletes mated with Nordic-looking business executives; ethereal dancers articulated with rough butchers; pole-vault champions joined with playwrights in decline. The ruin is frequented by men of every social status: widowers, married men, bachelors, sterile men, men with children, revolutionary workers, varicocele sufferers, electricians, habitual vagrants, lawyers, lunatics, opera singers, pop music singers, chess players, ambassadors, transvestites, construction workers, paraplegics, sculptors, journalists, musicians, sugarcane cutters, waiters, lifeguards, composers, HIV-positives, gardeners, aviators. Bit by bit, they all put in an appearance at the ruin: men of every size, age, race, taste, family background, habit, religion, culture, social extraction, political and philosophical tendency (some of them, the majority — being normal, after all — are happily free of any political or philosophical tendency).

Victorio begins to infer from all this that sex may be the only form of true democracy that can exist in the world. Or perhaps he reasons that it would be best to conclude that any revolution that boasts of being democratic should begin with sex.

One morning at daybreak Victorio is accosted by a blond marvel who must measure at least six foot three. He looks like a Yankee marine, in the best sense of the words marine and Yankee, which is in the aesthetic sense; anyone would say that a whole government department had been created to select these handsome, coarse fellows, all the more handsome, the coarser they are. The marvel's eyes are gray, his hair is storybook-yellow, his body is a wonder, for it is muscular yet refined and elastic, devoid of the stupid artificiality that comes from working out in the gym. His hard expression, that of an outlaw or a policeman (two sides of the same coin, either capable of turning into the other) makes him even more interesting to someone with aristocratic tastes. As always happens in such cases, his only visible imperfection makes the rest of his perfections stand out: the absence of one of his front teeth lends his smile a hint of ingenuousness and the same time makes it menacing; innocence allied with pitilessness yields the most longed-for and effective of aphrodisiacs.

He stands next to Victorio and opens his fly. What projects forth from it into the half-darkness of the ruins is not any old member, but the bodily image of human jubilation. He doesn't pee and he doesn't turn his fierce gaze in any particular direction. Nor does he need to. Luckily no one has arrived yet at the ruin. Emboldened by an attack of mysticism that has much in common with Spinoza's philosophy, Victorio approaches him resolutely, like someone going to a long-awaited encounter with the divinity. Except, when he is about to take that profusion into his hands, the bugger knowingly puts his prick away, flashes his broken smile (which is not broken, but admirable), and says, "Come with me."

"Where to?" asks Victorio, his hopes raised.

Without answering, he pulls out his wallet and shows a badge (ostensible or real): National Police. "A word to the wise . . . ," the bugger insists with a whistle that escapes through the gap in his front teeth.

"Well, I'm not wise, and I don't have to go anywhere with you," Victorio replies, frightened.

"Cut the bullshit, faggot, you're going wherever I take you." He grabs Victorio by the arm and forces him to walk in front. "Who's ever seen a faggot with a will of his own? You're coming with me to the police station right now."

Victorio offers resistance, so the policeman twists his arm. A sharp pain rises along Victorio's whole arm, up to his shoulder and the middle of his back.

"What's the matter, *mamita,* don't wanna go?"

Victorio cannot keep the tears from welling in his eyes.

Solicitously, the bugger smiles again, "All right, then, what'll you give me in exchange?"

"Nothing that could be worth your while," Victorio swears, and he's telling the truth: he can't think of anything he might own that would hold the slightest attraction for this good old boy.

"So you don't have anything? Really? And what about that ring?"

Victorio instinctively hides his hand. The sonofabitch is talking about the engagement ring that belonged to La Pucha, Hortensia, his mother: a massive gold betrothal ring studded with tiny legitimate diamonds, which she gave to him shortly before she died, begging him never to lose it. The ring has become so much a part of Victorio that he has forgotten about it, the way you might forget about your organs or your breath. "I can't give it to you," he says, or begs, imploringly, "it's a keepsake of my mother, who's dead."

"You don't say? Fuck, you're gonna make me cry!" taking up the hard tone again, he shoves Victorio. "Come on, you little shit of a queer, I'm gonna give you a keepsake of your dead *mamita*."

He pushes and shoves Victorio out of the collapsed building. The faggots begin arriving, but when they see the bugger shoving the poor fairy into the street they all disappear like shadows among the shadows of the ruins, transforming themselves into statues, into half-demolished walls, into cracked columns and broken doors. "Ah," thinks Victorio, "the lack of solidarity of all queers in every ruin!"

Victorio resists until he finds himself coming dangerously close to the police station. Then he yanks off the ring and hands it to the glorious delinquent. His beautiful smile, made more beautiful by the absence of his front tooth, is all the payment he gets for handing over his mother's ring. Victorio then decides to collect his volume of Saint-Simon, his crude black bag, and whatever is left of his life, and move away from the ruins on Calle 114, the street formerly known as General Lee.

5

Slowly Havana is cloaked by that dirty, dusty, diffuse veil of dejection, lethargy, and dismay that is dusk. The dark night (of the body and of the soul). Every time dusk falls, Havana begins its rapid process of disappearance. The electricity is cut off. Life seems to float suspended, or it really is suspended; it halts in time. All there is left to do is to wait.

Voices are heard: "When will the lights come on?" and people's spirits close up like withered flowers in a dry vase. Illusions flee — the few that still remain.

The lights go out, and for a few seconds Victorio has the sensation that he has gone blind, until his pupils adapt. The darkness torments him and makes him happy. These are the times when he enjoys his greatest freedom. Since every single person in Havana suffers from the blackout, Victorio loses any particularity, any personal traits; he ceases to be who he is, transformed into a shadow puppet.

However, he says that blackouts are the best times to pee and shit. In the middle of the shadowy thickness, out come the old newspaper, the invariable bushes, the abandoned building where some of the most peremptory and basic needs of the body are carried out.

On many occasions he goes to urinate in an empty lawn or a demolished building, and he experiences the succinct happiness of a sudden humid sea breeze that caresses and awakens his sleeping prick. Fantasy immediately begins its onslaught. That is when torsos, thighs, hands, feet, mouths, necks begin their parade: a parade of images that does not have to be exotic, for it could be a dance movement from Baryshnikov's best years, a close-up shot of a Catalan soccer star, the smile of a Mexican singer, the airborne body of a famous jumper, or perhaps nothing more (and this is already enough, perhaps too much) than a chest half-glimpsed through one of the windows that so abound in this city, impotently open to let in a breeze that refuses to circulate.

His hand shakes out the last drops of urine; and it keeps on going, shaking it more than the case demands, moving into a search for a rhythm, back-and-forth-and-back-and-forth, slowly, very slowly, because, like all pleasures, this one has its torturous aspect, and because going slowly yields more opportunity for fantasy. His hand languidly moves his root. His other hand also moves languidly, from nipples to neck, from mouth to testicles. One of his fingers, the middle one, slips down his ass and makes circles, circles, and pushes inside, opens the anus, continuing the circles, circles, more circles. Scenes of great tenderness come into his imagination, in which his body is not only being pleasured, but at the same time being loved.

Victorio does not know why he has never felt loved. Since the time he woke up to sexuality, he has known that his body served to relieve needs, to satisfy instincts, but never to awaken passions. Mirrors have never been able to explain to him the reason for such a conclusive fact. He has looked long at himself in them, but the damned mirrors have never sent him any message. Victorio cannot be characterized as beautiful, but he isn't what you would call an ugly man either, making him, in this most important aspect of life, like the majority of people: that is, he stays on the mediocre sidelines where no one stands out. He even believes that some parts of his body are frankly beautiful, like his fleshy, feminine, rosy lips, which look like those of La Pucha, Hortensia, his mother; or his hands, which have always looked like an adolescent's. He knows he has a dainty, shapely back. Of course he also has some ugly parts. His eyes, for example:

small, dark, skittish; or his thighs and calves, which are too skinny. And how many ordinary, everyday people, who haven't partaken of either ugliness or beauty, have conquered the love of another and experienced the supreme good of a meaningful caress?

Victorio has never had the good fortune of going to bed with anyone. No man has bothered to tell him he loves him, or to give him the kiss that would tell him he needs him, he desires him, he loves him. No one has shown an interest in passing the back of his hand over Victorio's cheeks. No one has gone to the trouble of dedicating an affectionate, desirous smile to him. No one has given him a flower, a compass, a sprig of orange jasmine. On the gloom-shrouded nights of the poor quarters of Havana, he carries on the lot of the lonely. He caresses himself, imagines great passions. He tells himself how much he loves him, and searches for pleasure at his own hand, in unfamiliar gardens and furtive nooks. He has no idea on how many walls and trees he has left the whitish marks of futile offerings.

He does not know and could not have explained whether Havana has more windows than other cities; but he is tempted to maintain that no other place has so many windows left so audaciously open. Here is one of the characteristics, he deduces, that no one should overlook in this city: the omnipotence of windows, the brazenness of windows. No blinds, no shades, no curtains. The windows are genially open to the street, to the midsummer heat, to the slightest breeze, to the lack of any breeze, to the hope of a breeze, to the faith that a possible thunderstorm might mitigate the persistently sultry weather for some short time. Windows open to the impertinence of glances: not only the shameless glances thrown by passersby, but the no less shameless gazes of those who, from dark interiors, spy on those passersby.

These windows are the best way the people of Havana have

found to be ubiquitous, to live in several places at the same time. Your house shelters you, the walls support you, the roof protects you, doors and windows provide the necessary separation, distance, and independence. A house seeks privacy, the needed seclusion; but who ever said that the people of Havana want to close themselves off? They don't like isolation, and they detest privacy. Some say, rightly or wrongly, that the sea provides more than enough exclusion and withdrawal. Anchored in the Gulf of Mexico, they explain until they tire of explaining, the Island itself symbolizes confinement on a grand scale, the sea as imprisonment and as disease.

Yet, true as it is that one tires, one collapses in exhaustion from all this talk about the sea, seclusion, and insularity, others must be onto something as well when they insist that the people of Havana do not live in the world, that for the people of Havana, the world does not exist. The people of Havana live in Havana. Not even in Havana: they live in the four streets that make up their little neighborhood, and humanity is composed of fifty or sixty neighbors, and fifty or sixty more who occasionally walk through those broken streets, worn away by sea, sun, and cyclones, by the humiliations of time. These incandescent streets are enough to make your eyes burn.

But wouldn't it be better to abandon all these fruitless explanations? The truth is that the people of Havana are as avid for gazes as they are for wind and weather, and if they take shelter under a roof and behind walls, it is because the sun loves to torment Havana more than any other city. The house flees toward the street, or the street takes over the house. Windows have been one of the ways the people of Havana have found to be sure that they possess a space on the map made by cartographers.

Victorio is also certain that there is no other city where you can see so many bodies through the windows. Men and women loll about naked, voluptuous, in front of windows thrown wide open. You walk innocently along the street and your eyes stray to the interiors. You observe the secrets of the houses and of everything that goes on in them. Not only the parade of naked and generally beautiful, gorgeous bodies, but also arguments, intimate conversations, adoring looks, painful moments, weeping, eating dinner, basic needs, festivity, mourning, cleansings with scented water, white flowers, powdered eggshell, and chinaberry branches.

And listening. The pleasure of listening in. Victorio walks down the street hearing the music that blasts from the open windows. Turned up all the way, mixing in with the voices of conversations, arguments, prayers, jeers, incantations, and jokes. Laughter, riotous belly laughs. Any childishness is motive enough for a laugh.

And not just watching and listening; smelling, too. The aroma of flowers wafts through the windows, of so many flowers, set out to please the saints and spirits (good and bad); the cheap perfumes used in cleansings; shrill colognes (Sietepotencias, Florida Water); buckets full of ice water. And the smell of cooking.

All that is missing is the touch. To caress the extraordinary surface of a person's back, lustrous with sweat, to kiss those avid lips, lips trying to form words they never come to utter. You have to listen to conversations, enter the dance, sleep on the riverbank under a night white with stars, "make love" (a French metaphor — that is, a rational and therefore inadequate one), screw, shaft, get it on (Caribbean metaphors — irrational, that is, on target) on the Malecón seawall, facing the immense sea, with the horizon laden with hope; you have to live in the *here and now,* because tomorrow . . .

Does anyone know anything about tomorrow? In a city where History has eliminated pleasures of every sort (with the dreadful solemnity that History always displays), could it be that anything — the slightest, the most puerile, the stupidest, the rudest thing — might finally turn into a delicate, urgent pleasure?

And then, there's hunger. If Victorio is wandering in some distant district and can't get to the lunchroom of the Military Hospital or to the courtyard of the black woman, Alhelí, where he can listen to Arsenio Rodríguez songs and Marta Valdés boleros and enjoy well-prepared, providentially seasoned food, he can spend whole days *en blanco,* without a bite to eat, "in Blanco and Trocadero," as he says — and he is not far from the truth, since he has been hanging out around that famous street corner in recent days, walking around Colón (the neighborhood where whores used to live), around Prado, looking for anything he can put in his mouth. Sometimes he goes to a bakery on Calle O'Reilly, and the baker, a cheerful, jovial, fat mulatto who goes by the name Hierbabuena, gives him two or three loaves of bread. Victorio doesn't know why Hierbabuena hands him a bag full of loaves, on sight, without his having to ask for anything or put on a face like he's starving or start begging, he does it just like that.

There is also a pizzeria in Chinatown. Properly speaking, it isn't a pizzeria, just an improvised lunch counter: THE AUGUST MOON, CHINESE PIZZA TAKE-OUT, says the sign. The waitress, a young mestiza woman with a hint of Chinese ancestry, pretty, expressive, talkative, with curly red hair filled with colorful barrettes, fake flowers, and fake rubies, serves him the onion-and-Chinese-bean pizza with a smile and without being asked, and she turns her back without waiting to be paid, forgetting about Victorio (pretending to forget him?). He hangs around for a few minutes: he doesn't want to get carried away by his hopes, and then out of nowhere have somebody jab a finger at him and demand payment for the pizza. Victorio slowly saunters away, carefree, just in case, and puts on a "Who, me?" face, walking down Calle Zanja or up Calle Zanja (depending on your point of view), until the August Moon and its distantly Chinese waitress are lost to view. Sitting on one of the benches in the Parque de la Fraternidad, he makes short work of the onion-and-Chinese-bean pizza. His pleasure is not a whit different from what he would feel if he were to eat a fillet Chateaubriand accompanied by a good bottle of Ribera del Duero.

The sensation that Victorio experiences when he crosses the hell-holes known as Calle Dragones, Manrique, Campanario, Rayo, and San Nicolás to reach the Chinese restaurants is the same you would feel if you were to rise up from the depths of the sea. Sick and tired of darkness, what he needs is a bit of light. He takes Calle Zanja — wider, with a bit more traffic on it, and better lit than the rest. His objective would be to reach Calle Belascoaín, go up it to Calzada de la Reina, and sleep in the covered entrance to the Church of the Sacred Heart. Its excellent colonnade is very well protected, as if its boastful neo-Gothic architect had been benevolent enough to think of the homeless.

Today the marvelous waitress at the August Moon, her hair even more riotous and redder than usual, with more colorful barrettes, fake flowers and fake rubies than ever, serves him the onion-and-Chinese-bean pizza with a smile and without being asked. But something unexpected happens. From the black depths where we imagine the ovens and cooks must lurk, a man's voice shouts, "*China,* phone call for you," and the marvelous waitress at the August Moon, the Chinatown pizzeria, disappears through a narrow door that Victorio had never noticed before. Taking the girl's place is a toothless young man wearing a patch over one eye and a silk kimono. The changeover in the wait staff has caused a delay in service, and a small line has formed in front of the glass-lined lunch counter of the August Moon. The young man starts working quickly. He serves food and collects payments without smiling, with expert, machinelike movements. And so he turns to Victorio with a tone of voice that attempts to be friendly without succeeding: "Fifteen pesos, buddy."

"Right away," says Victorio, startled. He puts the pizza down on the counter and starts rummaging through his pockets. He isn't looking for money (he knows there isn't any there); he does it to gain time, to see if the distantly Chinese, red-haired waitress might return.

Time goes by, the waitress doesn't appear, and the toothless young man in the kimono looks at him through his single mistrustfully blinking eye. "Fifteen pesos, buddy," he repeats in a more peremptory voice.

Victorio smiles the smile of an innocent or an idiot, sees a bicycle taxi ride by, has an urge to climb on board and run away, but what kind of explanation could he give to the bicycle taxi driver? To continue his strategy of gaining time, he asks, "What do you have to drink?"

The young man in the kimono rivets on Victorio's eyes the steely stare of his uneven gaze, and unwillingly, reluctantly says, "Grape-flavored soda, and it isn't cold, buddy," and his voice comes out through his compressed lips in a furious hiss.

"Don't you have any ice?"

"Of course not, where do you think you're living? We're not in Paris, buddy." And he smiles a satisfied smile, for nothing excites a Cuban so much as reminding a fellow Cuban how bad life is and how far away Paris, Rome, Amsterdam, and New York are.

He isn't really toothless, Victorio discovers; it's just that his teeth are far too small. And he feels like explaining to the waiter that it should be easier to find ice in Cuba than enough grapes to make a soda. "Sure, give me a glass, what can you do! I've got to wash down this pizza."

The young man dips the glass in a bucket of soapy green water, then rinses it in another green bucket of soapy water. From a bottle he serves the dark, purplish-brown drink. "Now it'll be sixteen pesos, buddy."

Victorio nods and makes a gesture with his hand that is intended to instill calm in the waiter; he sips the warm soda: sweet, very sweet, it tastes as much like peach as it does grape. "How's La China?"

"Who's China?"

"The waitress."

"Her name isn't China, her name is Tuti."

"How's Tuti?"

The waiter doesn't answer. He is using a kind of bricklayer's spatula to lift the pizzas from the pans and put them on pieces of paper — outdated bureaucratic forms that are being used as napkins — and begins to distribute them. An old man reproaches the waiter for not giving him a ham pizza. The waiter insults him and shouts that the old man asked for a Neapolitan. The old man demands respect, using the appropriate tone of voice, and tries to explain that he couldn't have asked for a Neapolitan because he doesn't know what a Neapolitan pizza is.

Victorio takes advantage of the confusion: he runs away. He has done it so quickly and unexpectedly that it is only when he reaches the corner that he hears the dreaded cry, "Stop, thief!"

Victorio forces speed from his legs, which are not very fast, but are very hard-pressed by fear. Instead of continuing along Zanja, he turns into one of the bordering streets, which is darker and, fortunately, more desolate. He enters one of the buildings that are so plentiful here, one of those constructed by the Catalan master builders. He runs precipitously up the stairs two steps at a time (the elevator, one of those ancient models that looks like a cage or a confessional, undoubtedly stopped working years ago). If his intuition hasn't failed him, there should be a door leading to the rooftop terrace. A perfect silence accompanies him, and his feet barely touch the staircase steps, so as not to break the perfection of the silence. There is no light. On the last flight he stops running, since he now feels the power of invisibility. He discovers that he has lost the primitive bag with the photo of El Moro, the volume of Saint-Simon, the colored beach towel, in other words, the little bit of his history that he had kept. Only the key remains hanging around his neck. He climbs up slowly, terrified that all Havana will hear his pounding heart. His heart isn't where it should be, but scattered among his temples, Adam's apple, head, and the soles of his feet. The door to the terrace is closed with the wire of an undone clothes hanger. Victorio stands motionless, all his concentration on his ears: he is trying to decipher secrets and dangers from the silence that surrounds him. Apparently no one has followed him. No one could know where he is. He unties the wire and steps out into the night.

The indifferent calm of the breeze, the dark blue sky, the stubbornness of all these stars, the rooftops with their water tanks and weathered wooden shacks, the whole useless system of water pipes, and the other quite functional system of television antennas for entering into the world of soap operas and of having the world slip away with sweet swiftness. Victorio marches across the roofs, jumping from one building to the next. The rooftop path is another among the possible paths through Havana.

He climbs down the fire escape of a furniture store. He is standing in front of the funeral parlor on Zanja and Belascoaín, formerly Marcos Abreu. He is thinking that he'll continue walking rapidly to the covered entrance of the Reina church, and just then he sees the clown appear, the same one he had watched dancing that distant morning on the wooden scaffolding that had barely supported the building where he once lived. It isn't hard to recognize him, and it isn't hard to figure out that this is the same clown: there couldn't be two harlequins like this in the whole city of Havana. He's wearing tails again, a top hat, except this time the color of the suit is a luminous silken yellow, and his hair, his wig, is jet-black. His makeup, very nicely done, seems immune to the night's heat. His round nose is not red but black, creating an amusing contrast with his clothes.

The clown enters the funeral parlor.

Victorio follows him. In the vestibule he becomes disoriented. He has lost sight of the clown.

As luck would have it, there is only one chapel being used, and it is crowded. With some embarrassment, wrapped up in a timidity that gives him away, Victorio enters the chapel. Against the back wall, under the usual bronze crucifix, between two huge, theatrical candles (actually two electric bulbs in the form of candles dripping fake wax), he sees the gray coffin — poor-quality, decorated with flimsy little metal keys that open nothing and close nothing. By the coffin there is a line of armchairs, occupied by weepy women. A woman advanced in years, wearing an apron with a reproduction of a map of Sicily, serves coffee to another old woman, who is vigorously shaking her head no, and who takes the cup and drinks the coffee without ever ceasing to shake her head. Victorio is surprised by the old woman's gray hair, snared in one of those sequin-studded nets that no one wears anymore.

The hum of conversation rises like a pagan chant; you can even hear inappropriate words. The heat is so sweltering you can't tell if the people are crying or sweating. Most likely, they are crying and sweating with equal abandon.

Leaning against the glass window of the coffin, a young soldier weeps. Victorio thinks it ennobling to see a soldier weep, since it demonstrates the triumph of pain over impiety, the triumph of vulnerability over arrogance. A man, ready to kill, weeps before a woman who has died. Victorio comes closer, realizing that you couldn't call him a soldier yet. He's just a cadet. Despite his youth, his features already show the hardness, or perhaps better said, the inevitable intransigence of the future soldier. There is something severe in the high form of his eyes, in his beautiful nose, in his straight mouth, in his large manicured hands, in his wide shoulders. The truth is, not even his sobs can distance him from the image he gives of fanaticism and intolerance. Victorio feels tempted to assert that he is crying for a dead man or woman (his mother, he supposes), and that he will put the same ardor into killing his fellow man.

Victorio looks at the corpse. It is a woman, a little over forty years of age, tactfully made up, tranquil, about to smile. She looks beautiful, despite the way dead people have of seeming like inconvenient objects. Through her half-closed eyelids shine two pale amber crystals. Her mouth splits open beneath the incapable coquetry of rouge lipstick. From her nose, thinks Victorio, any second now, a thin stream of blood will flow.

A drum roll. All in yellow, the clown appears. A dizzying apparition. In one hand, the top hat; with the other, he pulls roses from the hat. There's no imagining how he can pull so many roses out of this little hat, much less how he is able to cover the gray coffin with flowers. And no telling whether the lights have really grown brighter or whether this is just a matter of suggestion. Everyone present presses back against the walls. The old clown looks like the caricature of an adolescent. He tosses roses. It is just a question of a few seconds, but it seems like an eternity; his presence lasts two, three seconds; then he disappears. The cadet, standing by his dead mother's coffin, manages to maintain his composure.

He is standing on the sidewalk, on the lookout for the clown, not really knowing why he is waiting for him or what he wants to do. He sees the clown leave the funeral parlor, sees him walk down the steps. He gets the impression that he is witnessing the apparition of some defeated divinity. The fellow leaving the funeral parlor in top hat and yellow tails isn't the one who, an instant ago, looked like an adolescent, laughing, dancing, capering about and handing out flowers. He looks different. Smaller, thin as a reed, gnarled, sinewy, wrinkled, his back bent double as if he were carrying a great weight, worn down by his years, the clown walks down the sidewalk in short, exhausted steps. You'd almost say he wasn't moving: that he couldn't move forward.

Part Two

1

Tuscan columns, Doric columns, Corinthian columns, Ionic columns. Made-up orders of columns. Smiling caryatids, frowning caryatids (comedy, tragedy). More columns, with art nouveau, art deco motifs. Solomonic columns. The remains of opera boxes with manneristic iron banisters and wooden hand railings with Greek, Roman, Byzantine decorations. Modernist scrolls. In the proscenium arch, the mixture of lion, goat, and serpent that form the Chimera, symbol of the glorious passions of the imagination. Next to the monster, beautiful Oshún levitates above her storm-tossed boat. The nine Muses hold the Virgin's mantle aloft, while black footmen lift the Muses' tunics. Busts of satyrs coexist with Isis and Buddha. A tiny gargoyle joins an angel. A nymph holds the noose for the Hanged Man of the Tarot deck. A mandrake is used in the birth of a small Belial.

Decorations by Tiffany and Lalique. Landscapes by Chartrand, Sanz Carta. Portraits by Romañach. Languid siesta scenes by Collazo. Portraits by Valderrama. In the friezes, grape leaves and olive branches alongside guava and chirimoya leaves, yagrumas, and palm trees. The lamps, the remains of lamps, range from the grand chandelier to unadorned lamps with solitary blue bulbs. Bowls in the form of mosques, with Islamic motifs. Six-candled candelabras, gigantic candlesticks.

Amid the destruction of the orchestra seating, a few seats can still be found in good order. No two chairs are alike. The upholstery is an intensely red moiré, though its darkness might, perhaps, be a result of the years, the dust, the fly droppings, and the other catastrophes to which all things constructed by man are prone. The backs of the chairs are in the form of crowns, masks, triumphal arches, while the chair arms are lions' claws simulating human arms, and human arms simulating lions' claws. The only thing that all the chairs have in common is the carved initials M and V, interlaced.

Plain, somber, italianate, the stage may be much larger than it appears to the naked eye; you might say the boards of the stage have shown the greatest courage in withstanding the calamities of the climate, the years, and so many maggots. The tatters of the curtain reveal that it was made from the same moiré as the seats. At the foot of the stage, a wooden pedestal supports a bronze bust of José Martí. Next to him: a set of century-old chains, like the ones the Spanish authorities once used in slave holds. Some backdrops and footlights are also still there, and you know that the lights exist only because of an excess of optimism; all that remains of them is their rusted skeletons.

Best of all, Victorio thinks, are the lavatories — perfectly preserved, with silvered mirrors, spotless glasses framed in bronze, unscathed stalls, luminous porcelain, and delicately embossed signs saying LADIES, GENTLEMEN, carved by some unknown artist, above doors made of pieces of precious wood, so precious that they still have the colors that pieces of wood have when they are precious. Behind the stage are the four dressing rooms, with their metal stars fixed to the doors, still able to reveal the glitter of sequins and glass beads.

Victorio has fallen asleep in one of the theater's dressing rooms, the first on the left, the only one that is unlocked. The other three have been sealed with massive padlocks linked to strong chains.

He has slept like an angel, one of those total sleeps that one imagines are so like death must be, sleeps in which there are no vicissitudes, or colors, or people, or memories, or residues of the day, in which there is nothing at all but the very act of sleeping, of leaving your body and all it contains, soul and spirit, abandoned to such an utter rest that you are only blessed with two or three sleeps like this in your entire life.

He doesn't know how long he has been sleeping: here's another special trait of this beneficial sleep. When he wakes up and finds himself in a room full of mirrors and light bulbs, flowers and masks, walking sticks and hats, and clothes of many colors, he doesn't think he has awakened but that he is just getting to the next stage of sleep, the most jubilant, no doubt. One of the pleasures of dreaming comes from its kinship with reality, just as one of the pleasures of reality derives from its kinship with dreams.

Music is what has awakened him, the playing of a flute. It sounds like a version for flute of "The Swan" by Saint-Saëns.

He has gotten up from the bed, actually a comfortable little antique *recamier,* and has walked around the ruins of the small, exquisite theater. He hasn't found anyone playing a flute yet, and he has come to think that there are two separate places, which are, at the same time, the same identical place: Havana and the ruins of the theater. And he has concluded that, like most paradoxes, that of the separation between city and ruined theater is a paradox only in appearance. There is no real contradiction. In the most intimate truth about reality, isn't this how things are, confused and unintelligible? You might argue that Havana derives from the ruins of the theater. Havana: a simple and enigmatic prolongation of this theater, known in an earlier era as the Pequeño Liceo of Havana, according to the spattered sign that is posted next to the dressing rooms. This impression seems to be the most mysterious and perhaps the most moving thing about it, for, given that it is nothing but the ruins of a theater, and a rather tiny one at that, probably built eighty or ninety years ago when the city had already been around for four centuries of epidemics, famines, ravages, and hardships, how can he possibly conclude that the city might have grown from the theater, around the theater, thinking of the theater, reproducing it in its street corners, walls, streets, parks, and buildings? Once you gain access to the ruins, you will inevitably imagine that you have entered the very heart of Havana. Victorio thinks of a hypothetical Genesis of the city in which it is written: *In the beginning was the theater.*

2

The sun's rays penetrate the cracks in the peaked roof above the stage. The sunbeams fall on the boards and stand out sharply, in varied, mysterious hues, incredible modulations that create varied zones onstage, circles and rings, well-defined spaces that no one would dare doubt were the work of expert lighting technicians.

From the orchestra seating, Victorio notices only two decorative items: a tomb on the far left, with a wreath of sepia-toned paper flowers and a wooden cross that reads GISELLE; on the right, a white grand piano, which is not, properly speaking, a decorative item. In one leap, one single, agile leap, Victorio hops onto the stage. He doesn't know whether his body is cutting through the sunbeams or being cut by them.

The music again. The same Saint-Saëns air, except that this time the music has dropped the polished agility of the flute, resounding instead with the blue stateliness of the oboe. The music seems to emanate from the old vestibule, back there, behind the frayed screens with country motifs.

Four clowns are playing four oboes. Clowns with curly mops of red hair, faces covered in white makeup, and a painted blue tear shining on each one's cheek. The four clowns have concentrated expressions that imply nothing but exhaustion. Seeing Victorio through the mirrors, the four elderly men stop playing and raise their weary heads. Victorio experiences a sense of joy that seems much like comfort and trust. These aren't four clowns or four elderly men, but a single old man dressed as Pierrot. An old man multiplied by the witchcraft of three glasses in three mirrors. The four are one, this one, the one and only clown. The same one who had danced across the timbers that once supported and united the old Royal Palm Hotel and the former palace on Calle Galiano; the one from the Military Hospital; the one he had encountered in the funeral parlor after running away when he stole a pizza in Chinatown.

"Good afternoon," says the clown. His voice has a lovely tenorino timbre that contradicts the centenarian age of his face, the emaciation of his tiny body, his wrinkled hands, like those of an aged child.

Victorio replies with a "Good afternoon" that almost sounds like a plea for help.

"You've had a good rest," the old man states, "and you certainly needed a lot of rest. Listen, friend, you fell down when you got to the corner of San Rafael and Belascoaín, and if I hadn't reached you in time I think you might have hit your head fatally against the curb. I though you were drunk at first, though your breath didn't smell of alcohol."

"I never drink, but I was worn out, or hungry."

"Yes, your breath didn't smell like alcohol, but it didn't smell like anything else, either, except a cavern, an empty stomach; your mouth was like a cave that even bats wouldn't dare to enter. I remember that I called you many times, and many times I heard the echo of my voice in the hidden corners of your innards."

Victorio can't help bursting out laughing. "How did I get here?" he asks as soon as his laughter allows him.

With outlandish seriousness, the old clown puts the oboe away in its case and asks, in studied tones, "Isn't it enough for you to know that you did get here, that I let you sleep in the same *recamier* where

Nijinsky, the greatest-enemy-of-the-law-of-gravity, once slept, that you traveled through your dreams for, I don't know, eight, nine days, as long as you must have gone without sleeping?"

"I'm grateful to you," replies Victorio.

The clown and the images that multiply him shake their heads. "No, no, son, there's nothing to be grateful for. Never thank me, understand? But tell me, what is your name?"

"Victorio," he replies, ashamed, as always.

The clown does not seem surprised by the odd name and asks no questions. "Mine is Fuco, Don Fuco. Well, you understand, my name isn't Don Fuco, but Don Fuco is what I'm called."

They walk past the screens. They head in among the remains of the orchestra seating. "How do you like it?" shouts the clown. "This is my kingdom, as you can see. Being a disciple of Baudelaire, after all, I like to surround myself with a lovable pestilence. I've been living here for years and I don't think there's anyone happier in the world."

"I never thought there could be a place like this anywhere in Havana," says Victorio.

"Because you don't know Havana. You're too young to know how many mysteries this terrifying city conceals." He makes a face that could signify terror or disgust, either one.

"Do you believe that's so?" and when he asks the question, Victorio involuntarily reproduces the clown's grimace.

"Believe? Not at all, I don't believe anything. I know it, I'm positive! There's no city so deceptive, my friend, as this hell we inhabit."

"What other cities do you know?" asks Victorio.

"None, just Havana, and if you want me to be sincere, that's enough and more than enough for me."

They've reached the stage. Don Fuco sits on the proscenium and looks around in satisfaction. Victorio remains standing, fascinated by the brilliant blue teardrop on the cheek of this aged Pierrot. "Didn't you ever want to travel?"

"Never. Do you want to know why? Simple! God, Mother Nature, or that Who-knows-what out there, made me be born in Havana; if I had gone on to Paris or New York, and had strolled along the Champs-Elysées or Fifth Avenue, what would have become of me when I came back? Tell me: I would have found that I was living in a small, crude city of no great consequence, a city with little history and too many pretensions. Out there, you've got Rome or Florence, where travelers are left gaping at the sight of Renaissance or Baroque buildings; no one would stop to look at a nineteenth-century building, but Havana never had a Renaissance, and our stones were so hard that they didn't allow for a very Baroque Baroque, so nineteenth-century is as far back as we go."

He pauses, sighs sadly. "So what would have become of me when I came back? I would have realized that the gods hadn't smiled on me; no, my friend, no, I think it's much better to discover the beauty this poor city of mine has to offer, rather than set out to find the beauty that others before me have discovered in the great cities. If I go see a performance of *Rigoletto* in La Scala of Milan or in the Vienna Opera, how could I return to these ruins? How would I have the nerve? Tell me, my boy, how would I have the nerve?"

Don Fuco massages his bare feet. "I'm tired, by God and all the devils. I don't think I can keep on going. I need a little Chinese ointment for my poor feet." He touches his chest with a gesture of helplessness and whispers, "Today I did the wicker basket routine. For me it's a tour de force now to curl myself up in a ball, turn myself into nothing, get into the basket, and make it dance to the 'Polovtsian Dances' from *Prince Igor*. I get out of breath, my heart stops, my blood suspends its circulation, my kidneys jump up all the way into my throat, and I am constantly overcome by the certainty that this will be the last time I'll be able to make myself so small that I can get into a basket made for storing vegetables. I'm old, my boy: very, very old. How old am I? A thousand, two thousand years, I think I must be at least that old. There are some days, like today, when I think I'm a survivor of infinite disasters, and it seems to me that I'm already returning along every road, that I've already experienced everything there is to experience, that I've seen and understood everything there is to see and understand, and everything there isn't to see or understand. I know my fate has been to live to see the triumph of mediocrity and bureaucrats, and to outlive the failure of the great enterprises of men, and there's nothing else, let me tell you, there's nothing else but that, the rest is silent. A long time ago I came to an incredibly important conclusion, I concluded that . . ."

The muttering dies down, turning into total silence. Victorio continues to be obsessed by the blue teardrop on the Pierrot's cheek. The light filtering down through the ceiling forms rings on the boards of the stage; and it softens, you can almost measure the way the light is losing intensity.

The clown doesn't seem to care about the arrival of night. "Today I went too far, I never should have danced inside that basket. It was too much, I overdid it."

Sitting on the proscenium, next to the motionless clown, like a marionette, Victorio inquires, "Why did you do it? Why did you dance inside the basket?"

Silence settles on the ruins of the Pequeño Liceo of Havana, with that special character that silence has amid ruins. Victorio comes to realize how far away, how far apart, how separate he is from the city. None of its endless rude noises reach them, nothing that is happening out there disturbs the peace of the devastated theater, as if the theater, and those within it, were floating in a spaceless space, an illusory dimension on top of the illusory island in the illusory continent on the illusory planet.

The lights work (twelve bulbs total) around the dressing-room mirror. The clown, minus his Pierrot outfit, dressed now in a green plush bathrobe and an ancient, ridiculous cap (from a production of *The Merchant of Venice,* he says, in which, he explains with a smile, he played an extraordinary Shylock), sits down before the illuminated mirror. He takes a long look at himself, concentrating on his old face, on his faded, watery eyes, and perhaps on the blue teardrop on his cheek. With a rapid gesture he tears off the Shylock cap: uncovering a gleaming bald pate, with a few sparse locks of indefinite color. His head is large and pear-shaped. He has the wide, domed forehead of someone who thinks and remembers much, the head of someone who has lived longer than expected.

He sticks his fingers into a jar of cold cream and, massaging his face with his fingers, uses it to remove the makeup. The labyrinth of wrinkles becomes more and more visible with each layer of makeup the cold cream takes away, until all that remains in the mirror is a corrugated, pathetic little face with miniscule eyes blurred by opaque clouds, and thin, colorless lips that betray his body's anemia and the lack of calcium in his yellow-green teeth.

"Time," he exclaims, "what's happening to me is time," and he makes a face at the mirror that cannot help but make you laugh. "I'm eternal, Victorio. Can you imagine what a horror it is to live forever? I don't know if anyone has ever been punished so hard." He rests his chin on his interlaced hands, leaning his elbows on the makeup table, and asserts, in his lovely tenorino voice, "Sometimes memories of the Roman Empire come to me, of the spread of the Goths, the French Revolution, the War of the Roses; I could swear I've met Galileo somewhere, and Mazarino, and Goethe, and I know I enjoyed myself in the brothels of Byzantium and the joints of New Orleans, and suffered under Napoleon, Lenin, Mussolini, Stalin, Machado: they're all one and the same, because, even though we thought that Mussolini, Lenin, Stalin, Machado died years ago, that's not true, they didn't die, that's just a supposition — it's what you think and what I understand, ingenuous as we are. We refuse to understand that the Tyrant is immortal, the Tyrant is reincarnated whenever he wants, in whatever body and voice he wants, that wizard, that dog, that Malignant One: he's reincarnated in every man who loves power, and when I suffer from these attacks of eternity, like today, and start thinking that I'll never find any rest, I get an urge to lie down on the ground like that character in Melville, and shout to everybody, to each and every one, 'I would prefer not to!'"

The clown is now an insignificant little old man staring at himself in the mirror. And then, as if he were making fun of himself, of this deplorable image, he lights up the mirror with another mocking grimace, and stands up with difficulty, bent over, taking short steps, like someone who can no longer bear the weight of life.

The clown lights a thick taper of yellow wax, stuck in a metal candlestick. He asks, "Would you like to drink some orange juice?"

Night is beginning to fall. The dressing room has tall, narrow, elongated windows with blue panes, thanks to which the sifted light of dusk creates a fictional atmosphere.

"The only value to be desired is that of artifice," says the clown, while reaching into a cabinet for a crude glass with red lettering that reads EL RON DE CUBA, and setting it down on the small makeup table. Then he takes out two glasses made of amber crystal, perhaps from Murano. "Well, of course, it's Murano; it isn't likely you could find any other crystal like this. It comes from the glass furnaces on that island, that lagoon and those marshes," and he takes out a pitcher, too, which he fills with cool water. While he pours the water into the crude glass with the lettering, he sings in his well-timbered tenorino voice,

Anywhere out of the world . . .

and he hands Victorio the ugly glass that holds the water, and orders, "Drink!"

And Victorio drinks the cool water.

Then the clown pours the water from the crude glass into one of the elaborate amber crystals that seem to be from Murano, and again orders, "Drink!"

And Victorio drinks the water, which now, in the new, ornate, elegant glass, is no longer water, but luscious, thick, delicate orange juice. Without realizing that he is trying to get all the enjoyment he can from the freshness and sweetness of the oranges, Victorio cannot help closing his eyes. For one brief moment he forgets about the clown, about Nijinsky's dressing room, and about the theater. The moment is brief, but no less intense, for all that. He forgets about himself. The great reality, or rather, the great truth is the juice of the orange.

The clown places the empty glass on the makeup table. He asks, he orders, "Come with me!"

Is it night already? The stage looks like a black cage. It is transformed by the light from the taper in the candlestick.

"There are not many people who know that this theater existed, exists, in Havana, and even fewer know who might have been its owner — what man, or woman, had the idea of constructing this hidden wonder. You, my boy, must no doubt be thinking of one of the

great Cuban families, Gómez-Mena, Falla-Bonet, Bacardí-Bosch . . .
A crass mistake! Those distinguished lineages had nothing to do with
the whimsical little theater. What happened was much stranger, more
like a fairy tale, to tell you the truth. At the turn of this century, on a
pleasure trip to Havana — which wasn't really a pleasure trip, but a
journey of star-crossed love — a Russian beauty arrived here: the
young, wealthy princess Marina Volkhovskoy, part poetess, part
painter, part violinist, and all adventurer, who dedicated long hours
to writing romantic verses, or painting in pastels, or playing the Ty-
rolean Steiner that her father had given her for a birthday present. I
mentioned star-crossed love, and I think all great loves are star-crossed,
no? Because, ay! my boy, what happened was that, on one birthday,
the princess met a god. The god appeared in a concert hall in the unexpected form of a forty-year-old black dandy, timid yet arrogant,
who could handle a violin like no one else. He was a god who came
from Cuba, named Claudio, married to a German noblewoman, and
employed as a chamber musician by Wilhelm II.

"So what happened to Marina when she saw and heard him?
Just what should have happened: Princess Volkhovskoy was overcome, paralyzed, couldn't even applaud his brilliant execution of the
Paganini theme. That night she couldn't sleep, nor any of the following nights. Every night the unlucky princess would go to the concert
hall and take the same seat, the last one on the far left of the first row,
ready to contemplate the black violinist's profile, perfect in so many
ways, and listen to his execution of the concerts, perfect in every way.
Then she would return to her palace, lock herself in her studio, and
rehearse and rehearse again polished pieces by Tartini, Francoeur,
Wieniawski, and even Johann Sebastian Bach's *Chaconne*. Dawn always found her with rings under her eyes, trembling, still playing.

"The next-to-the-last night, she did something daring: she stood
through his entire concert, applauded the violinist's own *Barcarolle*
without discretion, and after the final chord, she went up to him,

presented herself: *I am Princess Volkhovskoy,* speaking timidly yet arrogantly. She passed him a note and went back to her palace to wait, in the certainty that he would come. And indeed, the following afternoon the butler opened the great front door to let in the surprisingly black dandy, whom he led down a long corridor to the princess's studio. The violinist Claudio Brindis de Salas, black, from Havana, baron and cavalier of the Legion of Honor, at home in the houses of kings, entered with a distinguished gait, but he could not conserve his elegant indifference for long, for there stood the Russian beauty, completely nude, executing the *Barcarolle* without committing the slightest error. Amazed, without wasting a second, Brindis de Salas took off his own clothes, graciously picked up his violin, and accompanied the young woman in what must, beyond any doubt, have constituted (pity no critic was there; even more of a pity, there was no photographer) one of the most impassioned duets in the history of the violin."

Don Fuco looks around with half-closed eyes and lifts the candlestick, which projects gigantic shadows.

"Brindis returned to the Weimar kingdom. Princess Volkhovskoy packed her bags and went to Moscow, crossed the fields of Poland, the Black Forest, entered Switzerland, slept in Lugano, and arrived in Genoa, where she booked passage on a Greek schooner bound for the Antilles, reaching Havana several weeks later, where, horrified, she rented a room in the Plaza Hotel, amazed at the omnipresent heat, the intermingling of riches and putrefaction, the surprising sizes and colors of the flies and mosquitoes, the number of black dandies walking around the streets (she had come to believe that she was the only lucky woman), the kinds of stench that almost seemed like perfume, as well as the perfumes that smelled more like foul odors, the good and bad effluences that flowed from houses, from sewers, from coaches, from markets; she was surprised by that mixture of sumptuousness and destitution, the exquisiteness always bordering on frightfulness, the frightful quality that always surrounds splendor like a flock of vultures. She learned Spanish (a tender, divine language, a language of prayer, full of nuances) as quickly as she could, and set herself to finding out about that city, which she didn't understand, which she never understood, and which revolted and seduced her with equal delirium. She returned to Cuba every year, finally buying a lordly palace in El Vedado, around La Chorrera, near the sea (neither the Malecón seawall nor the avenue existed then, just the coral reefs and the sea), between the Hotel Trotcha and the Loynaz mansion. And in 1917, the year the Bolsheviks seized power, Princess Volkhovskoy, a White Russian after all, a cultured woman of good taste, a close friend of Nabokov, decided never to return to her homeland, and she gave thanks every day to Havana and to the Lord for the horrors from which she had been saved."

The clown moves the candlestick, passing it in front of Victorio's face. Staring with a long, deliberate look, he observes the vacillation of the flame.

"And so, my friend, in honor of her passion for the arts in general and for Brindis de Salas in particular, my friend Marina Volkhovskoy gratified her desire to build this shrine, where she and I were the only audience, together with an occasional guest, an occasional niece, the occasional ten or twelve Oblate nuns (her favorites), and, years later, with Monsignor Carlos Manuel de Céspedes, who at the time was not yet a monsignor but an educated young man, a voracious reader, a music lover, and a kindhearted student at the Seminary of San Carlos and San Ambrosio. Since the princess didn't like sharing her interests with anyone except for me (being her best friend) and Monsignor de Céspedes, she preferred not to let anyone know about her flow of riches, and she arranged it so that this theater never had a theatrical facade — no marquee, no outward showiness, no grandiose entrance hall; a long hallway, an unassuming door, half-hidden steps, . . . and heaven!

"Yes, heaven, because Anna Pavlova, the Great One, danced *The Dying Swan* here for her fellow countrywoman, the bishop, and me (Monsignor Céspedes hadn't yet begun to think about being born), just as Enrico Caruso sang the most outstanding pieces in his repertoire; and let me tell you, it turns out to be true what they say: 'Hear Caruso and then die.' And Sarah Bernhardt, that French-woman who was so French, so very French, that she dared to insinuate that we Cubans were 'Indians in frock-coats' just because we didn't applaud her as loudly as she had expected: hysterical, like any good actress, and French to top it off! That Frenchwoman, as I was saying, performed a selection of her best roles for an audience composed of the princess and your humble servant, and the truth is, she was an excellent actress, with a style that would be considered old-fashioned nowadays, but very convincing, very convincing, which proves once more that true art is neither old nor young, neither old-fashioned nor modern nor postmodern nor transmodern nor cutting-edge nor post-cutting-edge, in the words of the syphilitic rhetoric of critics who have nothing to say. It's art, period. Did you know, Victorio, that Maria Callas *did* visit Havana?

"Every version you might hear will tell you that the Diva never set foot on Cuban soil: since Havana belonged, as operatic territory, to her great rival Renata Tebaldi, the Cuban impresarios abstained from mortifying the latter by offering a contract to Callas, yet it is known that a beautiful, modest yacht anchored one morning in the Santa Fe moorage, where they've lately built what they call the

'Hemingway Marina.' The yacht was the *Tosca,* and it belonged to the fleet of the famous Greek shipowner, and the only passengers who disembarked were a young lady and a very elegant woman in a discreet, fresh blue dress, black kerchief on her head, dark glasses. A tugboat pilot who loved opera — don't look surprised, that's what life is like, my friend, a great confusion of paradoxes — the tugboat pilot and bel canto lover thought he recognized Callas in the goddess who was disembarking from the yacht, and he shouted *'Maria!'* and she didn't look at him. *'Maria!'* the pilot shouted again, and she turned an undaunted mask towards him. *'Maria?'* asked Maria with an ingenuous look, *'Non, non, monsieur, vous vous êtes trompé . . .'*

"And she didn't stay in any hotel: the enormous Cadillac that was waiting for her took her to a lovely chalet built of precious wood at a villa near the Baracoa beach, northwest of Havana. The villa belonged to Princess Volkhovskoy. Two days later, Maria, the Diva, the great Callas, gave a recital for the princess, and the princess had invited your humble servant, and Monsignor Carlos Manuel de Céspedes, and the Oblate Sisters, to accompany her in the Pequeño Liceo of Havana. The Cuban press never found out; the ridiculous world of society gossip never found out; we even hid the singer's name from Huberal Herrera himself, the pianist who accompanied her. He guessed, of course; nobody else could have a soprano with that timbre, a voice that came out of no part of her body, a voice that could only escape from her soul: it had to be her voice. Her voice! Callas! Good old Huberal Herrera preferred to keep his mouth shut out of fear that no one would believe him, and except for the people who arranged her trip and the people who heard her in the theater, the only one who knew about Maria Callas's Havana adventure was the great playwright and greater poet and storyteller, the magnificent giant of letters, Virgilio Piñera, who met her while she was walking along the Paseo del Prado, and without letting himself be impressed by her imperturbable expression and her *vous vous êtes trompé* — Piñera was as strong-willed as the Diva — he replied in his excellent French (which he pronounced, however, like a Haitian), *Oui, madame, moi aussi, je me suis trompé, je ne suis pas Virgilio Piñera, le poète cubain, je suis Alfred Germont . . .* , and, as Piñera told the story, Callas kept a serious look on her face but the Violetta Valéry hidden inside her awarded him with a smile."

The clown laughs. Uproariously.

Victorio thinks, *What odd teeth: yellow, or green, eaten away by time; they look like underwater fossils.*

The clown's eyes disappear. His body shakes with laughter.

"That wasn't the only case, my boy, not even the most flagrant. Diaghilev, Karsavina, and Nijinsky also stayed in the chalet built of precious wood at the Baracoa beach (not the First City of Cuba, but the other Baracoa, that little collection of shacks on the outskirts of Bauta). Karsavina and Nijinsky put on two unforgettable performances of *The Spectre of the Rose,* and Princess Marina Volkhovskoy and I had both begged so fervently for two (two!) performances of Nijinsky's classic piece. We watched the first one from front row center, but we were able to observe the second while hiding on the stage among the ropes, curtains, and decorations, because we both wanted to see how the genius, the greatest-enemy-of-the-law-of-gravity, made his great leap from a different perspective; and we wanted to see how the smile that the audience saw, the triumphant impassivity of his face, was transformed into a grimace of pain by the effort of that colossal, inhuman leap, an expression of anguish, of desperation; we wanted to see him fall, and see how all the others ran to him with concern and rubbing alcohol and damp towels. The princess and I were both interested in the splendor of genius. We were also attracted by its disagreeable dark side, its obstinate, demented side, without which its splendor would not be possible."

The clown raises his hands toward the candlelight. Victorio can see how his palms light up, full of wrinkled lines, hands that would drive the most brilliant palm reader insane. He can also see how the clown's smiling face falls into darkness.

"What fun we had with Anna Pavlova in her dressing room, which no one else used," he continues in his lovely tenorino voice, muted by his memories. "We saw Anna Pavlova cry, shout, bite her hands, beat her head against the walls, just minutes before going out and doing a glorious *Dying Swan* with all the aplomb and assurance of what she was: not a great ballerina, but a goddess possessed by the dance! And this theater likewise welcomed Pau Casals and Ella Fitzgerald, Antonin Artaud, Jean Marais (with Jean Cocteau), María Félix (with Jorge Negrete), and Michèle Morgan and Galina Ulanova and Celina González and Cora Vaucaire and Alicia Alonso and Miko Yana, the most famous of Japanese dancers."

"The locked door of the fourth dressing room, the first one going from right to left, the one with the largest sequined-and-tasseled star, belonged to Anna Pavlova, the Great One, during the four visits she made to Havana."

Don Fuco knocks on the door of the second dressing room and says, "This is where Lorenzo Nadal, better known as Lorenzo the Magnificent, got dressed, prepared, and practiced. He was not only the best pianist in the world, the man who has understood and interpreted the works of Chopin better than anyone else, but also the best

Cuban landscape painter ever, even though no one knows him for his piano playing or for his brush . . . Lorenzo, as magnificent as he is modest!"

At the third dressing room, he presses his ear against the door. "This one, in which you have put on such a virtuoso performance of sleep for the past several days, belonged, as you know, to Nijinsky during the times he visited us with Karsavina and Diaghilev."

He smiles sweetly. Victorio knows that the smile is not dedicated to him.

"It doesn't mean that they are the only ones who have used these dressing rooms, of course, yet on the other hand it does mean that they inaugurated them."

Don Fuco advances with difficulty toward the fourth dressing room, in front of which he kneels. His hand caresses the door with delight. He looks unsettled, nervous, fascinated. "This is the Dressing Room of the Grand Guignol," he says, or sings, in his clear, adolescent voice, now trembling, with a touch of mellifluence; "I know that this must be amazing for you, my boy."

"What's amazing is the story behind this theater," Victorio comments.

"Did you like it? Ah, well, another day I'll tell you a different story that will be just as true."

3

Afternoons, Victorio lies down on the boards of the stage and closes his eyes. He usually experiences a rare sensation. Not joy, though related to it. He thinks: *Happiness is like men, capricious; and like men, it possesses many faces, and does not have just one way of presenting itself.*

Afternoons, on the boards of the old stage, he closes his eyes with no intention of sleeping. This is the surest way of attracting the easily molded material from which memories are made. And he manages to calm himself and invoke his childhood in the little house in Marianao, in the Santa Felisa neighborhood.

He has been told that since the death of La Pucha, his father has been confined to a wheelchair. He remembers him as a tall, expressive, headstrong man of uncommon eloquence, able to carry on arguments about the most unforeseeable topics, a man for whom the words "life" and "revolution" designated an identical degree of certainty. Victorio always felt inadequate next to this man, with his strong smell of tobacco, who always looked older than he was, who at a certain stage in his life gave his son bear hugs that left saliva on his cheeks, and to whom he owed his name Victorio, the grounds for so many rude jokes among his schoolmates.

Papá Robespierre (as he and his sister had come to call him in revenge, years later) had struggled "for social justice, that man not be the bane of man." Luckily, when Victorio was little, Papá Robespierre was never home. He was first in line for self-sacrifice. He worked hard

101

as an administrator and spent most of his time in the hangars of Agricultural Fumigation. Like any good communist, he had no sense of
humor. He couldn't stand laughing at himself. Whatever the subject,
he would look for its solemn, serious side. When he was home, however, he cherished affection, even played with La Pucha, and took the
children skating in the park and bought them sodas, Guarina ice cream,
candy, toys, and cotton candy. Victorio remembers him in his olive-
green militia uniform, wearing the black beret with the tiny, waving
Cuban flag. Today the son doesn't know whether his father continues to dress like that, whether he is settled still in his old hopes. It has
been years since they've seen each other. Victorio is able to remember
him in the park, or anywhere, reading out loud, over and over again,
the same speeches by Lenin, and a few paragraphs that he had under-
lined in the Marxist-Leninist textbooks (Konstantinov and Afanasiev).
Papá Robespierre had belonged to the Popular Socialist Party, but he
had been a rebellious communist, one of those who could never rec-
oncile himself to the pact with Batista, and who felt great admiration
instead for the young lawyer Fidel Castro (the Boss, as he said) and
the "rebels" of the Sierra Maestra. During the assault on the Moncada barracks, in Santiago de Cuba, he suffered two excitations: the
news of the assault and the birth of his son, Victorio, who by miraculous coincidence was born that same Saint Anne's morning in 1953.

In the years following the attack on the barracks and the birth
of Victorio, Papá Robespierre left the Popular Socialist Party (or was
expelled from it; the truth was never learned), and devoted himself to
selling bonds to support the Movimiento 26 de Julio. A few years
later he couldn't go up into the Sierra Maestra to join the rebels, as
had been his desire, because La Pucha, Hortensia, his wife, not only
had little Victorio, but had become pregnant and miscarried a baby
girl. This misfortune left her with a serious imbalance of the nerves.
Papá Robespierre believed he had a civic duty to fulfill for his unhappy country; his fanaticism, however, did not let him lose sight of

the duty that he also had toward his unhappy wife. He behaved sensibly; he resolved not to forsake either country or wife: instead of going up into the Sierra, he devoted himself to the civilian struggle. Not only did he sell bonds for the 26 de Julio, he also bought arms and prepared and sent messages together with the weapons. He sent combatants to the mountains and plains where the battle was spreading. The second successful girl was born (another miracle) on January 9, 1959, barely twenty-four hours after the triumphant rebels entered Havana. For that reason, Papá Robespierre decided to name her Victoria (full name: Victoria Patria, though only a few people, thank God, knew this). The same name for both children, the name that so upset them and that made them put up with so many crude jokes at school. According to La Pucha, they were given the name by order of Papá Robespierre, no discussion, despite her tears and pleas.

La Pucha, superstitious as she was, considered it a disastrous name. As she tried to explain to her husband: "If a name means anything, it means the opposite of what it means."

"Balderdash!" replied Papá Robespierre, who believed in neither God nor superstitions, much less in women's tears or word games. And he insisted, "My son, my male, born weighing eight pounds on the day of a heroic action; my daughter, my female, the apple of my eye, born during the first days of Freedom, a citizen of the free city of a free country, not any old free country but the freest of the free, the First-Free-Territory-of-America, in the very heart of the Realm-of-Utopia."

And he wanted to prepare Victorio, above all, for the rigors of life and history. Although the adult who had been that child cannot remember anything about those days, he knows, he has been told, that he accompanied his father selling bonds for the 26 de Julio; that is why he often insists, sarcastically and inexorably, half joking and half serious, that he was born to go underground. He often repeats, "Since I was a child, I've been an outlaw."

103

After the triumph of the revolution, the fervent father started dressing the boy in little militia outfits that kept him bathed in sweat and covered his tender skin with rashes. As soon as Victorio was able to talk, Papá Robespierre made him learn anti-imperialist poems about the sugar harvest (Agustín Acosta) and poems praising the flag (Agustín Acosta, Bonifacio Byrne), and he taught him national anthems, war songs, verses about coal-mining girls with no white shoes, odes celebrating patriotic bravery, and more verses about freedom, the new era, and the birth of the New Man: Immaculate, Perfect, Spotless, Unstained, Pure, Pure as the era. He gave him toy rifles and targets that had, as their vulnerable bull's eyes, the Statue of Liberty (that hypocritical allegory), Donald Duck, President Eisenhower, Uncle Sam (those monstrous aberrations). "The Empire must be destroyed," he would exclaim in theatrical tones, scattering flecks of spit with every word, making excessive arm gestures that would almost always destroy one of the cheap porcelain decorations that La Pucha loved so much, purchased at La Quincallera or El Ten Cents. Papá Robespierre would take Victorio to stadiums where revolutionary meetings, baseball games, or both were being held. He would make him get up on the field inspectors' horses, and climb into the Fokker airplanes used to fumigate the crops. He wanted to teach him to be brave.

One of the methods that Papá Robespierre used to fortify Victorio's courage was to turn off all the lights in the house and leave him alone in that darkness for ten minutes. The old communist, the grave and circumspect admirer of Stalin (he never believed the horrors that were told about him) felt proud of his pedagogical method, which he had taken, he explained, from a text of Anton Makarenko. Papá Robespierre never knew what was all but inevitable: that during those ten minutes of blackout, Victorio felt a greater and greater terror every night; a terror that paralyzed him and that left him cowering in a corner of his room. His father was so absorbed in and fascinated by the creation of the New Man that he paid no attention to the sad, taciturn, and melancholy lad he was forming. Nor did he ever notice (he never noticed anything that was nearby and real) the only reason why Victorio was so delighted to accompany him to the Agricultural Fumigation hangars.

El Moro must have been close to eighteen years old. His skin was dark, his eyes Arabic, and his hair blue-black, hard, and steady. He was said to be the son of an Algerian revolutionary, an expert in economics who had graduated from the Sorbonne and was a confidant of Ahmed Ben Bella. In reality it doesn't matter where he got those traits, because beauty — Victorio thinks now — has no homeland. Victorio was impressed by El Moro's height, his walk, his ballet movements (he never seemed to set foot on the ground), his deep, light voice, his perfect Spanish with its distantly French *r*s, his smile, whiter than you ever could have imagined. "Come on, boy, let's go fly," he was always saying to Victorio-as-a-child, by way of greeting. El Moro would go up in one of those ancient Fokkers and he might have become the most daring man you might have imagined. He played around in the sky, turning loops like an overconfident bird, making Papá Robespierre and the rest of the workers there curse over and over, "That degenerate Moro, the day you least expect it he's going to kill himself, and the worst part is: he'll screw up the best plane we've got, that *sonofabitch-Moro-faggot*."

That's what they said. The truth was otherwise: their words of reproof bore no relation to their smiles of approval, their indulgent expressions, the pride that burst through their phrases of condemnation; they called him *faggot, sonofabitch,* while smiling approvingly at the loops he turned in the air with such ease. Loops and loops and loops, mysterious *S*s. He would get lost in the clouds and reappear like a glorious bird. El Moro stood for happiness, freedom from care, intrepidity, generosity, beauty. Victorio doesn't even need to close his eyes to see him again like the first time, that afternoon, when he and his father had gone to the airfield. It was lunchtime. The workers were taking advantage of the little free time they had to organize ball games. El Moro was bare-chested and wearing his camouflage militia pants. He was in the center of the field, in the middle of a leap, stock-still (in every leap there is an instant of eternity), with a concentrated expression and arms upraised. He was going for a ball that was far too high. Victorio saw no ball. All he saw was him, El Moro, and that was enough. And is enough, and will be enough, he thinks. He saw, he sees, he will see a young man, motionless in midair, who could not reach the ball and did not need to return to earth to start running. All these years later, Victorio can glimpse El Moro supporting himself with one arm so that the rest of his body can climb up a fence and get over to the other side. This isn't really a memory. It's something more: an obsessive, motionless scene, a still photo. An instant of eternity. Time has not, has never been able to undo the scene. Victorio remembers that the game ended and that El Moro came up to them, sweaty, smiling, greeting Papá Robespierre with respect, and noticed the boy. He asked the father, "What, your lieutenant?" and patted the boy's head with such a rough gesture that it became tender.

Lying down on the boards, with his eyes closed, in the ruins of the theater that becomes confused with Havana, Victorio thinks he has always known, since he was a small child, how many ways there are to find charm in things. Then, it was the matter of a man's body. Large, dark hands, dirty hands with fingernails darkened by the grease of Fokker engines. A big nose, broken, like a boxer's. Purplish lips, Algerian, wet, smiling, split by a delicate scar (as a child, he himself said, he had a harelip: they operated on him in Paris). Dark nipples, turgid, ringed by the rebelliousness of thin, downy hair and bluish blackness. The way one muscle stood out, one which, Victorio learned much later, was called the serratus. The gesture with which he shooed an insect or dried a drop of sweat that was dripping down his hair into his temple. The round navel — rather crude (that is to say, classic). The hairy black underarms. The way he had of turning toward a tree, opening his legs, unbuttoning his fly, pissing. Scratching his toes. Saying good-bye. Singing hit songs. Spitting with his tongue pressed against his teeth. Cleaning his ears with the nail of his little finger. A curse word, or just a simple gesture, meaning nothing. Come on, boy, let's fly!

Victorio wonders whether things are the way they are, or the way the multiple whims of memory reset them. In the theater which, according to the clown, saw the agony of Pavlova and heard the peerless voice of Callas and knew the enchanted dancing of Alonso and observed the way in which Nijinsky prepared for *The Spectre of the Rose,* Victorio becomes certain once more that El Moro is still there, saying nothing, leaning against the tree. The tree, too, is the same one as ever. The Algerian is peeling and sucking on a piece of sugarcane; the syrup spills from the corners of his mouth, reaches his chin, dampens his chest, his stomach, his pants. Again Victorio sees El Moro's wet pants. Not only wet with cane syrup. His sweat is forming a dark band around his waist. There's the smell of cane syrup. And the strong smell of the Algerian's sweat. And the aroma of damp earth. As he did in his dainty child's bed, Victorio curls up into a ball. He keeps his eyes closed, and feels protected.

Now she is a pile of bones kept in the ossuary of the family crypt, but back then La Pucha, Hortensia, Victorio's mother, was a quiet, discreet woman. She had large eyes, subtly almond-shaped, as if some impossible Chinese blood had flowed through her Cantabrian veins.

107

Her skin was white, the skin of the daughter of an emigrant from the north of Spain, and her body, like herself, was obliging and lovely. Victorio remembers her slender, graceful hands, the hands of a princess, not of the seamstress that she actually was. She spent the whole livelong day sewing dresses for weddings and *quinceañeras.* Unlike Papá Robespierre, for La Pucha, Hortensia, his mother, the only true politics was affection and the only country was the family. Victorio thinks that at some time his mother must have loved Papá Robespierre's resolute eyes and the vigor of his body and spirit. She must have loved him, Victorio doesn't have the slightest doubt about it. It's just that her youthful passion must have turned, over the years, into mere acquiescence, into nostalgia, and of course into much more pity for him than she ever would have allowed herself to feel toward her own self.

Victorio-as-a-child withdraws from the bustle and partying of his extended family. He walks along the coastline, littered with sargasso. The sea breeze, the sky, and he form the same matter. Something is becoming vast, everlasting, that is to say, indestructible and eternal. His body grows huge and comes to fill all that can be seen and not seen, all that can be heard and not heard, all that can be touched and not touched, all that can be tasted and not tasted. On the beach, you are anywhere in the world. Say one word, you've said them all. Any song you sing is every song.

Other forgotten moments of wonderfully rich times come back to him. Not the sort of moments that are generally taken to be wonderfully rich. No great occasions. Nothing of the sort. Just plain happiness. Running through the streets in the thunderstorms of May. Eating *manzano* bananas. Sticking his hands in the mud and feeling the contact with the wet earth. Getting mango fibers stuck in his teeth. Sliding down the hill on a palm-bark sled. Listening to Grandfather

Don Inés sing old songs on his stool in the courtyard, after a bath, while the sun is going down and the road is cooling off. Stealing the *malanga* fritters that Grandmother Emilia would hide in the pantry. Sticking his finger in the meringue icing on the cake. Scratching his back against the rough edge of the door. Skinny-dipping in the river. Running his hand over trembling skin. Drinking coconut milk. Peeling mandarins with his teeth. Sitting in the sand to witness the sunset. Leaping as if the possibility of flight were really possible.

He opens his eyes. Total silence over the ruins of the Pequeño Liceo of Havana. The ruins are suspended over the face of the abyss and hover over the surface of the waters.

Victorio thinks about his father. Papá Robespierre always thought that traitorous sons are no sons at all. *Traitors to what?* he wonders. Victorio doesn't think he has betrayed anyone. It has been a long time since he would have liked to tell the incorruptible Papá Robespierre that he never betrayed anyone. He would have liked to have asked him if he, the Jacobin among Jacobins, could imagine that his son had different desires and needs, that he thought differently, that he was (he is!) different. Why, in that world of discipline and soldiers, have they never been able to understand variety? Why does everyone have to wear the same clothes, sing the same song, and worship the same idols?

On the quiet stage, the persistent beams of the sun, entering through cracks in the ceiling, are once more at play. He finds the ruinous orchestra seats facing him, and he feels a desire to recite the famous verses of Gastón Baquero,

La mañana pregona que no existe la nada.
Sal con el pie derecho a saborear el día.
Vive y nada más! Este día es tan bello,
que nos olvidamos de que tenemos huesos.

Morning proclaims that nothingness does not exist.
Step on out with your right foot first to savor the day.
Be alive, and nothing more! This day is so beautiful,
we might just forget that we have bones.

He enters the bathroom. He disrobes. The contact with the water awakens him. As in his dreams, he feels his body's communion with the water. He rubs his skin with a sea sponge that revives forgotten sensations. He accepts the shower with gratitude, which translates into a mixture of dynamism and sleepiness. Again he experiences the elated way his body has of enjoying, and repaying, its contact with water and soap. Each muscle has its moments of glory. His skin allows the intoxicating rapture of warm water to flow over it.

Yo tengo ya la casita
que tanto te prometí . . .

Now I have that little house
I've promised you so much . . .

He finds a blue silk kimono with apple trees and Fujiyamas in various pastel colors, very Japanese. It occurs to Victorio that it must be a costume from some production of *Madame Butterfly*. The kimono reminds him of the house robe he used to wear, in spite of heat and custom, in his little room on Calle Galiano.

And where is the clown? It has been awhile since he last heard music from either oboe or flute. Unlike other kinds of loneliness, the sensation that there is no one else here in the ruins is a discovery and a joy.

He has no idea what time of day it is, but the sun is coming through the blue windowpanes of his dressing room. He climbs on top of a piece of furniture and opens the window.

The sea. The empty Malecón seawall disappears into the distance. It must be early. The excessive sun and exaggerated heat turn the seawall into a searing stone altar. No skiff is out fishing at this impossible hour; no fisherman would risk it. There aren't any children swimming, either. No bather would be so suicidal. At most, some German from northern Germany, or some Norwegian, or some Swede might lie down on the wall to bathe in this sun, so much more insolent than any sun they would ever find in Hamburg, Molde, or Stockholm. This is the precise time when the sea is so tranquil that it allows the sun to multiply into endless suns and form a multitude of mirrors. Entering the sea means wandering among flashes of light: the brilliance of the sun and the brilliance of its reflections. Along the horizon he seems to see a sand barge passing, the long arms of its cranes now dormant. It is also possible that there is no boat out there, neither sand barge nor cargo ship: everyone is familiar with the falsehoods created by the complicity between horizon and light.

Even the wide avenue lining the Malecón, built on land won from the sea, is empty. Not even cars whiz by at this hour. Victorio experiences the sensation that this city is not his. Havana becomes a foreign, malevolent, reticent, remote city. Too much loneliness, disconnection, exile, incomprehension, abdication, anger, and injustice seems to have settled between Havana and Victorio. He knows that he is in Havana and not in Havana. This sensation of being exiled within his own city is not new. For many years he has felt alienated, observed and observing, an outsider, excluded, cut off, out of place. For far too long Victorio has wandered through Havana without recognizing it as belonging to him, and even more seriously, without Havana seeming to recognize him as belonging to it. So the sensation that assails him now at the window turns out not to be that of the exile-who-still-lives-in-the-same-place; its is something more subtle: at the blue windows of Nijinsky's dressing room, in the ruins of a theater unknown until now, he has a feeling that there is not only an unfathomable spiritual distance between himself and Havana, but that a physical distance has also been established, as if the ruins were not in Havana but in some more distant, some much more distant point, in land salvaged from the limits of geographies and histories.

The city becomes completely effaced, disappearing without disappearing: fleeting, ghostly, like the cathedral of Rouen in the famous paintings by Monet.

He tries to open the other dressing rooms. He can't. Chains and padlocks keep them closed tight. He returns to the stage, where the play of light and shadow has lessened. Where do you enter and exit from this theater?

For the moment, he doesn't want to go anywhere else, though it is always good to know where the exits are; it is even useful to track down the exit to the Champs-Elysées, to keep evacuation doors well marked. One sometimes has a need to escape, even from Edens and empyreans, from nirvanas and idyllic gardens (as the Quintero brothers might have written). Without doors that say EXIT, SALIDA, SORTIE, in bright red lights, as anyone knows, the glories of Paradise can turn into the torments of Inferno. And from this place, it seems, there is no exit. No matter how much Victorio goes over the ruins, he cannot discover a door to Havana. He walks from one end to the other, feeling the walls and murals; and those doors that do not lead to bathrooms or dressing rooms turn out to be purely decorative, doors opening onto adobe walls.

Victorio feels no fear. Unlike other times when he has felt closed in and locked up, over so many cloistered years, the ruins of the theater do not induce claustrophobia in him. This walled-in ruin is the least walled-in place he has ever known.

4

The days pass by. Victorio, however, is living a single, gigantic, happy day. Here among so much history he finally feels at home. He is annoyed and enchanted by Don Fuco's delirious stories. Victorio loves watching him rehearse the acts, so ridiculous and so beautiful, that he will later perform in funeral chapels, hospitals, on the street, in cemeteries and old age homes. "Any place where grief is to be found," the clown specifies, "and there are lots of these places, to tell the truth. The first rule on this island is to suffer, as if it were an offense to enjoy life, a crime against the nation. No, no, you can't take pleasure in the delights of life, you have to suffer, for who-knows-what future. We can't be frivolous, we can't be frivolous, we can't be frivolous!" And then, as if he had just made a great discovery, he adds, "The worst part is what always happens next: some people suffer and others don't. I can't imagine presidents and ideologues, ministers and subministers, presidents of corporations, ideological-journalists-of-renown eating our horrendous daily bread from the corner store, which isn't bread but some poor idea of bread, or living in shacks made from rotting wooden planks that let in the damp when the first three raindrops fall in the summer rainy season, and let's not even get into the hurricanes of September or October. No, I can't imagine high-and-mighty presidents suffering through heat and blackouts, or searching desperately for an antibiotic that can't be found in any pharmacy."

"As always," Victorio adds, "presidents, ministers, generals, and commanders-in-chief live in palaces with their gardens and swimming pools, they get around in extraordinary cars, they partake of the most exquisite delicacies."

"You don't have to be a minister . . ." says Don Fuco, and he leaves the sentence unfinished.

The clown would like to eat nothing but salt bread (if only he could have some bread sprinkled with seeds!) soaked in olive oil. "That alone would be enough to live on, bread and olive oil, well-seasoned olives. And a good red wine, of course, an aged wine from the banks of the Duero," he adds with a wink and the roguish melancholy of an old connoisseur. "The oil should be extra virgin," Don Fuco expertly clarifies, "low in acidity, unfiltered, deliciously bitter, if possible from Baena, from the Núñez de Prado family."

Don Fuco's lips and his nostalgic pupils gleam, his hands raise in a false gesture of pleasure. But he makes do with the daily ration that he receives, sometimes, from the nuns at the Santovenia Old Age Home or at the Convent of the Immaculate Conception, and sometimes from his friends, the cooks at the Calixto García Hospital, the Emergency Hospital, or the Covadonga Hospital. Don Fuco has managed to get hold of some plastic containers that hold the heat very well, and with them he brings lunch and dinner to the ruins of the theater every day, where they graciously give him their leftovers. The rations are not abundant, but there is enough to share, especially because they put plenty of bread in his covered basket. The bread is made with little flour and almost no grease ("The miracle of the loaves!" the clown remarks ironically), with almost no flavor or substance, yet it's enough to keep your stomach busy and to trick the phantoms of hunger. Yellowish and smacking of jute, the rice also tastes heavenly in the china plates. At the hospitals they usually serve a lot of stews and a lot of soup, and every now and then a bit of fried fish chock-full of fishbones. Some of the old age homes, on the other hand, being under the care of the Vatican nunciature and the Spanish embassy, offer fried chicken and now and again a little roast beef. Don Fuco brings dessert from Chaca's. And the coffee — made from ground roast chickpeas, with lots of sugar to ward off fainting spells — keeps all day in a huge metal Chinese thermos with pagodas painted in black on its sides.

For Victorio, the food that Don Fuco finds is plenty. They eat on worn-out white linen tablecloths. They use silverware with Marina Volkhovskoy's monogram. Victorio is surprised to find, amid these ruins, the Chelsea china and the silver cutlery with the imperial coat of arms and the two initials.

"It isn't the same to eat on a clay plate as on fine china, my friend," the clown declares in a feigned didactic voice; "the china makes it so that flavors don't lose their virtue, just as the Murano crystal enhances the bouquet of wines and liquors."

In the ruins of the old theater, time goes by differently. It isn't that it seems to happen more rapidly or less so, that it quickens, slows down, or stops. Nothing of the kind. Victorio is thinking about another quality of time, which belongs to the theater alone, ineffably, as if one minute, neither more nor less than the sixty seconds of a single minute, could enclose all the hours of the day and all the days of a month and all the months of a year and all the years of a century.

Best of all are the magic classes that Don Fuco gives Victorio, for then the student, naïve and bewildered, but fascinated, too, experiences an even more intense excitement that involves not only time but space; and it is as if, in these moments, time and space, those two mysterious qualities, depended on Victorio.

For example, Don Fuco has an hourglass. It is an hourglass that, in principle, works like any other hourglass. Yet when Don Fuco holds the ancient timepiece in his hands, it violates the laws that Newton deduced, and also breaks the stringent direction of time (older and more established than Mr. Newton's laws): instead of falling, the sand rises, moving from the lower to the upper space, as if the world had turned upside down and the North Pole had transformed into the South Pole.

Likewise, Don Fuco has a hat — that ancient, ridiculous cap of Shylock — from which doves do not fly, but into which they are instead attracted. The entire stage is suddenly covered with white doves, and Don Fuco has to do nothing more than hold out the Shylock cap for there to be a beating of wings, and the birds come to the hat, and disappear within it.

He also has a torch whose flame is lit with the clown's breath, and a large mirror in which you don't see yourself as you are, but as you would like to be. He keeps, moreover, a player piano or organ. He has a gold-and-red cape that can make those who wear it disappear, and a black armchair for taking journeys merely by closing your eyes.

5

A graceful light filters in through the tall window and finds a way to soften the darkness inside the ruins of the theater. Silence — capricious, impulsive — reigns, despite the distant laughter that arrives from who-knows-where. There is also some sort of conversation present in the background, some sort of faraway music, the sound of a television. Or of the wind.

"It's so tiresome, it's too too difficult," sighs Don Fuco, "to live in the Land-of-Forgetting and struggle against it at the same time. Against forgetting, I mean. I'm sure you understand me. There's a reason why the ancients, in their ever-wise way, claimed that Lethe, the goddess of forgetting, was born of Eris, the goddess of discord, who also engendered two other children that were therefore Lethe's brothers: Hypnos, sleep, and Thanatos, death. Like everything else in this life, there's more than one side to forgetting." A few seconds later, a certain pitying tone can be heard in his voice. "In this country we suffer from every possible type of forgetting, don't you think?"

"I've never thought about it," Victorio responds. "To me, forgetting seems like a solution to the frightfulness of life."

"Don't be vulgar, my friend," the clown replies in disgust. "If there's anything you should avoid in life, it's triteness. Let's go back to the starting point: there's forgetting, and there's forgetting." And he laughs, knowing he's made a trite remark.

"Please, don't get sibylline on me," exclaims the other, amused, feeling bold, vulgarly sibylline.

"The Sibyl was a woman inspired by the gods." And he laughs. "Thanks for the flattery, I don't deserve it."

Victorio looks at his hands. His hands tremble, as if they held the solution to all the world's problems.

"I said, and said rightly, that there's forgetting, and there's forgetting, and that phrase is a useful bit of foolishness. Sometimes, forgetting mitigates the frightfulness of life, to use your words, Victorio, my friend, though they're a little overblown, for my taste — I'm a man who doesn't care much for epics or tragedies, as you might have noticed; I love the comic sketch, and miniature beauty at its peak — sometimes forgetting assuages the horror, I repeat, and that kind of forgetting is not merely beneficial but indispensable. Remembering the Holocaust is, I suppose, a basic obligation, or, better put, a civil obligation, given that we must bear that horror in mind: among other things, to prevent it from being repeated."

He raises a hand closed into a fist and strikes the floor. Then he raises both hands, smooth as resting wings. A lovely smile lights his face.

"Remembering the Holocaust is extremely important: there is something else, my friend, that is also very important, and that something is never to forget certain pleasures. Yes, Victorio, really listen to that glorious word: *plea–sure.*" (He exaggerates the word, pronouncing it with his whole mouth and tongue, as if to savor it.) "It would never occur to a satisfied, contented man, a man unmoved by fear, to lock up someone else, or to rob someone else, or kill someone else, don't you think? Ponder that for a while, but you don't have to try too hard, it doesn't take much effort, and you'll see that the reason for all sorts of slavery, tyranny, holocausts, assassinations, repressions, wars, has to be sought in a shortage of happiness. The man who's fascinated by grasping for power, the man who's fascinated by exercising power,

118

and who holds on to power like a life raft: the man, my friend, who wants to dominate everyone else, who thinks of himself as the chosen-of-the-gods, who sincerely believes (let's concede that he's sincere, at least) that 'he has been called for a higher mission'; whatever he might look like: grandiose or insignificant, when it comes right down to it, that man is an unhappy wretch, and worse, a slave, and even a poor devil. If only he wouldn't screw everybody else so much!"

After this invective, Don Fuco seems to choke, and he is overcome by a coughing fit. When he manages to quiet the cough, he flutters a maddeningly white handkerchief around his mouth, leaving a scent of fine perfume in the air. He clears his throat. He seems to calm down. His voice has taken on the unclouded tone of familiarity. A long silence arises in the ruins of the theater, all over the city. He shrugs his shoulders. He doesn't laugh. But laughter trembles in his hands, shines in his eyes, echoes in his words, emphasizes the pallor of his skin, his lips, and, together with the afternoon wind, stirs his thin gray hair.

"I wonder whether forgetting has something to do with the climate; what do you think?" he asks without caring in the slightest about the answer. "The climate always seems to be the easiest solution: this damp heat, ay! All it lets you do is stretch out in a hammock, under a mango tree, with your fan and your glass of lemonade. This heat that has us all sunk into lethargy! Lethargy! You'd think they made up the word just for this disastrous island stuck between the Gulf of Mexico and the Caribbean Sea. So, did you know that the word 'lethargy,' just like its cousin, 'lethargic,' comes from Lethe, the goddess of forgetting, as I just said? This is one thing, my friend, on which we have to agree with the heads of state: it is necessary to remember! It must have been Renan, I'm not sure — you know, forgetting is like a virus, a curse placed on the blood — who said that nations are formed by the memories of their great deeds." He raises one hand to his lips and studies Victorio with merry attentiveness. "It seems to me I'm simplifying, if not ruining, Renan's notion, but I suppose he'd be willing to forgive me. I simply want to insist on my main idea: to dominate, heads of state legitimize themselves through heroes and their heroism, and they emphasize the brave side, the indomitable side of the people they want to subjugate, and they constantly remind them of great feats (which they exaggerate more often than not, or, let's go ahead and say it, which they invent) such as heroic acts that never happened, that were really shabby little acts that were converted through the sinister art of rewriting history into heroic acts, because, let's concede this once and for all: History is also Literature. My God, even a small child could see that much: something that never happened, told by someone who was never there."

He pauses briefly. He strums his fingers. Breathes deeply. The smell of the sea grows more intense as dusk falls. He has another coughing fit; he brings his hands to his mouth and pulls out a bone and a flower.

"That's how it is!" the clown whispers, categorically, without giving Victorio any idea what he is referring to.

> *Modesta diosa del final del día*
> *tarde consoladora, amiga grata . . .*
>
> Modest goddess of the close of day,
> consoling twilight, cherished friend . . .

recites Don Fuco in his finest register. "A lovely poem by Julia, the least well known of the Pérez sisters," he notes, and returns to silence.

"It is hard not to notice," he says at last, "that heads of state always endeavor to recall sad times, to recall heroic acts, acts of sacrifice, to go back to eras when things were very unhappy, and to emphasize heroes and martyrs, people who suffered or gave their lives. And what happens? Well, in comparison, the present looks like a panacea. Imagine, friend, if I spent the whole afternoon telling you for hours on end about the persecution of the Christians under Nero, or the history of the African slave trade, or if I spent hours some pathetic afternoon reminding you how much the Cuban people suffered under the resettlement program planned by the most sadly famous Majorcan of all Majorcans, Valeriano Weyler, you'd think your life right now were some sort of kingdom of good fortune . . . isn't it true? So I've come to the conclusion that human happiness must be sought elsewhere, that we shouldn't compare ourselves with unhappy people but with happy ones; that we shouldn't remember disasters, but the glorious good times."

Now the clown is the caricature of a head of state, touching his neck with both hands, clearing his throat. He emits a sound, a repeated syllable (pa, pa, pa), perhaps in order to check the quality of his voice.

"The beauty of the world tries to stay proportionate to the wickedness of men," he emphasizes, while opening the dressing room used by Anna Pavlova, the Great One.

Don Fuco is pale and haggard. Is something the matter with him? The dressing room in none too large, and seems much smaller because of the amount of furniture and objects that can be guessed at in the shadows. The clown takes off his shoes and places them in a basket that is tight against the wall, next to the door. Since Victorio is already barefoot, he follows him without worrying. He feels overtaken by a cheerful fear that excites him. Don Fuco turns on the light. Hundreds of sparkles flash in Victorio's eyes. As he adapts to the excessive brightness, the first thing he discovers is the great number of dresses that are hanging in the room. Dresses from every era, in every color, form, and fabric. Morning, afternoon, and evening dresses. Dresses that reflect the profusion of light in sequins, glass beads, and jewels. Dresses that turn into mighty sources of light. Victorio realizes that there are also books, jewels, papers, and objects.

★

"This is where the country's relics are kept, and kept well: the clothes of Rita Montaner, Barbarito Diez, Beny Moré, Celia Cruz, Alicia Alonso; here are the manuscripts of so many famous authors, the guitars of María Teresa Vera, Manuel Corona, Pablo Milanés, and Marta Valdés, the piano of Lecuona, keepsakes of Alicia Rico, Candita Quintana, Esther Borja, Miriam Acevedo, Iris Burguet, and Blanquita Becerra, the bloodstained shirt of Julio Antonio Mella, the likewise bloodstained tablecloth of the Lamadrid family on which Julián del Casal died, paintings by Portocarrero, Amelia, Tomás Sánchez, Acosta León, Raúl Martínez, works by Ñica Eiriz; there are lots of relics here, my friend, and if I don't mention all of them it's because I don't want to overwhelm you. But I also know that some things are missing. I dream, for example, of getting Pablo Quevedo's crystal-clear voice, though as you surely know he left no recordings behind; I wish I could have the taste of sapodilla, the smell of rain, the morning dew from the Valle de Viñales; I wish I could store the tears of some of those who took to the sea in 1994 in those unstable rafts, I wish I could keep samples of the tragic farewells in airports, the echoing of horses' hooves at the Battle of Mal Tiempo. What I need is all the relics of our country — not the ones that are considered sacred, but the others, the real ones, the profane relics, the ones that aren't epic, that don't serve as weapons of war."

6

It is much easier to get out of the theater than Victorio had guessed. All you have to do is lay down on Giselle's tomb; the weight of your body sets a complicated-looking deus ex machina in motion, lowering you into the basement, from which you can walk through narrow hallways and corridors to a small door that opens under a staircase.

This discovery takes place on one of the many days when people are marching for who-knows-what political cause. This will be the first time Victorio has left the theater since the night he arrived. He has to accompany Don Fuco to the Colón Cemetery. Chaca, a great old friend of Don Fuco, has died. The news has saddened the clown, who avers that he cannot make the trip alone. He doesn't wear his clown costume. He has given Victorio a worn leather satchel, like the ones that family doctors carried many years ago.

When he descends like Giselle in her tomb and trails through long, dark corridors, Victorio is dazzled by the brightness. He has passed through the caressing darkness into the provocative light. The walls look scorched by the excesses of light. Throughout the northern hemisphere, he thinks, fall must be beginning now, and in Havana there aren't any dead leaves (which means, among many other things, that no Jacques Prévert would write *"c'est une chanson qui nous ressemble. . ."*), no evening lights, no cool breezes, no drizzle as cool as the breezes, none of that melancholy so characteristic of fall, a melancholy that makes you want to cry and laugh. Throughout the southern hemisphere, spring must be beginning now, and in Havana there aren't any tulips, lilies, or narcissi, no migratory birds are arriving, the sun isn't burning again after long months of white and gray, because here the sun is always burning. And you don't feel the kind of desire to laugh that is frankly a desire to really laugh out loud without hiding your tears or concealing your nostalgia. No Marquis of Bradomín will come here to announce that "the cheerful and uneven ringing of the mule bells" awakens "an echo in the flowering olive grove."

It isn't spring. Or fall, either. Havana lies at a latitude that lacks any transformations. It occurred to them to locate this city on the motionless side of the world. And since it is always the same and is unfamiliar with change, to him the city feels defeated, shattered, much more so than others that are older than it and that have been just as punished by history, yet not tormented by anything quite so baneful as immobility.

Victorio has just rediscovered Havana, after a length of time that he would find it hard to specify. He discovers it in all its ugly beauty, its uncouth elegance. Since Victorio has never left the Island and doesn't know what it feels like to return, he hasn't been able to experience the true sensation of rediscovering Havana.

Together with Don Fuco he is walking into the narrow, filthy streets, not with the sorrowful emotions of someone who is coming back, but with the tingling joy of someone who is going away. It isn't spring, or fall, either; nevertheless, the day hasn't turned out hot. A breeze rustles the tops of the trees and carries the scent of the cemetery, which comes from mixing various scents, such as that of earth combined with the sweet smell of fresh-cut flowers. The breeze comes laden with revolutionary slogans or threats broadcast on loudspeakers: "Whosoever attempts to take over Cuba will reap only the dust of her soil drenched in blood, if he does not perish in the battle. We will drown ourselves in the sea before we consent to be anyone's slaves. Dear imperialists, we are absolutely unafraid of you. In this country, the order for combat is always standing. We are an invincible people. Men die, the party is immortal. Country or death. Socialism or death."

A funeral cortege enters through the huge, eclectic front gate of the Colón Cemetery. Other corteges are waiting at the round chapel for their dead to be absolved. Don Fuco and Victorio wander among marble statues — Christs with compassionate gazes, tearful angels, imploring virgins. Victorio comes to experience the great serenity that always overtakes him in cemeteries.

At last, at three o'clock sharp, here comes the cortege of the old and famous pastry maker Chaca, the Saintly Pastry Maker, as they called her, famous for her desserts, well loved in her neighborhood of Cayo Hueso, especially around the house near Callejón del Hammel where, until yesterday, people of all sorts, of every race and religion, of the most diverse cultures, would gather every afternoon to eat desserts that Chaca handed out with a smile, with that naïve expression of hers, as if she were unaware of the quality of the desserts she was giving away.

Chaca's retinue consists of a veritable multitude of blacks, Chinese, whites, mulattos, embraced by the shared misfortune of their great loss. Some of the women raise blue-sleeved wrists and sing,

Yemayá azezú, azezú Yemayá . . .

Others instead sing quietly and say their rosaries and recite Our Fathers, while there are a few who recite the twenty-third Psalm.

When she reaches the open grave, one old black woman breaks

a large clay water jug. The explosion of water blesses the ground and walls of the grave, while the old woman lifts a song in an African language.

The coffin descends into the pit with slow composure. It is felt hitting the ground, and a powerful silence spreads. It is as if everyone there were waiting for what, in the rapture of a moment, was about to happen.

With surprising agility, leaping from tomb to tomb on the tips of his ballet slippers, Don Fuco appears. This time his suit and mushroom hat are an effective sea blue. His face is coated with white makeup, and his tremendous nose gleams seashell pink. He is spinning a blue ball on the tip of his index finger. On the recently placed lid of the Saintly Pastry Maker's tomb, Don Fuco performs virtuoso *entrechats* worthy of Nijinsky, the greatest-enemy-of-the-law-of-gravity, while passing the ball from one hand to the other, and from his hands to his head.

Victorio cannot get over his astonishment at seeing the old man accomplish such feats with that aged old body, tormented by years, drudgery, and dearth. The clown's smile does not even waver from the effort. When he finishes his *entrechats,* he adopts the pose of Giovanni da Bologna's *Flying Mercury,* with the addition of the ball, which spins on the tip of his foot, raised in attitude.

Victorio finds him leaning against a pedestal that supports an archangel with fallen wings and an imploring expression. Sweating, eyes closed, Don Fuco now seems to have doubled in age. "I can't go on," he exclaims. "I'm dead, this is too much for my age." He opens his eyes and blinks several times as if the daylight bothered him. "Does it do any good?" the clown asks. "I had to do it," — Don

Fuco's voice seems to emerge from the depths of a vault, devoid of tonality — "for her, for Chaca, the finest pastry maker in the world. I don't think anyone on the planet made desserts like she did, and she gave them away, friend; she never charged a penny. She said her business was to sweeten the palate. 'Life is very bitter, Fuco,' she'd tell me, all serious, 'sweet and bitter are the most important tastes in life,' and she'd laugh, and Chaca's smile would be as sweet as her pastries, and I'd see her spend days and nights making her sponge cakes, custards, *boniatillos, cremes, majaretes,* lemon and orange pastries, *arroz con leche;* she'd give away baskets of sweets through the little window that she opens next to the door of her house.

Don Fuco looks despairingly at Victorio. The white base of his makeup is dissolving in his sweat. His teeth are no longer pearls, but green bits of underwater fossils. He has asked for a moment alone, so Victorio lets Don Fuco rest on one of the benches in the catacombs of the mausoleum for immigrants from the town of Ortigueira, and wanders aimlessly around the cemetery, which is the best way to walk through a cemetery.

Victorio likes to visit cemeteries. He enjoys the morbid pleasure of reading tombstones and epitaphs and sorrowful, genteel, and shocking verses, and of looking at names and calculating ages from the dates etched in marble. The sky has now clouded over. The clouds rush past rapidly, low and reddish. Wind rustles the treetops, stirs the faded flowers in the flower boxes, and carries the smells of jasmine, stagnant water, and earth from one end of the cemetery to the other.

Victorio enters the southern part of the cemetery, that is, the poor side, the broad and neglected region of anonymous stucco and cement tombs, the side with no mediating angels, no mourning women, no interceding virgins, no open books, no marble statues, no pietàs, and no Christs. This is an extensive region where the only luxuries are flower boxes with crude epitaphs in lettering that the rain undertakes to erase, where sometimes not even flower boxes exist: just jelly jars or olive oil cans filled with water and wildflowers.

Then he sees Salma. She is sitting on a tomb, and her eyes are red from crying. Her tears, however, do not keep her face from lighting up with a lovely smile when she notices Victorio's presence, and she shouts, "Triumpho!" as if she were at an amusement park. "Ay, Triumpho, Triumphito, what a surprise, you!"

He couldn't have imagined how a woman like Salma would be able to remember him just from seeing him once, when they had shared nothing but a bowl of soup and a few hours together one rainy night.

In one graceful leap, the young woman stands up. She plants a kiss on his cheek. He notes that she has cut her hair: now she is wearing it very short, pageboy style, so the white shocks of hair have disappeared from her head. "You look prettier this way," he observes, touching her head.

"It's so hot, you, this city's enough to roast you, so the less you have on top, don't you think?"

"What are you doing here?" he inquires.

"My mother," she says, still smiling.

"Your mother what?"

"She parked the cart."

"What do you mean?"

"Eh! What's wrong with you? What has 'parked the cart' always meant in Cuba-la-Bella, Triumpho? Or did you just get here from up North?"

"No, that's not it, Salma."

She keeps silent for a few seconds. "If you only knew, you, the phrase seems so right to me, 'park the cart'! I even think it's true, true-as-true; it's like life is this big old cart, this huge, heavy cart that they give you when you're born, like the ones the Chinese pull Europeans around with in the streets of China, yeah: you're born and they tell

128

you, 'Come on, here you go!' and bam! they foist the cart on you, and then you have to drag it around all your life, your whole life long, childhood, adulthood, old age, from when you open your eyes in the morning till you close them at night, and longer, because even when you have them closed you're still dragging your jalopy around. You think you're sleeping and resting, but wrong, boy, fucking wrong: you're still dragging that old cart from one end to the other, and it's getting heavier all the time, more loaded, because everything that happens in your life, you pile it on the old wagon they foisted on you when you were born, and so you go on for days and days, through cities and cities, bustling around the streets of life, till one day, one day you get sick and tired — you get sick of everything after a while — and you shout, 'This is the end, goddam it. I can't go on. I'm tired,' and you go, peacefully, you park the cart and wham! Zap! You disappear!"

Victorio can't help smiling. "So, your mother decided to park the cart."

"She got tired, Triumphito, she got tired, poor woman, I understand her: she couldn't go on, she was too sad."

"What did she die of?"

"Nothing, you. I'd say she died of grief, that she was too sad and her cart had gotten too heavy. The thing was, my aunt Migdalia, my father's sister, had come by my house to visit, by pure coincidence. She thought my mother looked sick, so she took her to her house in the Sierra del Arzobispo. I had disappeared — nothing new, you know? I did that a lot; you understand, Triumpho, life isn't easy, not easy at all, is it? And whenever I'd come back home my mother was always there and she'd make me some soup, so when I didn't see her that day, what a surprise! I practically went crazy, running around to every hospital I could think of, until my aunt Mary came to get me. My mother had already fallen into a coma, the doctors were talking about cerebral hemorrhages and blood irrigations, and I don't know what all. Baloney, you! The only thing doctors understand are the mechanics, the pathologies, the anatomies — veins this, liver that, respiratory tract and kidneys the other, bullshit, boy! A doctor couldn't tell you if you had sadness, or grief, or desperation, or a cart that was so heavy you just got tired, all because sadness and grief and desperation and heavy carts don't leak or hurt or get inflamed or broken; exhaustion doesn't get infected; weariness doesn't flow through your arteries, bitterness isn't made of lymph; resentment isn't composed of cells, and they can't amputate your cart, isn't that so, Triumpho? Triumphito? My mother died because she was too sad. First, my father's lousy exile. My father who used to play the New York clubs with the jazz greats. I never told Mother that my father had gotten remarried to a Dominican bolero singer, a famous woman, a lovely mulatta, Ligia Minaya was her name, a former judge who had left the law and Santo Domingo behind her to sing boleros in New York, a beautiful mulatta, that Minaya, being Dominican after all, you know? with long dresses, incredibly long, cheerful-green or malicious-green, the same shade as a bottle of Cerveza Presidente, tight dresses and enormous earrings with fake aquamarines and black gloves up to her elbows, and scandalous Dior perfumes; and I also didn't tell her that my father had, has, three sons with her, three handsome mulattos, just imagine, sons of a Dominican mulatta and a Cuban mulatto, yes, Triumpho, my half-brothers on the Dominican side in Queens, New York, capital-of-the-whole-wide-universe."

Salma's eyes are red again; she is blinking nervously. She rubs her hands sweetly along the lid of the vault, as if she were caressing her mother, and, leaning over, she kisses the shoddy granite.

"Did your brother leave?"

"Yes, child, didn't I tell you?"

"No."

"Oh, well, sorry. The night you came over, she said he was away in Viñales, remember?" She pauses before continuing. "She was lying, and lying the way you ought to lie: knowing that you're telling a lie. Chichi, my brother, hooked up with an Italian prince. I don't know if he's a prince, but he is Italian, and I know that he's into selling artworks, and he's one of the key men for those auctions they have in New York, so if he isn't a prince it doesn't matter, because as for money he's got more than enough, and he's not ugly either, mid-forties, looks like Marcello Mastroianni when Mastroianni was forty-ish, not a bad-looking guy, you; and as for Chichi, my brother, what can I tell you? Beautiful, gorgeous, divine — I wish that for just one holiday I could look like him: black hair, green eyes, long lashes, a gymnast's body without ever seeing the inside of a gym; a round, lush ass like two loaves, two real loaves, not the kind they sell in the corner store, bread kneaded with love and fine flour, and his prick is so beautiful and appetizing, it seems like it was made from honey, condensed milk, and fresh yuca dough. That's why he's been so lucky, Triumpho, because he's pretty. Beauty is the first kind of luck and it attracts all the other kinds of luck, don't you think? My little brother conquers men and women without saying a word, without doing a thing, just by appearing. The lucky bastard's got magnetism, he was born to be admired and loved, and the first woman who loved him was always my mother, more than she loved me, much more than she loved me — and just imagine if my brother Chichi isn't beautiful, because I don't mind that she loved him more, and that's because I love him more myself than anyone else in this nasty world. I'd get upset with him, I'd say terrible things to him because he'd leave home and make my mother suffer, and as soon as he looked at me with his smile or took off his clothes in front of me with that skin of his, more delicious than a *buñuelo* with slices of guava, I'd break down crying, we'd break down crying, my mother would cry, too, the two of us would be there crying, and he could do whatever he wanted with us, with his smile and his green eyes, his white, white, white skin like a *buñuelo* before you fry it, his innocent little face, his I-didn't-break-the-plate face."

Salma sighs. She gives Victorio another kiss on the cheek. "It's so good to find you, Triumphito! Some people disappear, others reappear, that's life." Two tears escape her eyes: her lips try to give the lie to them with a wonderful smile. "Yes, Triumphito dear, my brother Chichi left, went away, ran off, deserted, cut out, beat it, took off running, set out for a better life. He's not the only one, you, not the first and not the last. In Cuba everybody wants to go, getting on a plane is synonymous with winning the lottery. The only solution? Leave the Island. What do you think, Triumpho, Triumphito?"

He shrugs his shoulders. "Nothing, I don't think anything, what do you want me to think? I'm getting tired, too, girl, real tired of dragging my cart from one place to the next. Yes, Salma, I also suffer from terminal weariness and terror in the blood. My sister also ran off, she lives in St. Petersburg — no, don't be alarmed, not St. Petersburg, Russia — my sister isn't crazy; she lives in a clean, handsome town in Florida, a tranquil, maybe too tranquil, sedate town on the west coast, near Tampa. They built a museum there dedicated to Salvador Dalí, and another Museum of Fine Arts where Victoria, my sister, works as a guard, a *museum attendant.*"

"Divided families, sick country," Salma reasons.

Victorio pats her head, her masculine haircut. "Goodness, what a tremendous discovery!" he exclaims in the middle of an explosive laugh.

She pays no attention to his mockery. "My brother left for Rome and I fooled my mother, I told her Chichi was wandering around Cuba, that's why every night when I got home from work, you know, I'd ask her about my brother, 'And Chichi?' and she'd answer that he was going around, over here, over there; in Holguín, she'd tell me, Gibara, Guardalavaca, Marea del Portillo, and she'd run out of tourist centers, lots of occasions she mentioned the same place two or three times. Listen, Triumpho, if I had painted a map with the trip that Chichi was making according to my mother, it would have been the craziest itinerary, totally absurd, a lie, pure lies, bullshit, bullshit and lies. We both knew we were lying, we both knew that Chichi was in Rome in a marvelous penthouse near the Quirinal Palace where you can see the city and a half, all the way to the Vatican. There were two Chichis, Triumpho: the real Chichi that we never talked about and who we'd probably never see again, and the fake Chichi, the wanderer who was traveling all over the island, the Isle of Crap, the Screwed-over Archipelago, and nobody can put up with so much sadness, or live by fakery all the fucking time; the sadness and the fakery pile up on your cart, and your cart starts to get heavy, and heavy, and heavier, and too heavy, too fucking heavy! All that sadness makes it just too plain heavy, and you're not a mule or a cart horse. That's what happened to my mother, she was a smart little woman, her, she said 'That's enough!' and decided to park the cart. She realized she was never going to reach my brother with that cart, you, and just see if they haven't gotten tired of trying to fool us with that bitch of a phrase that all-roads-lead-to-Rome."

Don Fuco's appearance brings about a mixture of shock and joy in Salma. The clown is dressed as a sultan in a bad Hollywood movie: Damascus clothing, red turban sprinkled with false rubies, black slippers embroidered with green and gold thread. "And this charming lady?" he asks in his singsong countertenor voice.

Salma bows majestically as if she were truly standing before a sultan. It is obvious that this act of playful seriousness pleases the clown, who looks Salma over from top to bottom, searching, interested, amused. "I need," he exclaims, "a woman like the great Asmania, the consort of Pailock the Great, who would be willing to let herself disappear."

Salma laughs. "If you are able to make me appear again, I wouldn't have any problem with that," she replies, enchanted.

The clown nods. He makes short leaps, minute cabrioles that demonstrate the agility of his feet.

"If you would be kind enough to make me appear, I would be brave enough to let myself disappear," Salma insists. And she dances like a little girl.

Part Three

1

It would be safe to say that Salma feels she has entered a palace, one of the splendid palaces that Victorio only dreams about. Don Fuco proudly shows her around the place, and he squeezes her chin now and then as if she were a little girl.

The first thing she does is sit on the toilet and allow her intestines to empty themselves luxuriously, in a manner very close to religious ecstasy. Second thing, she takes a shower. Salma experiences enormous pleasure when her skin comes in contact with perfumed soap and water that is warm from hours of sitting in the sun-baked pipes. Fascinated, blissful, she sings

> *En la comarca de Su Majestad,*
> *todos repiten lo que dice el rey,*
> *él les da el agua, les da el vino y el pan*
> *pero más tarde les cobra la ley . . .*

> In the country of His Majesty
> everybody repeats what the king has to say,
> he gives them their water, their wine, and their bread,
> but later his laws will make them all pay . . .

From somewhere not far off a flute rises to accompany her voice. She sings with more brio. She steps out of the bath wet and naked, and enters the former dressing room, still singing. She finds Victorio and Don Fuco sitting on the floor Japanese-style around a table that is set with a tea service of the finest china, which they are using to serve linden, chamomile, and peppermint tea, piping hot.

"Just the thing for sultry weather," the clown explains.

Sweet, transparent, the liquid slides down her throat. One of those immortal old General Electric fans is running, a model from the Second World War. The dressing room is cooled down not only by the air blowing from the fan, but by the humming of its motor.

"My God, I never thought I could get away from Havana without getting away from Havana," Salma says, laughing, and making Don Fuco and Victorio laugh. Then, naked as she is, shameless or innocent, indifferent or childlike, she goes to the window and looks with careful admiration at Don Fuco's telescope.

Salma's presence in the ruins of the theater is another blessing for Victorio. Like a young girl, she is always cheerful and ready for any kind of game. Victorio likes to repeat, "I swear on my mother's grave that happiness exists," with an ingenuity that time and misfortune cannot bend.

For Salma, the matter is rather more simple: she feels joy, and all the rest — the reasons, explanations, relations, implications, interrogations — makes no sense.

Every morning, Salma and Victorio enjoy Don Fuco's rehearsals, watching him prepare his show. After a long meditation and concentration practice, they see him stand up, walk to center stage, sing, dance, recite poems, and perform acrobatic acts. Don Fuco imitates famous actors such as Buster Keaton, Chaplin, Cantinflas, Jacques Tati, Groucho Marx, Fernandel, and Totó. He manipulates a marionette that is a perfect reproduction of Louis Armstrong, and sings

"What a Wonderful World" with the identical voice and explosive smile of the black jazz musician.

However, the most wonderful thing is that his imitations never attempt to be exact. Don Fuco never ceases to be Don Fuco. When he is doing an imitation, he makes it obvious that he is doing an imitation; he isn't the other, but someone parodying the other. The result is an intelligent and very funny appropriation of the other, because he performs a masterly sleight of hand, which is that when he imitates one of the greats of comedy or song, you get the idea that the greats of comedy or song were the ones who had been imitating him. When, for example, he dresses in black and covers his face with unflappable white makeup, you would swear that it was Buster Keaton who had tried pretending to be Don Fuco. The confusion is astounding, entertaining! Some mornings they find themselves watching Greta Garbo in *Anna Karenina,* Giulietta Masina in *La Strada,* Lucille Ball in *I Love Lucy,* and even Rosalind Russell in *Auntie Mame.* On the stage appears the man whom Don Fuco considers the greatest tenor of the twentieth century, Alfredo Kraus. They see Arturo Toscanini appear, directing an orchestra of puppets. Fred Astaire dances with that elegant air he has of a latter-day marquis, a marquis of dance, and his feet fly over the boards, accompanied by a Ginger Rogers with a wooden body, strings, and a gauze dress. Ella Fitzgerald sings. Juliette Gréco and Amalia Rodrigues sing. On a few mornings he attains the dramatic weight of María Casares or John Gielgud. Don Fuco climbs onto the stage and is transfigured, rejuvenated; he looks nothing like the little old man who moves slowly and walks with difficulty through the ruins. And how well he handles the marionettes! He picks up a puppet and you can't tell who is moving whom.

Evenings, at the moment when the sun begins its slow retreat and the city melts away among shadows and sea mists of improbable colors, Salma and Victorio watch Don Fuco descend like Giselle in her tomb. They watch him leave. And they experience the sharp pangs of nostalgia. They know — they think they know — where he is going. He'll go to old age homes, hospitals, funeral parlors. He'll wander the most poverty-stricken streets in the city (and there are lots of poverty-stricken streets, more and more of them). He'll disappear in among the horrors of the underclass neighborhoods — El Husillo, La Timba, El Romerillo, and Zamora. He'll walk down the bridge in La Lisa, searching for the specters and *güijes* that live along the banks of the Río Quibú.

2

"Confession is a basic human need," Victorio says during one of these lonely afternoons. His voice takes on a feigned tone of ingenuousness, and it is clear that he wants to rid the phrase of its hint of ridiculous theological wisdom.

Salma nods in agreement, though she doesn't seem to be paying attention. They lie down on the boards of the stage, in the languidness of the afternoon, which for some mysterious reason is not hot. Actually, the days and nights in the theater are never hot; a breeze is always blowing here, as if these ruins were not in Havana but in the ideal meridian of an ideal geography.

Victorio says, "When I was little, my mother used to send me to a neighbor woman's house for milk. To get to her house, near the obelisk, I had to walk along the old railroad line, which passed behind the Maternity Hospital and ran through a region of backyards, pastures, stables, orchards, woods, and darkness. The shadows induced a paralyzing terror in me. I couldn't keep going; I thought I couldn't keep going; it's the same thing. Night sounds awakened to assail me. Crickets, spiders, and owls transformed their cries into shrieks and yells. Near the vinegar store, long, dark arms would always reach out to touch me, and I could hear a voice, a voice calling for me. I'd close my eyes, I could only keep going with my eyes closed, and of course I'd trip and fall in every pothole that dotted the ground; I'd hurt my legs and hands, and get up again, and become paralyzed again. I'd

recite the prayer my grandmother had taught me to ward off fear —
a useless prayer, naturally; in moments of terror, nothing does any
good. The neighbor woman lived in a little wooden house fenced off
by prickly pear cactus. The ugliest woman in the world, I used to
think. A kerosene stove had exploded in the poor woman's face while
she was cooking, and the fire, its tongues of flame, its fury, its pitilessness remained fixed forever on the perplexed face of my mother's
friend. She used to kiss me with her astounded eyes and twisted
mouth; I could feel the crags on her face, the wickedness of the
flames on her cheeks. She'd kiss me and ask me questions I didn't
know how to answer; she'd give me the jug of milk, and I'd begin the
journey home: the same arms, the same voices, the same way I had
of closing my eyelids, but now I not only had to watch my balance,
I had to balance myself with the milk jug, and when I got home my
mother never knew, never could know, what kind of battles her son
had survived."

Salma stands up, raises a hand, and declares, "Well, the paths I
was on when I was a kid were dark, but not at all like yours, and that's
the truth. They were shadowy dark, the nasty streets of the part of
Havana where I was born, by the will of God or the Devil. And me,
I associated fear with eyes — not my own eyes, you, but other
people's eyes, you know? Lots of pairs of eyes peering through window blinds, because, ay, everybody in Havana looks, know what I
mean? And the thing isn't that everybody looks, it's that everybody
judges you. They look so they can make comments, so they can catch
you. That's it: their eyes, you, their eyes like knives, their eyes sticking in your flesh, you, their eyes looking for some weakness so that
later they can tell where they found the lips of the wound, tell where
your tumors were throbbing, tell where you were hiding your weak-
nesses, so they can disclose what's about to break at any moment. Me,

just imagine! Ay, Triumphito, me, I was a girl who always had my heart between my legs. I found out real young that the center of my life throbs there, nothing else had any importance, I didn't care about the rest of my body, I hardly knew what my fingers were doing when they used to look for refuge in that damp, hungry, greedy orifice. I'd give myself pleasure, till one day, or one night, I don't know which, you, I discovered that other fingers could give me even more pleasure than my own. Fusilazo taught me — that was the nickname we'd given to my cousin Iván: Fusilazo, Gunshot, he was the one who taught me this glorious little detail. Fusilazo would come visit with his mother from Los Baños de Elguea where they lived, and we'd go get in the same bed, you, to sleep together, and as soon as we heard our mothers snoring and my brother Chichi breathing heavily, I'd open my legs so that Fusilazo could hold out his hand and let his fingers disappear into that soaking wet hole, damp with the promise of pleasure, the hole that I called 'my real-true-heart.' And Fusilazo, my cousin, he called that heart 'your mouth-down-there.' I remember him telling me, 'Let's play geography. Me, Fusilazo, I'll be Punta Brava, and you be Hoyo Colorado.' I'd start opening my legs, that is to say, my real-true-heart, to every finger that felt like penetrating it. And guess what happened, you. I discovered something so-so-so-so marvelous that I figure it must be the best, the most beautiful find of my life: I discovered something better than my own pleasure, which was the pleasure of others; since my eyes adjusted quickly to the darkness in the room, I could make out the expression of satisfaction on my cousin Fusilazo's face while he was hungrily digging into the inner secrets of my real-true-heart, and I could see his prick sticking straight up like some triumphant flagpole, a pole that I caressed with my hands to induce that magnificent eruption from all its inner volcanoes. And what do you think happened then, you? His happiness turned toward me like the dazzling light from a streetlamp reflected in the water of a mirror."

★

"I have never, girl, listen to me: never! known love," Victorio states categorically, and he tries to conceal with a smile the self-pity that sometimes attacks him. "I have never felt the delicious anguish, the gentle desperation of love, of that tormenting happiness, that ambrosia-sweet poison, that cotton-candy knife, no less deadly for all its sweetness. No, my friend, I have never known the serene disquiet with which one waits for one's beloved. And what's worse, much worse: nobody's ever waited for me with that kind of disquieted seren-ity, with the intention of disquieting my own serenity. I've never awak-ened anxiety in anyone; I've never managed to turn anyone's reason into outrage; nothing, no being, human or divine, has been struck down to his knees by lustiness before me; no loving words have ever called out for me; no angels have ever appeared at the bends in my paths — and the world, you know, is full of angels, isn't it? I, Salma, my sweet friend, have never seen my body gleaming in another man's eyes; no one's lips have ever sung the praises of any part of me; no lips have ever wanted to join with mine; no hands have desired to know the softness of my skin. I've never known love — never, neither my own nor that of other men. I've never learned what Stendhal meant by the crystallization of love. And perhaps — I've thought a lot about this — the first of my sexual experiences set the tone for all those that would follow. One can never know if things will turn out in life the way they do in superstitions, in cards, in essays, or in books."

"How old would I have been? Fourteen, fifteen years, not more. The Painter's Son was brushing up against seventeen, which is just the age for pushing hard on every door and shoving them all wide open without thinking about it. His father, the Painter, had the job of whitewashing all the poor houses in the neighborhood of Santa

Felisa. The Painter's Son helped his father, cleaning his brushes, preparing the paint, handing him paint cans, holding ladders, cleaning up the few drops that the Painter — good painter that he was! — allowed to hit the ground. I remember that when they were working, both the Painter and the Painter's Son wore only cut-off pants, and I'd look at the epiphany that was the body of the Painter's Son: God makes Himself manifest in all creation, Salma, and seventeen-year-old bodies are the parts of creation that are the worthiest vehicles for revealing the Creator. Maybe it was because of that business about the Divine Light needing perfection to reveal perfection. I admired that body as if I already understood what it really was: a sacred image. For some mysterious reason, beautiful bodies always catch sight of the bedazzled gazes that they induce around the world, no matter how slyly they are stolen; and sometimes reason isn't what calls their attention to those gazes, but some sign in their own skins, in their own forms. Something exists in themselves that's quick to let them know when the clockwork of admiration has been set in motion. And, even though it isn't always clear whether you can talk about a virtue of their bodies for catching sight of those gazes — because fascinated gazes must also have their own vivid intensities — the thing is, sweet Salma, that I was sure that the body of the Painter's Son was aware of the depth of devotion with which it was encompassed by the gaze of that boy of fourteen or fifteen years, not more, whose house he was painting; because, for some other just and mysterious reason, beautiful bodies, like God, also have the inevitable component of perversity. And I know, Salma, that you'd like to hear an example of that perversity, so let me tell you that the Painter's Son used to pee without closing the bathroom door, and he'd direct his gushing urine into the precise center of the toilet bowl, right where the water is the deepest, and in that way he managed to intensify the exultant noise of the flowing stream, since, for some reason, even though he was just brushing up on seventeen years old, the Painter's

Son understood what kind of wicked conjectures and disquieting certainties a powerful stream of urine can awaken in someone who is devoted to hanging around, to listening intently near the bathroom; and I also can't help but point out that I, being all of fifteen or fourteen years old, not more, knew how to make myself disquieted, and I knew how to decipher the coded language of a stream of urine."

"Ay, Triumpho, my Triumphito, let me tell you, after those nights with Fusilazo, my cousin from Los Baños de Elguea, I started looking for other guys who would find pleasure in me and who would spread their pleasure to me. I went around the stinking streets, you, looking for somebody I could satisfy so as to satisfy myself, and there were lots of guys ready to give me a scrap of satisfaction in passing. And as you might have guessed, the time came when doing it with their fingers wasn't enough for them. I remember the shopkeeper from the corner store, a guy they call Cuartobate, Heavy Hitter, a black man, sixty, seventy years old — older than the palm grove in Anafe, you, tall as a palm tree, brawny as a two-hundred-year-old ceiba. He carried me to the backroom of his store one afternoon, and there, on top of the sacks of rice and beans and brown sugar and the cans of mackerel, he let me know that fingers aren't the only things good for entering my 'heart,' my 'mouth-down-there.' He lay me down on a sack of rice, you, and I swear, Cuartobate, that old black man, looked like a Romeo when he was naked in my arms. I'll never forget the amazing size of his manhood, I'll never forget how he could pick me up with practically just one finger, or how, with that third arm of his, he tore me up inside, like he was ripping up a flimsy piece of tissue paper, like he had stuck some blessedly lit torch all the way into the wellspring of my guts, and set fire to my insides and to each and every one of my organs: a sweet fire, a fire that didn't do me any harm. I didn't suffer, you, I didn't suffer. All I had to do was look at Cuartobate's face — the black shopkeeper, sixty, seventy years old, older than the palm grove in Anafe, like I said — because as long as the old guy was on top of me, burying the most important member of his body in my insides, he was young again, you, I swear it, he was transfigured into the adolescent he must have been once upon a time. Each movement, each thrust of his yearning, took a ton of years off of him. He turned back into the fabulous black dockworker he had been in the thirties, back when Machado was in power, I guess, or maybe the Pentarquía, what do I know. And that old guy Cuartobate's recovered youth, and his attitude, the intensity of his pleasure, completely erased my pain, if there was any pain. That was when I learned the morbid joy he got from screwing the little white girl who could have been his granddaughter — what am I saying, his great-granddaughter! And there I was, full of thanks, grateful for the satisfaction that his satisfaction stirred in me, kissing his great big hands, which weren't hardened any longer by his years of hard work, which had turned back into the hands of a strapping lad on the Havana docks. I kissed his bronze arms, molded by unloading sacks of sugar, nice and young again, bronze again, crisscrossed by veins that were pumping his twenty-year-old's blood, you. I kissed his neck, his rejuvenated cheeks, and I let my mouth disappear in his great big mouth, in Cuartobate's broad lips, with their taste of tobacco and rum that so excited me. I mixed my sweat with the sweat of his body that came and came and tasted of jute, sugar, grass, flour, earth, onion, garlic, and sweat."

"By that time Hortensia, La Pucha, my mother, was already letting me go to the movies alone; well, actually, she'd let me go to the Lido, which was two blocks from home," Victorio resumed. "One night, pretending to be fearless, I risked sneaking off, with a pounding heart that made the risk even more attractive, all the way to Cine

Avenida, which was a little bit farther, around Calle 41, out past the Tropicana. I remember they were showing a Jacques Tati movie, *Monsieur Hulot's Holiday,* and I always loved — I still love — Jacques Tati. The theater was almost empty, as it usually is whenever the movie they're showing is fabulous. And since it was empty, it was easy for me to distinguish the close-cropped, powerful head of the Painter's Son, trying to get together with another female head. Indeed, the boy had apparently taken his girlfriend to the movies, and of course the last thing they had on their minds was to enjoy watching that hilarious actor — tall, extravagant, ridiculous, expressionless, with his little cap and his odd walk — while he walked around in the sand on the beach without saying a word, until at the end he set off a festival of fireworks. Then I remember that, after the show was over, I walked back with the cheerful kind of calm that movies leave you feeling when they've seduced you, going down the streets that lead to the Tropicana cabaret; and the thing is, right next to the Show Under the Stars there was (or is) an entrance to a narrow little alley where I could take a shortcut, which meant getting home more quickly so that I could pretend to my mother that I hadn't gone to the Cine Avenida but to the Lido. Besides, the good thing about the alley was (or is) that it was dark, that it was lit up from time to time by the colorful lights from the show, and it was also fun to listen to the deafening bands from the cabaret, the obligatorily cheerful, obligatorily likable voices of Miriam Socarrás (the most-beautiful-mulatta-in-the-world) and the other emcees and singers, who'd say, 'Welcome to *Tropicana, el* cabaret *más esplendido* in the world!' — you know how stupid or full of shit we Cubans are: for us, everything about Cuba is the most splendid, the greatest, the most beautiful, the most heroic in the world; and on the night that I'm telling you about, sweet Salma, when I was walking down the Tropicana alley, as everybody called it, I saw a figure leaning against one of the black walls that surround the cabaret, behind the clumps of oleander. At first I didn't recognize him, until the flashing red and blue lights whipped past to the easy drumbeat of tourist music, and revealed the frowning face of the Painter's Son. He didn't have to call to me for me to come obediently over to him, through the disobedient vegetation of woody ferns, garden malangas, rosebushes, and long-rooted poplars that were painted in the carnivalesque colors of the lights emanating from the cabaret. The Painter's Son had his fly open, and overflowing through it was his blessed bloom, the noblest part of his body; and his right hand was engaged in bringing a cigarette to his mouth — yes, he smoked, despite his youth — while his left hand gently moved that magnanimous prick, yes, affectionately, carefully, lightly; and I want you to know, sweet Salma, that the Painter's Son never looked at me, he didn't seem to notice I was there until I was standing close by and could hear, from the Tropicana, the most-beautiful-cabaret-in-the-world, the paradise-under-the-stars, the lovely voice of Manuel 'Puntillita' Licea singing 'El Son de la Puntillita'; and so it was that the Painter's Son tossed his cigarette away, took me by the waist, undid my belt, pulled down my pants, and I didn't get to see him but I knew that he was spitting on one of his hands and smearing his prick with saliva; I felt the coolness of the night and the heat of the prick of the Painter's Son on my bottom — a prick that was probing, searching, and since it couldn't find the place to stick in right away, the Painter's Son used his other hand, his fingers, to orient it, in such a way that one of his fingers penetrated my virgin ass, my little fifteen-year-old ass, and cleared the path, and his prick slipped in ruthlessly, almost scornfully, with a sense of victory and superiority, and I experienced a pain that wasn't pain: an intense, shooting pain that felt strangely more and more like delight. And what did I learn, sweet Salma? I learned that this was the only pain that tended toward pleasure until it was transformed into satisfaction, absolute satisfaction;

and the Painter's Son forced me to lean forward, he wrapped my waist in his arms, I felt his exhalation against the nape of my neck, the fire of his breathing, while Manuel Licea was singing

¡Ay, nena de mi vida, la puntillita . . . !

Ay, my darling little girl, the tip . . . !

while the Painter's Son was moving yearningly on top of me, for a few minutes, and I could tell he was coming because of the intensity of his panting and because I felt when his cum hit me in my darkest depths. Then he pulled out his dick, shook it hard a few times until it let out the last drop of cum, plucked a few poppy leaves to clean himself off, calm, satisfied, put his member back in his underwear, buttoned up his fly, lit a cigarette, started walking, went away, and while the audience was applauding for Miguel 'Puntillita' Licea, the Painter's Son left without turning a glance, a smile, a curse in my direction, *sans me parler, sans me regarder,* as the poet would say."

"The eyes were out and about: as soon as I left the backroom of the corner store, the whole neighborhood knew that I had been in the arms of Cuartobate, the black giant, the old shopkeeper, and that was when I understood the pernicious power of eyes that spy through the blinds of thousands and thousands of windows. That afternoon I realized it, you: every step, every gesture, every act had been observed, meticulously spied upon, precisely recorded — and not to do good, to tell the truth, but to screw you and screw you and embitter the milk of your life. That's right, Triumpho, they accused Cuartobate, the poor, magnanimous black shopkeeper, of corrupting minors. I denied it all, my love, denied it and denied it: I may have been a young thing but I was nobody's fool, and without my accusation, you'll understand, there wasn't any case, except that my reputation as a whore stuck so hard that not even the Chinese doctor could have gotten rid of it for me. My reputation was that of a whore, and the eyes that grew more and more bloodshot from watching me, the eyes that pursued me everywhere, other people's eyes, were like the eyes of the devil. And what was I supposed to do, you, in a case like that? How could I explain to them that I wasn't a whore, that I didn't charge a penny, that all I wanted was for them to take pleasure in me, that my reward was seeing them find joy? Come on, tell me: how could I explain to them that at heart it really was an act of generosity? Fourteen years old and already Salma was a whore, the whore of all whores. They gave me a horrible nickname, Triumpho, it gives me the chills just to think of it: they called me Isabelita-Bite-and-Run; that's why I erased the name Isabelita from my life. Around that time I saw a movie with a gorgeous Mexican actress and I took her name, Salma. I called myself Salma. Ay, Triumpho, my brother Chichi got into so many fights on my account . . . !

"That's how things were, terriblehorriblebloodcurdling, until El Negro Piedad, better known as Sacredshroud, showed up, and all the gossip stopped — at least, they stopped gossiping at the top of their lungs; their eyes didn't close or even move away from the blinds of all those windows: no, no way, they kept on floodlighting me; and El Negro Piedad, better known as Sacredshroud, protected me like a brother — an incestuous brother, that is. Incestuous and mercenary, because he was the one who set a fee for my satisfactions. And at first, to be honest, it didn't bother me, not at all, it didn't bother me at all: old Spaniards, Italians, Germans, white as white frogs, with spots all over their skin, cultured, with cultured sweat, strange-smelling sweat, sweat from ancient civilizations, sweat that dated from the Roman Empire and the Middle Ages — that's what El Negro Piedad, better known as Sacredshroud, told me — sweat that came from exhausted civilizations, sweat from Carthage and Tyre and Cyprus; old tourists with stinking breath, cultured breath, some of them with limp pricks that they called penises, old men with the stench of the Renaissance, throwing themselves on top of me and satisfying the boredom of Europe through me; and then, to top it all off, they'd leave El Negro Piedad, better known as Sacredshroud, the bright green of real bills — dollars, you, hard cash, freely convertible, *money-money,* that I could use to buy my mother her powdered milk, her toothpaste, her soap, her oregano, her nose drops, her deodorant, her oil, her detergent, her almond butter, her nutmeg, her shampoo, her blood pressure medicine, her 'red rags' — that's what they call beef in the black market, her mosquito repellent, and her Viennese pastry, which they sell for a lot of money, ay, you, for lots and lots of money, at Pain de Paris . . ."

3

"Why don't we go into the locked dressing rooms?" asks Salma.

They are alone. The clown has gone off clowning at a school for the mentally and physically handicapped.

Victorio tells her, no, they shouldn't enter any locked rooms: Pandora's great sin was curiosity.

She doesn't know who Pandora was, and doesn't care; she explains that she doesn't see what harm it could do to anyone to open a locked door in a building in ruins.

He tries to convince her, bringing up all the arguments about being well-educated, of having good manners.

Salma makes fun of him and counters with an equally large number of arguments: the truth is, if they are going to live in this old theater, they should get to know every inch of it.

Salma, of course, is like a little girl, and little girls tend to be hardheaded, so Victorio points out to her that the keys are hanging next to the handless clock, so she should open and go in whenever she wants; he'll stay.

She acts offended, and growls, "All right, I'll go by myself, after all, I don't need anybody to go with me, I was born by myself and I'll die by myself" (tone of dramatic comedy).

"Find something you can use to defend yourself," he warns malevolently.

She laughs defiantly and specifies that she walks with Martí, that Martí defends her wherever she might go and wherever there is danger, that trenches made of stone (or bronze) are better than trenches made of ideas.

Victorio sees that she is, in fact, holding the bronze bust of José Martí. He hears her footsteps moving off toward the other dressing rooms. It isn't that he has no curiosity. He'd also like to know what's hidden there; it's just that he knows how to control his curiosity, because there is something even stronger in him, which is fear, the fear of the unknown.

And Victorio, who lies outstretched on the *recamier,* tries to read; he cannot concentrate on what he is reading; he wonders what Salma will find when she opens the door to the dressing room of the Guignol. So the best thing, the most intelligent thing to do, he thinks, is to drop his book and go see; after all, she's right, if you live on a planet, it's so you can get to know it as well as possible. He sticks the leather bookmark in the book, stands up, and leaves the dressing room. He hasn't taken two steps when he runs into Salma. "What happened?" he asks.

She trembles, doesn't reply right away. "The Guignol's dressing room was full of people; well, not people: full of dead people," she says.

"Dead people?"

"That's what you heard, dead people, you, corpses hanging from the ceiling."

Victorio goes to the Guignol's dressing room but doesn't dare open it. No, Salma's lying, she's gotten carried away by her imagination. He returns to her, has her lie down on the *recamier* with her head on his lap. "Tell me about the dead people."

"What dead people?" she asks innocently.

To triumph in Hollywood: to have a house like Shirley MacLaine's, up on a hill, with wide decks projecting out over the

Pacific coast, the way she saw it in a magazine article (*Hola?* *Vanidades? Marie Claire?*), to have a young, rich, handsome husband, Andy Garcia or Benicio Del Toro, if possible, to be as fought over by casting directors as Julia Roberts.

In dreams that are not dreams, she envisions herself on the high seas. The Virgin — golden, radiant, blinding — appears on high. Salma becomes aware of a colossal force that is freeing her from the water and lifting her up toward the resplendent figure, so that Salma melds with the Virgin's radiance. She is certain that she is disappearing, devoured by the glare. A voice that is not a voice, of course, music that is not music either (how to explain it?) blesses her and gives her patience, and for a few moments, Salma learns what substance comprises salvation. The only terrible thing is that this kind of understanding is composed of substances that are far too fragile: fleetingness and forgetting. Afterward, all that remains in her are a few sensations, the intuition of the sort of happiness that dissolves, disappears into the folds of sleep or the traps of wakefulness, just like the image of the Virgin herself, above the deep sea of her aspirations.

Victorio holds her tight, as if he could save her from what has already happened.

"That night, I almost merged with the Virgin's radiance, and I heard *'Salma!'* Again I heard my name, and at first I thought it was Her, all goodness and love, calling me, *'Salma!'* until, when I was already too close to her incandescent glow, I realized it wasn't the Virgin's voice, and my fantasies fell apart in confusion and shadow."

She opened her eyes. "Salma!" Her mother was leaning over her. "El Negro Piedad is looking for you, darling, El Negro Piedad is looking for you," her mother was whispering.

Salma didn't move for several seconds; she was having a hard time understanding what her mother meant by those words. She got up, naked as she was, stretched, yawned, looked at herself in the mirror, and opened the door. Preceded by the penetrating fragrance of Kenzo cologne, El Negro Piedad appeared. Dressed in white. Linen shirt, linen pants, leather slippers. Alert almond eyes, gentle, smiling lips, hair cut very short. That night he wore no Santería necklaces. Tall, strong, handsome and sacred as an *orisha*. So tall, he always had to lean over to kiss Salma's lips. With the fingers of his right hand, he played with the short hairs between her legs, while with his left hand he squeezed her nipple.

"What are you doing here, guy? Didn't you say we'd have today off?" Salma asked, exaggerating her sleepiness.

He knelt to plant a kiss on Salma's navel. "There's this thing, angel, called 'imponderables,'" he pointed out, sitting down on the creaky bed. He didn't look at Salma's mother, didn't greet her, didn't notice her: he never did, as if the woman didn't exist. "We have to get going quick. Dress up."

Salma shut her eyes. Perhaps she was invoking the image of the Virgin; all she could see, however, was the light of fleeting fireworks, so she opened her eyes to the only possible reality. "Ay, sweetheart, I feel like the Cuban flag, tattered and shredded!" she exclaimed piteously.

"Well, sew the flag back together, angel, because our country looks down on us with pride; call on all your womanly strength, put on a pretty dress, comb your hair, put on some perfume, don't forget your crystal slippers, and away we go! With your charm, that's all it'll take." And he stuck out his tongue in a not exactly childish way.

Salma couldn't answer him. If El Negro Piedad ordered something, opposing him would be futile, even dangerous. She called on all her strength and began to get dressed. She felt her mother's almost useless eyes on her; they saw little, or saw nothing, but they couldn't hide their fright at what they thought they saw. She tried to pretend that she felt happy to have an excuse for going out. She improvised a glad expression.

"I even went so far as to sing,

> In the country of His Majesty
> everybody repeats what the king has to say . . .

while I stuffed myself into a tailored green dress, a crazy dress, you, shocking, provocative, a plunging neckline, it left my shoulders bare, and it isn't that I have pretty shoulders: I have young shoulders, and sometimes youth is more important than beauty, don't you think?"

For lack of jewelry, she wrapped a silk scarf around her neck, in open defiance of the heat of a Havana night. She wore black patent leather shoes with thin heels, an ancient pair from her aunt Mary. She piled on the makeup with a touch of exaggeration, outlined her eyes, rouged her cheeks, and crimsoned her lips like an aged coquette who needs to seduce an adolescent. She meant to make fun of El Negro Piedad, better known as Sacredshroud. She really didn't like excessive makeup; she loved the pallor of her face, her uncolored lips, her wide, masculine eyebrows, as well as the permanent dark circles under her eyes, which she thought lent her the air of a Mexican vamp — though men no longer liked vamps, Mexican or otherwise, but rather robust, buxom, ridiculously healthy women. She combed her long black hair with its white, or golden, or rather, golden-white highlights, and she did it up and kept it in place with a tortoiseshell hair band; and she put on a Givenchy fragrance, Fleur d'Interdit, the gift of a businessman from Bilbao who was in town selling detergent. Finally she put on her sunglasses, an excellent knockoff of Dior, which didn't make her feel any more elegant, but did make her feel safer and better masked, like a rock singer at a concert in New York's Central Park. She turned toward El Negro Piedad, better known as Sacredshroud, with her arms upraised, as if she were finishing a musical number, an odd and outdated imitation of Doris Day.

Standing up, El Negro Piedad, Sacredshroud, couldn't help laughing; he tried to control himself, which could have seemed more insulting. "You look like the countess of Revilla de Camargo," he exclaimed, doubtless having no idea who María Luisa Gómez-Mena had been.

She cared little about El Negro Piedad's joke, much less who the countess might have been. The only thing she wanted was for this torture to end, and to come back home and go to sleep on her creaking bed in the old Van Dyck photography studio.

On the ground floor of the Cacique Inn Hotel, one of the newest and most elegant hotels in the city, in El Vedado, on one of the banks of the Almendares River, close by the sea, there was (or is) the Sweet Feeling Café. As usual, even though it wasn't a weekend, the café was fairly full and bustling. It was decorated with old automobiles (Chevrolets, Fords, Buicks . . .), with helicopters, illuminated record players, neon lights, very good-looking waitresses and waiters dressed up as Natalie Wood, Sal Mineo, and Elvis Presley, with mixed perfumes and mixed drinks, and loud boleros played at top volume. This was a place where you could bask in nostalgia for the mythical Havana of Beny Moré, of El Chori and Marlon Brando, or of a Hemingway who looked more like Humphrey Bogart in *To Have and Have Not*. The results, however, couldn't have been more counterproductive. A tourist who entered the Sweet Feeling Café could have been in any city in the world. The atmosphere would be vaguely reminiscent of Havana. The Havana of clichés. As all the old-timers, who had worn linen guayaberas and savored expensive cigars in Vuelta Abajo, liked to explain, Havana in the fifties had never been like this. Havana today, much less so. There was something affected about this cheap stage design. What did Cuba's austere capital, with its dirty, desolate, dark, stifling, poor nights, have in common with this flashy production piece of colors, lights, loud music, cell phones, shimmering fabric, mojitos and Cuba libres, drunken sprees, and lots and lots of hundred-dollar bills?

Salma makes it clear that she didn't waste her precious time wondering about serious and difficult-to-answer questions. Once she had found herself there, in the Sweet Feeling Café, she'd forgotten the wretchedness of every day, the daily hunger, the dreams, and the fact that she had felt like sleeping. She'd forget everything that was bad about her life, or about life. As much as she had needed pleasure as well as money, she didn't feel capable of framing questions that might hinder delights and deals. She'd close her eyes and turn to face any feeling of estrangement or guilt.

"I felt like Cinderella on the night of the ball, and I couldn't care less if I got caught at midnight and my gown turned to rags."

Victorio takes on the role of prosecutor and reproaches her in tones of admonishment. "Eleven million Cubans were suffering while you were off having a great time in a realm of make-believe and partying."

"So? That's their problem," Salma replies, not getting the joke. "You learn to be an egotist in this life; and if not, tell me, who the hell else was going to worry about me?"

For Salma, entering the Sweet Feeling Café came to signify what entering through the door for Oscar nominees does to a Hollywood actress on the night of the award ceremony. A preamble, she believed, to what awaited her when her turn came to go out into the world. Cinderella or Salma Hayek. Same difference. Beautiful-elegant-powerful-magnetic. She and the world, both transformed: she'd leave behind the filthy, gloomy streets, descend the marble staircase, step onto the red carpet, and find herself in the middle of a festival of multicolored lights. From the moment when the maitre d' came over to greet them, all courtesy and dressed-up formality, Salma would correct her way of talking, smiling, looking, gesticulating, walking, and breathing.

"Three men were waiting for us that night," she tells Victorio.

At one of the best tables in the Sweet Feeling Café, three ruddy, red-faced men with blond hair and transparent eyes, all over sixty, one of them weighing well over three hundred pounds, sat sweating in spite of the air conditioning, and from their gestures and tones of voice, they must have been drinking Havana Club and Coca-Cola for quite some time. They greeted Sacredshroud in English, with exaggerated friendliness. In perfect English, so slightly accented that everyone who heard him was astonished, El Negro Piedad introduced Salma. She lowered her chin almost against her chest and cast her Lauren Bacall look. She stretched out her hands and wiggled her fingers like little wings. She recited the usual phrase, the one El Negro had taught her, *Jao du yu du?* which he always corrected, *How do you do?*

"I really should explain, Triumpho," Salma said, doubling over with laughter, "that one of my tricks was to pretend I was less educated than I am, and you know I'm a dunce. Sometimes I went so far that I came off like a real fool, a borderline idiot, you, and the thing is, my intuition told me, I thought I knew, that the only thing men's stupidity would appreciate would be the stupidity of women; that a male, being an idiot after all, would never put up with females who were smarter than him. That was the great lesson of Marilyn Monroe, the most womanly of all women, and Isabelita-Salma humbly adapted it to her tarnished circumstances."

The three men kissed her hands, raised the volume of their guffaws as if she had made a joke, and invited the pair to sit. Salma cast two glances: a naïve one toward the foreigners, and a complicitous one at El Negro Piedad, better known as Sacredshroud. From his glance, she would know whose side to sit at. Quickly, furtively, he moved his attractive, playful almond eyes; that was all she needed: she sat next to the old blond who weighed more than three hundred pounds. "Salma, Salma!" shouted the ruddy blonds, clapping as if the name were worthy of applause.

"They're from Hamburg — Germans," El Negro Piedad, better known as Sacredshroud, informed her with a smile meant to throw off those who didn't understand Spanish.

"I swear, that blond King Kong would rather have a hamburger with *cachú* —"

"*Ketchup*," he corrected.

"— and lots of cheese, you," she exclaimed in rapid, exaggerated Cuban Spanish, Cuban-Cuban, so there wouldn't be any chance that they could understand her, and she gave another smile for the same objective.

"*We are very happy,*" El Negro Piedad, better known as Sacredshroud, said in English, and he gazed at Salma with an endearing, sweet, happy, loving look, explaining to her in an undertone, "You're going to have to put up with that disgusting-fat-old-Nazi-from-Hamburg, my little whore — the guy's loaded with bills that have all the zeroes you could imagine."

She returned his affectionate smile and smoothly replied, "You're a son of a bitch, Negro, a disgusting, rotten shroud."

"A son of a bitch who'll lift you out of poverty," he replied tenderly.

"You'll wear me out with this lousy miserable life!" she insisted with just as much apparent adulation in her voice. "If I keep on going to bed with these German and Turkish gorillas, I'll end up preferring women, *chinito*."

"That's what I'm here for, to keep you from losing your taste for men, little girl. And let's stop talking Spanish — it's very bad manners, because these gentlemen are European and therefore very well mannered."

"If they have good manners, then I'm Princess Martha Louise of Norway, you — go fuck yourself, what the hell language do you want me to speak, my pimp?"

"Just shut up and smile, that clever tongue of yours is meant for other things. The only language you need, you can smile and speak it with another mouth, my love," he said, smoothly, and he filled their glasses with rum and improvised toast after toast, like a perfect Muscovite.

"Go see if you can find me something to smoke," threatened Salma, who didn't smoke, "because no sober woman in her right mind would touch that King Kong or the prosthesis between his legs."

Meanwhile, the Germans — enchanted, astonished, affable — were gazing at them with the faces of expeditionaries who had just disembarked in some godforsaken landing in the Amazonian jungle; faces of how-can-it-be-that-these-natives-speak-like-humans; in sum, Baron von Humboldt faces. On the stage, a contortionist was mistreating her body to the rhythm of a guaracha with a disco beat. She was forming bizarre figures with her feet, and with her mouth she was taking the dollars handed to her by the generous and respectable members of the drunken public. The Fat German rested his heavy arm on Salma's naked shoulders; she sank into her seat in embarrassment. Furious, she breathed the piercing smell of sweat from his Aryan underarm: a smell that she knew well, a smell that, for reasons she did not understand, was shared by every single European she had been unfortunate enough to have.

"Yes," Victorio admits, "I know that smell: piercing, ancient, the smell of Alexander the Great, of gladiators, of Vikings, of Kublai

Khan, of Louis XIV, a smell that has haunted their armpits since the fall of the Roman Empire, since the Middle Ages and the Crusades. In a strange, obscure way that smell is related to the Dawn of Humanity; it's also that, since they have been eating good meat, sausages and hams, and drinking excellent wines and dark beers, from the invention of the wheel up to our own day, the smell of those European underarms has achieved a pinnacle of intensity and absolute stench."

Salma is not listening to Victorio's reflections. She is telling how El Negro Piedad, better known as Sacredshroud, then draped his arms over the shoulders of the other two Germans. Of course, she knew El Negro very well, and she was certain that he was wearing Lapidus in his beatific armpits. The exquisite Europeans stank like stables; the third-world Chinese-mulatto smelled of celestial fragrances.

Meanwhile, the Fat German was giving Salma his own glass to drink from, and squeezing her against him. She felt herself sinking into a filthy, wet mattress. The conversation was all in English. Salma explains to Victorio that she would laugh whenever she guessed that she should laugh, and nod whenever she guessed she should nod. She appeared interested, and of course she looked ridiculous for laughing and appearing interested. She was sober and tired: a fatal combination. The tiredness sharpened her senses. She drank as little as possible. She couldn't bear alcoholic beverages. She found alcoholics even harder to bear. She profoundly hated drinkers and smokers. El Negro Piedad shared her ethics; he never drank, under any circumstances; he didn't smoke tobacco, much less marijuana; he didn't snort coke, and didn't go for any of the artificial paradises. He could be happy without resorting to artificial means, as he would almost humbly say. And the truth was that, when he left the cabarets, the clubs, the hotels, the discos, El Negro Piedad, better known as Sacredshroud, led a radically austere life of physical exercise, meditation, asanas, yin-yang, incense, healthy diets, and things like that. An Afro-Cuban Buddhist, he liked to call himself, serious and smiling.

El Negro had advised (ordered) Salma never to drink while she was working. She had no need for such a recommendation; drinking made her very queasy, so, like him, she pretended to drink and pretended she was getting drunk. "They call that 'playing dead to see what kind of funeral you'll get,'" Salma says sarcastically. If the Germans, Spaniards, and Italians hadn't been concentrating so hard on their own pleasure, they would have noticed that the level of the rum in Salma's and El Negro's glasses never varied. They would have noticed, moreover, that there was something fake about their cheerfulness. Sometimes El Negro could even seem like a real drunk — delirious, grinning broadly, making clumsy moves. Salma, who knew him, admired his histrionics and would tell him, "You should have been an actor." You could see his intelligence, the clarity of thought in his eyes, because his eyes were always watchful. Without losing their cheerfulness and childish grace, his eyes observed, measured, calculated. Sometimes Salma thought that his eyes never came into play, not even at the moment he was making love with her — another thing that he accomplished, according to Salma, with unparalleled virtuosity.

"The Afro-Cuban Buddhist," she says, "can prolong his pleasure or cut it short according to his whims. He has total control over his body and his emotions, you; every one of his members, including the vigorous manhood between his legs, responds to his will. I've never known a man who was so unbreakable, so invulnerable, so confident of himself and of the path he's on."

As soon as the "clients" went away, El Negro Piedad, better known as Sacredshroud, would regain his composure. At those moments he seemed almost melancholy. Salma could have sworn that under his libertine appearance lurked the soul of a Quaker, or something even more serious and mysterious and unknown.

"I don't know, you, I don't know who he is, who's hiding behind the unbeatable body of El Negro Piedad."

At that very instant, while the Fat German, the one with the strong smell under his arms, was squeezing her against him, Salma in turn sneaked a peek at El Negro sitting, playful and affectionate, with the other two Germans from Hamburg; generous, eager to please, he let himself be admired ingenuously, humbly, as if he didn't understand why they were admiring him.

The contortionist had disappeared from the stage to make room for a fat and hideous bolero singer, her hair done up in a bun with golden ribbons, wearing a lamé dress that was also gold and spangled with sequins, wearing so much makeup she could barely move, with beads of sweat on top of the makeup. Thank God, the *bolerista*'s voice was imposing, extraordinary, sweet, caressing, between declamation and singing. Electrified by the singer's voice, the audience fell into a churchly silence. All eyes were on the hideous fat lady, because their eyes were not "seeing," their eyes were "hearing," along with the rest of their senses. Salma took advantage of this to run off to the bathroom; she had been peeing in her underpants for some time. She walked past the bar — crowded, bustling. She was about to cut through to the hallway leading to the bathrooms, when a tall, lovely black woman, dressed all in blue like the Virgin of Regla, stopped her by her arm: "Don't go," she ordered.

"Is the fox on the loose?" asked Salma, knowing full well that the answer would be in the affirmative.

"And how, *china,* so get lost!" the woman replied.

Salma noticed that, yes, there was a certain commotion around the ladies' room. Yep, the police had started up their harassment again. They were doing it without inviting people's attention, so as not to alarm the tourists. But once you got inside the bathroom — Salma knew from experience — they'd shove you, insult you, mistreat you, take away your identity card, and you'd spend the night on a gray, gray granite bench in a police station, and given a fine and police file. "Go ahead, honey, run tell the others," demanded the beautiful black woman in the blue dress.

Salma went up to the first table she saw, pretended that she knew the young woman who was enjoying a good time there, and whispered in her ear, "Listen, girl, the fox is on the loose."

The young woman got up and went in turn to another table, while Salma continued with the cheek-kisses and the whispers: "Listen, girl (or boy, depending), the fox is on the loose." A general mobilization of boys and girls followed, all kissing others, whether they knew them or not, and declaring that the fox was on the loose, while the *bolerista* intoned in her enchanting voice,

Habrá paz y felicidad en nuestro querer . . .

Our love will find us peace and happiness . . .

Salma sank back into her seat. El Negro Piedad, better known as Sacredshroud, already suspected the news. "The fox?"

"Ugh, loose," replied Salma in a sigh mixed with anger, exhaustion, loathing, even a desire to cry. "The fox is loose and no rest for the prey."

Sacredshroud didn't even blink.

She repeated her gesture of annoyance: she was sick of the police always running after them, as if they were the cause of the problem.

"It's the same old story," Salma explains to Victorio, "like the guy who threw out the sofa where his wife had committed adultery."

"Come on! Let's go!" Without losing his composure, El Negro Piedad directed the Germans in his delicious English; she saw him smiling, fascinating, handsome, sure of himself, tipsy from all the rum he hadn't drunk. Salma couldn't imagine what fib he was inventing;

she knew that they stood up and that, in the company of the Germans (Salma has never been able to understand how such horrendously ugly people could allow themselves the luxury of being racists), they left the Sweet Feeling Café, and the "fox" couldn't stop them.

"In Cuba, you know, Triumpho, in Cuba-la-Bella, the greatest-of-the-Great Antilles, the most-beautiful-land-seen-by-human-eyes, the Heart-of-Our-America, the First-Free-Territory-of-America, we Cubans have always been third-class, or fourth-class, or fifth-class citizens," Salma observes without lowering her voice, since inside the ruins of the Pequeño Liceo of Havana there is no point in being afraid. "You know," and she points at Victorio with an admonishing index finger, "that hotel rooms are off-limits to us Cubans, whether it's a luxury hotel or a mediocre dive." Her eyes are gleaming with bitterness. "Not even with money," she insists indignantly, "not even with money! We can't rent a room in any hotel that has more than half a star."

El Negro Piedad, better known as Sacredshroud, clever as he is, kept two rooms permanently rented in the house of Kyra Kyralina. She couldn't really have been named Kyra Kyralina, of course; no one knew the real name of the sad Rumanian soprano who was married to a Cuban who had studied chemical engineering at the University of Bucharest. She had been living in Havana for more than thirty years, directing a choir called Danubian Nights, Aficionados of Bel Canto. No one knew how Kyra Kyralina had come to live in a penthouse with nine bedrooms, rooftop terraces, a swimming pool, and ocean views, which before the revolution had belonged to a poet of agreeable love verses who came from a moneyed family, an obsolete modernist, enormously popular among the readers of *Vanidades*, an undistinguished rival of José Ángel Buesa. Kyra Kyralina had set up the two rooms in the former servants' quarters for rental, and they had no reason to envy the rooms of the Hotel Nacional or of any of the Meliá hotels that were springing up every day in ever-greater profusion all around the city. Black porcelain bathrooms, curtains, air conditioning, first-class furniture, round bed, strategically placed mirrors, telephone, minibar, cable television, framed reproductions of paintings by Dutch masters, and music from Radio Taíno, the tourists' station. The only detail that spoke of the owner's origins was, on the night table, a small bronze statue of Nicolae Ceausescu.

Kyra Kyralina received them with an arpeggio of laughter; her soprano voice was very feeble now, and she endeavored to make her "Rumanian" Spanish seem italianate instead. The expected gold tooth shone in the back of her mouth, a sign of Slavic or Soviet influences; she wore her hair saffron red, her fingers weighed down with rings, and her nails so long and blackened that they seemed false; a black velveteen ribbon hid the wrinkles on her neck; her incredibly high heels contrasted with her silk house robe with enormous flowers in an astonishing yellow. She always made this operatic kind of entrance.

While Salma walked into one room with the Fat German, she saw Sacredshroud entering the other room with the other pair. "That was the first time," she reveals to Victorio, "that I saw El Negro go off with a man, much less with two."

Once they were in the room, the Fat German's plan was to kiss her. She turned aside — coquettishly, of course, so as not to offend him. "First, a spot of rum," she asked, with a *fille mal gardée* look on her face, and since she could see that the fellow didn't understand her, she tried to use her English: "Primero, *ferst, yoo an mee, wee dreenk ron, oll rye?*"

The German couldn't restrain his laughter; his swollen belly leapt and vibrated as if it were pumped full of some kind of explosive gas. He understood what she needed, however. Salma prepared a drink of rum and, on the sly, as she had seen it done in so many movies, dropped in two diazepam pills. *Dear Virgin, make him fall asleep quickly,* she prayed. She let the pills dissolve. She pretended she was drinking, and gave the German several sips, using all the charm she could summon. "*Bebe rápido,* mye mann, hurree hurree drinkit queek, mye hansohm mann." He obeyed; he was drowning in laughter. Salma laughed, too. She began the slow game of stripping his clothes off of him. The German's body boasted an unreal whiteness, so white he was almost pink, like a species of pig, Salma thought. His protruding tits fell on top of his equally protruding belly. The German was a sweaty, hairless hulk that roused her to a sudden hatred, which she attempted to convert into greater sweetness. His pelvis, too, was nearly hairless, and the few short hairs he had were blond, nearly white. She was surprised, and not unpleasantly (the truth be told), by the enormous magnitude of his virilely Prussian member, so youthful and impertinent that it seemed to have nothing in common with the rest of his obese body.

"His member attained a rare state of perfection, of beauty," she exclaims.

"They say that's how Germans are, that there's a similarity between pure Germans and pure blacks. Let's see what the fans of racial discrimination have to say about that," Victorio replies.

Lying down, the Fat German looked like one of those volcanic islands that erupt in the middle of the ocean. "Closs yoor ice," she told him in her daintiest voice. He understood her and closed his eyes. She began to knead the German's splendid masculinity. Between his age, his exhaustion, and the alcohol he had drunk, Salma wasn't able to make the prodigy completely hard. Luckily, she thought. She still thinks. She caressed his equally enormous, healthy, handsome balls. She petted him affectionately as a dove. Her hand ran without malice over his thighs, his calves, the slenderest parts of that body; over his monumental belly, his arms with their gangly muscles. Her sweet hand was attempting not to excite him but to make him drowsy. At last, at some point she heard his regular, deep breaths, turning into snores. With great relief, she rose from the bed, looked at herself in the mirror, sad and contented, anguished and happy. "This has been a great day, Salma, my little Salmita," she tried to assure the disconsolate image in the mirror. She heard his perfect, harmonious, sonorous German snores and got ready to leave. She quietly opened the door. Outside in the hallway it seemed silent enough. The darkness made her feel safe. She turned back to look upon the volcanic island in the white, round ocean of the bed. She saw the clothes lying in disarray on the carpeted floor. A sudden idea hit her. She closed the door. She went to the Fat German's pants and looked in his back pockets for the billfold. There it was, big and made of high-quality leather. She opened it. It was stuffed with credit cards and hundred-dollar bills. Salma took two of the bills. She stood there for a few seconds, uncertain. She returned one bill to the billfold and hid the other in her shoe. She went back to the door. The fat old European was sleeping delightfully, his mouth open, his eyes not entirely shut. Salma left the room in absolute silence. She reached the elevator door with her heart pounding. It took centuries for the elevator to arrive. She entered, feeling certain that someone would call out to her or grab her by the arm. Kyra Kyralina might sing a middle C of alarm. Nothing happened. The elevator brought her calmly down to the bottom floor, to the parking garage. Agile and silent, Salma made it to the sidewalk. She ran to the corner. Finding herself free and blessed by the streetlamps on Calle Linea, she looked up at the dark night sky and said, "Forgive me, dear Virgin, he has more than I do." It was an attempt to justify herself before that immensity, animated by uncountable galaxies.

★

Victorio caresses Salma's head. It has gotten late in the ruined playhouse. The last shafts of light are again falling to good effect on the boards of the stage and plunging it into an implausible atmosphere of chiaroscuros. Whether out of fear or out of nostalgia, Salma sings

> *No le abras la puerta*
> *a tu soledad,*
> *la siudad está muerta,*
> *pero qué más da . . .*

> Don't open up the door
> to your loneliness,
> the city is dead,
> but why should you care . . .

Sometimes she likes to pick up the bronze bust of José Martí, as she does now, and hold it high, brandishing it as if she had a grenade in her hand. "With this bronze head," she declares, "there won't be an enemy left alive. Trenches made of stone are better than trenches made of ideas," she repeats. She sighs and caresses the bronze head. "I wish I could have gone back home!" Salma says after an incalculable time. "Walk in like nothing had happened, pour a bucket of cold water over my sweaty body, eat a bowl of vegetable soup, talk with my mother, ask about Chichi, go to sleep!"

What kept her from going home was her greater fear of running into El Negro Piedad. Salma would head off to Cuatro Caminos and wander around the farmers' market, and from there to La Esquina de Tejas, where a shoeshine boy (specializing in white shoes) would talk with her, and an herb seller, tall as a palm tree, with beautiful, gleaming jet-black skin, and the old-age-blue eyes of a prophetess, would give Salma a few twigs of *vencedor* and tell her, "May you find tranquillity, my daughter." Salma would continue down to Calle Agua

Dulce. In the old Quinta Dependencia clinic she'd mix in with the patients and spend the day in the cool shade of lemon, mango, and avocado trees. One afternoon she felt so reckless that she dared to walk up Belascoaín, turn onto Calle Reina, and go into the church.

"It was," she says, "as if I had come to the end of a well-planned trip."

She entered not knowing why, and yet with a sense of hope.

"Hope?"

Salma shrugs.

She didn't usually enter churches. She felt overawed and somehow protected by the somber silence of the nave, the solemn odor of incense, the humid coolness emanating from the walls, the lovely colors into which the sun seemed to break through the stained-glass windows above the high altar. She wanted to approach the crucified Christ on the high altar, with that lovely face of desperate resignation and those eyes, which couldn't understand the reason for so much suffering, turned heavenward. She tried to cross herself. She couldn't remember whether you did it with the right hand or the left, whether you did it starting from forehead to heart or from heart to forehead. A woman was sleeping on the front pew. It caught her eye that the woman was not badly dressed or dirty and that she had with her an immense leather suitcase covered in old stickers for Air France, Pan American, KLM, Aerovías Q, as well as that she was keeping the light from the stained-glass windows off her face with a beautiful silk shawl. The image of the sleeping woman made Salma feel the burden of her exhaustion. An uncontrollable urge came over her to lie down on one of those comfortable church pews and sleep, too, sleep, sleep, sleep, that's it, sleep. She found a half-hidden pew under a column on which you could see a Christ praying on the Mount of Olives. Moved as much by hope as by exhaustion, she lay down on the pew.

"I fell asleep, Triumphito, and that was when I dreamed of you and of my brother Chichi. A very odd dream, because I had only seen you once, and if you're wondering how I knew it was you, let me tell you: simple, you, real simple. We were standing in the rain, just like on that night, sheltered under the arch in the city wall; I had lost a shoe and I was looking for it, and you told me, 'Don't look for it, it doesn't matter anymore,' and suddenly we were standing on the seashore — I don't know how or why, you, you know what dreams are like, don't you? And there was a rowboat by the shore, with some man in it I didn't recognize, and my brother Chichi, who hugged me, happy like crazy, you, so happy that his happiness seemed like sadness."

Salma tells how she and Victorio entered the warm water, walked all the way to the boat, and Chichi and the oarsman together helped them get aboard. The sea was calm. They lost sight of the shore. The lights of Havana seemed like remote glimmerings from other distant cosmic agglomerations. They found themselves in a black, impotent hole. The sea at night seemed nothing like the sea in the daytime; the sea at night is like an abyss: there are unfathomable chasms within it. There was nothing in the sea other than night. They felt it, they knew it. There was no way to search in their memories for this darkest darkness, impossible to resort to the storehouse of memory where darknesses, lived and not lived, are hoarded. No matter how long you searched and searched, you'd never find a darkness comparable to this. The darkness of the sea is a one-of-a-kind darkness, unlike any other. Even in the gloomiest site on earth, you still have your feet and the solid ground, and you still have certainty there under the soles of your shoes; the gloomiest site at sea is much gloomier than the murkiest places on earth. To top it off, it lacks conviction and firmness. There is no darkness, real or imaginary, anything like the darkness of the sea. Not only is it total, it is also aimless. Salma folds her arms over her crossed legs, huddling as if she felt cold. She feels cold, and afraid.

"Yes, I felt afraid, Triumpho, but not afraid of drowning. You, I remember you were sitting there calmly, holding my shoe in your hand."

Salma says that at some point they saw lots of boats, barges, smashed rowboats, broken rafts shattered from long voyages, inner tubes from trucks, all traveling along with them. Silent beings were following the same route. Chichi nervously ordered, "Don't look at them, don't pay any attention, don't even think of looking, keep your gaze straight ahead, let's mind our own business."

"They were drowned men, Triumphito. I don't know why we knew that they were drowned, but they were."

Drowned men, who came out to guide navigators along a good route and ended up guiding them to the worst. Yet they were not evil spirits: their intentions weren't bad. They tried to help, only they couldn't. How much can you expect from an army of dead rafters?

"In the blackness of one of the rafts, I thought I could make out a little girl, and she was singing, and I couldn't hear the song, and you were sobbing, Triumphito, and I couldn't hear your sobs — it was awful! — and we tried to touch each other but our hands passed through our bodies like they were passing through air or through light, and that was when I felt a soft pressure on my shoulder."

A young woman, as young as Salma, perhaps younger, practically a girl, told her, "Come, please, don't stay there." Salma saw that it was a nun wearing a white habit and a silver crucifix. She understood that they had turned on the lights in the church, perhaps to begin the Mass, and that the nave was filling with poorly dressed old people, taking tenuous, sullen steps, steps that, after so many failures of history, had lost all hope for human justice and sought the ever more comforting help of a God: because men, no matter how much they try to paint themselves as men of the gods, always betray; the gods, never.

Perplexed, not totally awake, Salma rose from the pew. She followed the nun through one of the tall side doors. They came out into the lovely cloister, where the vegetation possessed the urgent green of patios where the sun barely shines, where the humidity of Havana becomes even more humid. Salma admired the radiance of the worn stone paving. They went up a lateral staircase that also gleamed. They reached a dining room. At one of the tables she saw the woman with the suitcase and the silk shawl. Salma smiled and greeted her like an old friend. With a gesture of disappointment, or of exhaustion, weariness, or debility, the woman attempted to respond to her signal: she could barely close her mouth.

The nun pointed out a table to Selma, and ordered her sweetly, "You will have some lentil stew." The nun brought a bread basket and served a large bowl of lentils with vegetables, beef, ham, and the strong flavor of onions and garlic. For Salma, it tasted like heaven. In a large polished, elegant crystal glass, Salma savored a tamarind drink for the first time in her life. The nun watched her eat with a smile of approval, perhaps with a touch of superiority: sometimes, practicing charity makes us see how much we have and how fortunate we are compared with those who receive our gifts. Salma didn't know how to thank her. She took the hundred-dollar bill from her shoe and, when the nun was looking the other way, placed it under her empty plate.

"Would you mind telling me," Salma asks, quickly forgetting the story she has been recounting and looking at her hands with a baffled expression on her face, "what they mean when they say that the present isn't important, and that the only thing that matters is the future?"

Victorio smiles, shrugs, makes faces that are supposed to mean that he doesn't understand either.

"The present time is for the struggle: the future is ours! In other words, what we get is the struggle, because the future is nothing, and if it is anything, nobody knows anything about it, so the really-real reality is struggle and what's really ours is *nothing!* Unreality!"

"That statement," Victorio points out, "reminds me of the posters that storekeepers used to hang in their store windows (in the remote era when storekeepers owned their own stores), the posters that said 'No credit today; we only give credit tomorrow,' with the result that every time you went to the store, today was today, and to-morrow would come tomorrow, and as for buying something on credit: never! It's the same thing, it certainly is: 'The present time is for the struggle,' but nobody could guess how long that struggle might last, and as for 'the future is ours,' ugh! You can't touch, you can't grab, you can't know the future!"

"And what do you think they mean when they ask you to bleed yourself dry in the present so that you can have a better future?"

"Well, I don't know, I don't know, the storekeepers were just making a joke, they were using the charm of humor to make the point that they'd never sell anything on credit. I don't think it's likely that the spiritual guides of the people have the objective in mind, be-cause, you know, as far as jokes, humor, and laughter go — no, they don't go in for happiness, for making people laugh."

"Are they trying to lull us to sleep, like the Christians with their story of heaven?"

"That must be it. Look, don't rack your brain over it; we suffer enough from those fine folks without having to put ourselves in their places, too, and trying to understand what they do and why. I think they just like power, and anybody who gets a taste of power will in-vent the most preposterous formulas in order to hold on to it."

"Hey, you, you're catching on."

"Sometimes an angel enlightens me. I was ten or eleven years old when my mamá took me to catechism behind Papá Robespierre's back. Right there in the chapel of the San Rafael hospice–clinic, a tender little old nun, the Platonic idea of a nun, from the Carmelite order, would be my guess, prepared me for my First Communion. I didn't understand that religion. I never understood religion — not that one, and not any other, either, to tell the truth. It isn't that I don't believe in God. I've always been too vulnerable not to believe in God; but on the other hand, I did understand that every religion was quite a ways beneath my concept of God. For example, how could you believe in that strange separation between the 'vale of tears' here and the 'promised paradise' to come? It's clear, it's utterly clear: if I was born — I thought, I think, I'll always think — if I was born, I had to be happy here and now, and not have to go around hoping for some doubtful paradise. But I always liked the church's pomp, Bach's music, Mozart's *Requiem,* Giotto's paintings, Tiepolo's apotheosis, Bernini's colonnade, Narciso Tomé's *Transparente,* the potent silence of the naves, Michelangelo's *Pietà,* the smell of incense: sure, because all those things speak of the soul, of the spirit, of the unitive way and all that, right; all these things are able to get straight to the senses. So, fine, and then what happened? Ah! Well, one day the revolution triumphed and they started getting rid of the churches and for heaven they substituted 'the future,' for 'the next world' they gave us unforeseeable futures, utopian futures, just as illusory as 'the promised paradise,' that is to say: come on, guys, start suffering! Put up stoically with the hardships of the present, because the good stuff is coming after you all die, and after your children's children's children die! Bullshit. For God they substituted the Idea, the Ideal, History, how should I know what all! For the saints, they substituted the heroes. Ay, poor heroes! I don't know if the saints wanted to be saints, or the heroes, heroes. They couldn't have cared, it couldn't have mattered to them, and you know why? Because their present was for the struggle, and the future that was in store for them was sainthood or heroism, that is, nothingness. Nothingness! Doesn't it make you laugh? Did you ever believe that fraud? And what can you tell me about equality, the idea that we're all equal? Be honest, doesn't it make you laugh?"

★

Salma says that she left the church, faced the night, and felt that her eyes shone with unaccustomed peace, that her lips formed a sedate smile, that her arms were swinging placidly, and that her footsteps were taking on a long, slow rhythm.

Salma says that her whole being radiated a harmony which, like all harmonies, was apparent to everyone.

"Ay, Triumpho, I swear to you that when I walked the whole length of Calle Reina, all the pedestrians made way for me reverently, the young guys that passed by looked at me respectfully, the rudest fellows bowed to greet me."

Salma judged herself happily immaterial, as if she weren't walking down one of the filthiest streets in one of the filthiest cities. She was walking on air, that is, on heaven: a touch of the divine had rubbed off on her. She had nothing to do with the shortcomings, the poverty, the misfortunes of Havana.

This blessedness came crashing noisily, painfully to the ground when she reached the corner where the old Van Dyck photography studio stood. Salma says that she looked in every direction: in every cranny she sensed the lurking shadow of El Negro Piedad. Once more she saw the Fat German lying on the bed like an immense volcanic island rising up in the ocean. She reproached herself for her recklessness in venturing home; but since she had come this far, and was already here, the best thing to do would be to go in quickly, without thinking twice about it.

Salma says that the door was ajar and the room was dark. She turned on the flickering light of the porcelain Buddha lamp. *Mamá*, she called, *Mamá*. A pointless call, given that the house was a photography studio converted into a single room, with three dirty, disordered beds, and the doorless wardrobes, the cardboard boxes, the kerosene stove, the primitive Singer sewing machine. And the photographs, of course: the tinted photographs of so many unknown people, which served to hide the damp stains on the walls.

Her mother wasn't there. A shock: her mother wasn't there. A knot formed in the pit of her stomach, the knot that always formed when she foresaw some sort of danger. Mamá, damn it! she called again. She suffered the exact opposite of what she had just experienced on Calle Reina: now the law of gravity seemed to be multiplying, and something was calling her toward the floor, toward the ground. She turned off the miserable light of the lamp. Surrounded by darkness, she let herself sink onto the bed and wondered, "Now where do I go? What do I do?" She didn't have the slightest idea.

Salma goes to the spot where Don Fuco has hung the chains of Plácido, the poet. She returns with them tightened around her ankles and wrists. "A good magic act would be to break these chains," she says, and jingling, she sings again,

> *Y siempre fue así*
> *y eso tú lo sabes,*
> *que la libertad sólo existe*
> *cuando no es de nadie.*
> *Desde que existe el mundo*
> *hay una cosa cierta:*
> *unos hacen los muros*
> *y otros las puertas.*

That's the way it's always been,
you know it very well:
the only kind of freedom
is the kind nobody owns.
Long as the world's been 'round,
only one thing's been for sure:
some people put up walls
and others make the doors.

In the old photography studio, the dirt had accumulated, so it was clear that her mother had been gone for some time. A spider had even spun a web inside the coffee can. As for Salma herself, did she have any idea of how long she had been away from home, how long it had been since she had seen her mother?

She gathered water in a rusted olive oil can and took a bath with a bar of soap; in spite of it all, this consoled her. She lay down on the creaky old bed. She wanted to sleep, to disappear into dreams; whenever something was tormenting her, Salma only knew one way of avoiding reality, sleep. As soon as she lay down, naked and wet, she lost the link with the thing that was assailing her, the thing she wouldn't have dared to call "reality." She dreamed that her back was being caressed. Her back was being caressed so much that she stopped dreaming and woke up to find that, in fact, her back was being caressed. She opened her eyes. Sacredshroud was there, naked, on top of her. Salma says that she felt a shudder of joy, a delight which, she noticed, was composed of fear and pleasure — words that aren't as far separated as is usually supposed.

El Negro appeared tender. His dark almond eyes hadn't lost their constant gleam of childish cheerfulness. Sometimes, like now, Salma came to believe that Sacredshroud was really in love with her. His lips smiled. His whole irresistible body seemed to protect her. "My girl, my little lost girl," he formulated sweetly, so sweetly. He began to caress her backside, the loveliest part of her feminine body. Something told her he was not caressing it with his hands. She recalled how much he liked her skin to react visibly. "God," Salma thought, implored, cried, screamed, "why do I like it so much?" The scent of that one-of-a-kind breath reached her. His breath showed that El Negro's body was even more perfect on the inside. His tongue traced spirals around her ear, ran down her back, again reached her backside where it began to move more rapidly; it found the best, most secluded spot of her body, "your finest ass–pect," as he would say.

"How he liked to trace the outlines of my ass with his tongue!" she recalls, her voice glowing with something akin to pleasure, fear, and nostalgia.

He softly turned her over, looked at her with the clemency of his beautiful eyes, though he couldn't manage to make them reflect as much tenderness as he could demonstrate with his hands and the rest of his body. His mouth — hearty, humid, reddened — went to her small nipples. Salma's hands, apparently needing to feel hardness, went in search of the center of El Negro's body, the place where all his blood was concentrating. Realizing this, he moved his pelvis up so that she could touch it. He penetrated her with the amazing mixture of brutality and exquisiteness, of impiety and mercy, that was his most accomplished skill, his greatest refinement. The movements of his hips took on, as always, a rhythm that almost seemed like laziness, a torturous cadence, slow and musical. She never would have wanted it to stop, and El Negro Piedad, better known as Sacredshroud, never did stop. He enjoyed his absolute dominance over his gratification, over his rhythm, over his demon; and he had another divine gift or infernal grace as well: an awareness of the precise moment when he should let loose. He stayed on top of her for a while. He was very careful to respect the other's pleasure as long as possible. Then he straightened up; calmly, languidly he pulled out his long member, gleaming with many mixed essences, and wiped it on the sheet with gestures that never seemed disgusting.

"Even when he wiped his prick on the sheets he did it elegantly, you; he cleaned it carefully, meticulously, because he gave (or gives) a good fuck, like a good Cuban, and like a good Cuban he was (or is) squeamish: everything disgusts him."

He completed his hygienic operations, stared at Salma with

childish eyes, with amused and roguish eyes, and exclaimed, "So my little whore turned out to be a thief." He raised his heavy hand, and then and there he vented his fury on her face. Salma closed her eyes, because of the pain and because she was ready to let herself be beaten: what else could she do? Experience had taught her that she would come out the better for it if she didn't defend herself.

4

Don Fuco is massaging Chinese ointment into the soles of his feet. He says that this relieves the tensions in his body and soul, which is the same thing: body and soul are the same.

Salma is polishing the bronze bust of José Martí, because the clean bronze gleams like gold.

Victorio, who has remained lying down on the stage, stands up. He is seen marching to the back of the stage, where a feeble, distant light is being projected, creating an ominous set design on the tattered back curtain. Victorio lifts up his arms and recites in a powerful, lovely voice:

> *Dichoso el árbol que es apenas sensitivo,*
> *y más la piedra dura, porque ésta ya no siente,*
> *pues no hay dolor más grande que el dolor de ser vivo*
> *ni mayor pesadumbre que la vida consciente.*
>
> Happy is the tree, which can scarcely be called sensitive;
> happier still hard stone, because it is devoid of senses:
> for no grief can be greater than the grief of being alive,
> nor any sorrow greater than the life of consciousness.

He is making what he imagines to be an intelligent and theatrical pause before continuing the poem, when he hears his two companions laughing heartily. Salma collapses on the boards of the stage, her shoulders aquiver. Don Fuco laughs harder than Victorio has ever seen him laugh, his hands clasped in front of his face, without removing his gaze from Victorio, his eyes wide with surprise.

Victorio undergoes a series of confused reactions that take him from perplexity to disappointment, from disappointment to jubilation. For a few brief moments, he sees himself in the middle of the affected yet natural design of the stage. He has gone from reciting the pessimistic alexandrines of Rubén Darío to breaking out laughing, himself, enjoying himself at his own expense.

What is the reason behind their uncontrollable laughter at these serious verses? The humor does not lie, of course, in the magnificent alexandrines. Nor is there anything about Victorio — Victorio's seriousness, the pathos of his image half dissolved in shadow — that would move you to laughter. Perhaps the key is the way these two kinds of seriousness are conjoined. Maybe the grimness of the alexandrines, joined to the austerity of the performer, is what evokes the spark of humor, like two stones struck together. It could be a matter of the force evoked by the disillusionment of the verses, added to the force implicit in the sorrowful manner of the recitation, that somehow creates a force with the opposite sign. All that's certain is the forthright, enchanted, celebratory laughter, which relaxes the muscles of their bodies, the tension in their souls, the hardness of their spirits.

"You, sir, are a genuine clown," Don Fuco notes, "a real clown, a total clown, my friend."

Salma stares with a mixture of tenderness, amazement, and envy at this new Victorio, diminished by such overwhelming praise.

The ruins seem abandoned. Unpredictable, like everything else on this island, the days can bring rain or clear skies. Some days it rains while the sun still shines.

"It appears this will be a rainy year," Victorio deduces after a while.

"I think it'll be just the opposite, you," says Salma.

Without looking at any landscape other than the furious gray sea that can be glimpsed through the window in Anna Pavlova, the Great One's, dressing room, Don Fuco decides to devote himself to passing on his knowledge. At dawn each day they will stand before the master teacher, for long hours of arduous apprenticeship.

Salma learns the mystery of making roses and rabbits and doves disappear into hats, bags, and gift boxes. She dances with balls, fans, and umbrellas, and learns to shuffle cards in the air. She develops a routine in which she is Mata Hari, as played by Greta Garbo.

Victorio not only perfects the art of poems-so-serious-they-make-you-laugh, he learns the technique of Japanese dance, and is able to imitate Don Fuco, carrying out all his movements: as a samurai, as a geisha, as a small child, and as an old man. He can also enter the small wicker basket with the highly refined artistry that Don Fuco must have learned from Kazuo Ono himself.

Don Fuco tells them long stories about Pailock and Baro the Great. He shows them the art of the mime, which he learned in a Paris of the imagination at the hands of none other than the equally imaginary Marcel Marceau. How to make the most of facial expressions, glances, hand movements, the subtlety of the fingers. He reveals the secrets and nuances in the voice. He lectures on the unfathomable enigmas of chains of action; on the art of laughing and crying with authenticity.

"The spectator cannot catch sight of how much work each act takes us. As Alicia Alonso always says, one must master the technique in order to extend over it the illusion of ease. And so, in literature, music, acting, or dance, it is fatal if the reader, listener, or observer notices the work we are going through to attain what we attain."

Salma and Victorio are now able to recite verses from Shakespeare as if they were the commonest sort of speech; they are trying to understand the enigmas of the body. Don Fuco speaks to them of Stanislavsky, Meyerhold, Grotowski, Peter Brook. He teaches them how to receive applause, a rather more difficult discipline than most actors think: how to convert the applause into a second performance that will create a desire to come back to the show. They practice for long and productive hours, for glorious, amusing, joy-filled days.

Victorio has designed his own costume. He wants a Pierrot costume exactly like the one that Gilles wears in the famous painting by Watteau: baggy, overflowing at the collar, round, sleeves too long to be taken in, silk as white as mother-of-pearl, wide-brimmed hat, and white slippers decorated with big pink ribbons tied in bows. Victorio-Pierrot paints a blood-red tear on his left cheek.

Salma adores the joy, the shock that the upcoming practices will cause, and she asks, she insists that Don Fuco include them from now on in his shows. Her arguments are cruel and therefore unassailable. "All right, who's going to take care of this ruin when you're not here anymore? And tell me, who's going to go to the cemeteries when people are crying, and who's going to make people's lives easier — people who can't expect any other life — on an afternoon when they suddenly see a clown, a real clown, not one of those clowns that make them suffer? Old man, do you think you're going to live forever?"

Don Fuco laughs, lifts his hands, nods his head and accepts. And that is how Salma comes to be seen in a dark mask, a crimson leotard that she has decided to decorate with bursts of yellow, blue, orange, and mauve sequins on the breast and hips, and a felt hat with satin flowers, which, the old clown reveals, once belonged to Miriam Acevedo, the greatest actress from the Island.

When alone, however, as their debut approaches, Victorio grows restless, loses hope, says no, confesses to Salma that he's no clown, that he'll never be one, that he doesn't have buffoonery in him, that he doesn't know whether he'll be up to clowning before an audience whose reaction he cannot predict. "I've always run away from other people's gazes, Salma. I've always hid, ever since I was a little boy. In school, when they realized that I was feeble or clumsy or queer, as they liked to say, I could never stand it when they made fun of me. Their mordant gazes and mocking laughter wounded me like they were stabbing me with augers. I always wanted people to take me seriously, to look at me without laughing, without teasing. How do you suppose I could just stand there dressed like a clown in front of everybody? How am I, at my age, going to put up with things that I couldn't stand as a child?"

As if she had grown old during these seconds, as if she had become a very wise old woman, Salma makes no reply but limits herself to looking at him with eyes that light the darkness in the devastated stage of the Liceo. She seems to understand his arguments and more: she seems to understand what he is hiding, or what he himself doesn't know. Her hands caress Victorio's face. She sits down next to him. She hugs him like a mother, and like a mother she tells him, "My little boy, you're a little boy and you're mine," and she squeezes him in her arms and holds him to her bosom as if he really were some fellow out freezing in the rain. Victorio recalls that first meeting between the two of them, under the archway in the ancient city wall. He can even see the stray dog that was out there in the rain. "Who told you that acting like a clown makes you ridiculous? Have you ever stopped to think how many people make themselves ridiculous without ever dressing up as clowns?" She holds him even tighter, as if she wants to transfer her faith to him. "Ay, my angel, haven't you realized that there's too much ridiculousness and not enough clowning in this poor city of ours? Haven't you seen that we have too much mockery, trickery, nastiness, and not enough laughter and lucidity? My little boy, my poor little forty-six-year-old boy, don't you remember the story I told you about when I was an adolescent, when I discovered that bringing about pleasure in others is a greater pleasure than pursuing my own?"

Victorio nods, with his eyes closed.

"You can do it," she tries to convince him in her finest voice, barely a whisper, "you can do it, my boy, my angel, Victorio, I know you can dominate your demons and demonize your body and your words. You know why?"

But he is so bewildered by the fact that she has called him Victorio for the first time that he doesn't hear the question, much less the answer.

One day they have finished rehearsing an act that does not present too many complications, which they plan to perform, as a kind of test, in an old age home in El Palmar, a remote neighborhood of Marianao, out where the last houses give way to open fields.

Against the merry background music of a Vieuxtemps composition, originally written for piano and violin and adapted here for flute, Don Fuco comes onto the stage and pantomimes a man at table. His top hat serves as an imaginary dressing table, desk, workbench, shop counter, bar, console, and it is amazing how Don Fuco can leave it there suspended in midair, stuck in the air, and write on it, eat at it, sit on it, lean against it, use it as a stage on which he contorts his body in a strange dance that might be composed of Indian, Chinese, and Japanese elements as well as movements from the magnificent Martha Graham. To conclude, he falls down as if dead after a virtuoso *tour-en-l'air* with an *allongé* fall.

At that moment Salma enters in her sequin-spangled outfit, and covers up the clown's body with a black velveteen cloth. Victorio appears, reciting Rubén Darío's inimitable alexandrines. Victorio has managed to forget about the old folks and their nurses, and he recites the text with his eyes closed and arms upraised.

Some of the old people laugh and applaud timidly. Others neither laugh nor applaud. All of them, however, allow Salma to sit on their laps and sing a nursery song about a palace that has been destroyed and a king who has no subjects.

They don't go out every day. Maybe once a week. Sometimes not even that. They can't rush into it, just like that, so suddenly: they still have many things to learn and many fears to lose. "It is harder to make people laugh than to make them cry," says Fuco.

And they test themselves, they lose heart, they take heart, they grow bolder, they shrink with dread. One moment they're saying that nothing makes any sense, and an instant later they adopt the opposite opinion.

"A time will come when we take Havana by storm," says Salma, always the most likely to get carried away by her fantasies. Victorio and Don Fuco know that when she is inspired they have to let her be. "All three of us will go," she says, "all three dressed identically, you, to three different places, and we'll do the same act. We'll baffle everybody in Havana. They won't be able to figure out how a single clown can be in three places at once, and little by little they'll start joining us, others will come out, lots more people will want to discover their funny side, their clownishness, and in the end there'll be lots of us, hundreds, thousands, what do you think of that? A whole army of clowns."

"We have to start on the outskirts," Don Fuco declares. So they disappear out on the rocky alleyways of Zamora, in the marshes of El

Fanguito, in the unsanitary byways of El Husillo, in the dangerous shadows of La Jata, in the crammed quarters of Diezmero, in the remoteness of El Cotorro, among the wretched side streets of Pogolotti. They manage to infiltrate, during visiting hours, the big hospitals such as the Military Hospital, Covadonga, Emergency, Naval, Calixto García, Quinta Balear, Oncology, Mental Illnesses (Mazorra), and the Sanatorium in Santiago de las Vegas for those infected by the Epidemic of the Century. In each of them, they hear laughter from patients on the verge of death, and from the despairing sleepwalkers who treat the patients on the verge of death. They don't have trouble performing in Mazorra, because its director, a sensitive man, welcomes anything that can distract his tormented patients. They travel around as many funeral parlors as possible, whether run by the city, the province, or the nation. They attend burials in the Colón Cemetery, in the cemetery of La Lisa, in the Chinese cemetery, in the Jewish cemetery, the two in Guanabacoa. They visit old age homes. They enter the shelters where the victims of hurricanes and catastrophes have to wait, for year after pointless year, until their houses are rebuilt.

Since Don Fuco deems that misfortune is not always apparent, sometimes they approach the city center and go along the Malecón, the beaches of East Havana, the entrance to Cine Yara where the most beautiful boys in the world hang out, and the hangouts that line the Avenue of the Presidents (where the Fiat Bar, better known as the Repair Shop, has been closed by military decree). They venture into Catholic, Protestant, Adventist churches, Masonic temples, and Christian Science reading rooms. They put on performances at bus stops where passengers tend to spend whole hours of their fleeting lives waiting for an oversized bus called "the camel." They go to countless bars, above all to ugly, sorry, cagelike neighborhood bars, where a cheap alcohol called *chispetrén* is sold for Cuban pesos.

They travel to the fields where crops are being weeded or harvested, and where sugarcane is being cut in the same way it was two centuries ago. "Under the shimmering sun," as El Cucalambé would say. On the scorching mounds of red soil between the fields, Don Fuco puts on his shows during the lunch hour, when the people in the countryside take off their straw hats, wipe the sweat from their brows and chests, and leave their chores with a sigh of relief for a single hour of rest. They know that sweating in the countryside is not at all like sweating in the city. They likewise know the taste of the dust and the bad taste of the water. They curse the Cuban poets who would take any horror and turn it into an idyll, who sang about those infernos as if they were so many bucolic paradises. Victorio likes to recite ironically:

> ¡Qué lindo brillan los campos
> de mi Cuba idolatrada . . . !

> How beautifully the fields gleam
> in my beloved Cuba . . . !

No doubt about it, Romantic poets were blind to the flies, the mud, the buzzards, the sun, the mosquitoes, and the shit. Don Fuco points out, "It didn't occur to any of our nineteenth-century Romantics to stop and ask some of the slaves who were out here cutting cane what they thought about 'the fields of their beloved Cuba.' Did we have no Baudelaire who might have shown us the terrible beauty of carrion?"

They return to the highways and struggle to find the transportation that would take them back to the city, to their refuge in their ruined theater. The three of them can be heard singing, infected by Victorio's irony:

¡Qué linda la alborada,
qué primor,
cuando asoma en las montañas!
¡Qué linda se ve la sabana
con los rayitos del sol . . . !

How beautiful the dawn,
what a pretty show,
when it creeps upon the mountains!
How beautiful the savanna
in the new beams of the sun!

Every day they visit a new place. They travel from one side of
the city to the other. Along roads, streets, highways, and alleys. Rest-
lessly, in cars and trucks and bicycles and carts pulled by oxen. Salma
and Victorio come to know the good fortune of sleeping in secluded
parks, on damp romerillo bushes, under the disconcerting profusion
of stars. Too many stars keep you from getting a good night's sleep, as
Martí said long ago. They drink water from rivers that have not yet
been polluted. They eat fruit from the trees. They wake up in the
light of dawns whose colors they never would have imagined. They
take the combs from beehives without encountering danger, and savor the honey. They drink milk fresh from the cow. They don't care
that the countless varieties of butterflies and insects already have their
names: they classify them again with names that amuse them or that
they find more appropriate. The same for plants and flowers. And roads.
Byways. Estuaries. Savannas. Coves. Rivers. Channels. Palm groves.

They go into the sea whenever they have a chance. They enjoy
the danger.

Havana, like the sea and like the countryside, sometimes shows its
generous side. "Yes, it does have a generous side: the thing is to look

hard to find it." That is what Don Fuco insists. They are content to appreciate the personality of each street, the dialogue between buildings, the beauty hidden in new constructions and in ruins. They begin to appreciate the human side of the aggressive, anxious people of Havana. On long, interminable workdays, they crisscross the contradictions of that odious and lovable city. Havana has many faces. So do those who inhabit it.

Many days and lots of patience have taught them to dance, without music, on the gables of former palaces. Don Fuco has trained them to dance to the music in their memories. In addition, they have spent long hours practicing on the railings of the primitive opera boxes in the ruins of the theater. But now they are having their debut on the streets of Havana, in the old mansions where the moneyed families of Havana once lived. Not wishing to seem too outlandish, they have limited themselves to dressing in black, the only details being their very white makeup and two small felt hats.

They dance to the memory of a Debussy melody, so that their movements will be smooth and so that, for the moment, they will not run any risks that might prove fatal. This dance thus tends toward subtlety, with a touch of the indispensable voluptuousness that so pleases the public. From time to time Salma lifts her long skirt and shows off her thin, white, well-formed thighs.

The crowds that slowly form in the street shout, clap, or whistle. They're as likely to shout praises as insults.

Since they have learned to listen to the public's opinion to the same degree that they ignore it, they silently continue their dance, which is a parody of love. For them Havana then becomes the dance, the precarious balance and joyful danger of knowing that they could fall with any step in the dance, with any distraction. Havana, too, is a leap from gable to gable, with the elegance of two ballet dancers and the ridiculousness of two clowns. Reconciling elegance with ridiculousness has been an arduous task. Reconciling the two atop the gables of a ruined palace has been a rash deed. What is truly magical, however, is that they have learned to avoid the stones that the audience throws at them from the street, and to escape from the police without letting it look like they are running away. To transform a getaway into a disappearing act. Fear into bravery.

As Salma and Victorio pick up confidence and virtuosity they begin to add variety to the trio's acts. Don Fuco makes rabbits appear out of Victorio's hat and pulls scarves from Salma's ear. Victorio learns poems by Amado Nervo, Salvatore Quasimodo, T. S. Eliot, Pablo Neruda, Nicolás Guillén, Luis Cernuda, Cesare Pavese . . . After long, exhausting rehearsals, Salma can now dance like a marionette that mimics Maria Taglioni. Also dancing like a puppet, like an inanimate being created by the prodigious hands and imagination of Doctor Coppelius, Victorio plays the role of Josephine Baker or Fred Astaire to the rhythm of music that Salma wrests from the flute of Belisario López.

One night they bring their show to the Parque de los Filósofos, near a carnival of carousels and roller-coasters that has been set up alongside the Havana Amphitheater. They hang black curtains for a camera obscura from the trees. For lights, they have only a few large and ancient candles, fused forever to their intricate bronze candlesticks. Passersby begin to draw near, attracted by the strangeness of the improvised stage, until a sizable crowd of spectators has amassed around the ugly curtains.

A flute is heard, playing music. The melody is one that repeats, over and over, with disquieting insistence, a central motif. A Pierrot appears among the curtains. One blood-red tear shines on his cheek. It is a tear that seems to be made of tiny rubies. The Pierrot's attitude is one of sadness, dejection, and helplessness. This Pierrot has been subtle enough to understand that exaggerated tragedy can turn into comedy. He raises a hand and the music stops, while an odd voice is heard, saying:

> *No me mueve, mi Dios, para quererte*
> *el cielo que me tienes prometido . . .*
>
> I am not moved, my God, to love you
> by the heaven you have promised me . . .

The audience suffers its first confusion. The audience doesn't know if it should laugh. Until, happily, someone — the usual audacious soul — breaks the silence with the first guffaw. Emboldened, the rest of the audience follows. The poem is finished to a rousing choir of laughter.

Then an ambiguous figure enters, wrapped in a long cape of white feathers. The feathers shine white under the insufficient light of the candles. The silence now is impressive. The cape falls to the ground. From under it emerges an imitation, half tender and half grotesque, of the Blue Angel — that is, of Marlene Dietrich — singing "Lili Marleen." From the hat of this Dietrich, who evokes pity and therefore laughter, fly sparrows.

Now a young image of Death is advancing through the air; Dietrich's sparrows are attracted to her small hat. Death wears whiteface and phosphorescent bones painted on her black leotard. Dietrich begins to rise toward a meeting with Death, and when her song ends, they are joined in a single body. The resulting body is neither that of Dietrich nor of Death.

On the stage, the improvised space that serves them as a stage, a chair now sits. No one knows how it got there. The scant light of the candles dampens even more. The proportions of the chair grow, as if it has changed dimensions.

A long silence continues in the Park of the Philosophers. A useful silence. The body that contains both Dietrich and Death is lit with blue light. An adolescent body, covered only by white shorts. The steps with which he approaches the chair are slow, slow, incredibly slow. He sits down. His handsome back, the back of his neck, can be seen in staggering detail. The hypothetical stage is also lit up, perhaps because the adolescent has lifted his right arm with his palm open and turned toward the sky. White smoke is rising from his hand. From amid the smoke, which dissipates on high, appear domes, battlements, towers, arches, columns, windows, and balconies.

Half the audience applauds; the other half whistles in annoyance and shouts insults. A group of children stationed in the trees throw stones. Police sirens are heard. Police race toward the small crowd, who run away in terror at the sight of them. The police tear down the old curtains and put out the candles. "Hey, you there! Where the hell do you think this is?"

The Pierrot, Dietrich, and Death are forced into a police car. They are taken to the police station on Zanja, a place where the style is willfully ugly. There, on harsh benches of frightful granite, they spend the stifling late-night hours.

Though she is a member of the police, the lieutenant doesn't seem brutish. She is a little over twenty and capriciously beautiful, like all mulattas with yellow eyes. At five in the morning she orders them to leave, with the recommendation that they should wait until Carnival to start wearing masks.

★

"It is characteristic of any road to have roadblocks," says Don Fuco; "it is characteristic of any roadblock to grow larger and larger."

From that night on, everything gets harder. Entering hospitals, for example, becomes an odyssey. They have to use doctors' and nurses' gowns to enter unnoticed through the guarded doors. On many afternoons, in cemeteries and funeral parlors, they find themselves obliged to interrupt their performances so they can run away from the police.

They don't always manage to make people laugh. They are stoned in many workplaces. Expelled from gas stations and stores. Insulted and shooed away like enemies. Treated like lepers. As almost always is the case, incipient fame brings problems. Much more so in a city as envious as Havana, where fame is never forgiven; success, much less.

One morning they are not allowed to enter the Colón Cemetery. Two blue-uniformed guards call them over and lead them away to an office with tall windows opening onto a shining sea of tombs and mausoleums. The office is furnished in a savage Spanish renaissance style. The office smells of dust, dirty boxes, cockroaches, files, old papers, tobacco, and coffee. The secretary — a wax statue of a woman from the Havana of the thirties, complete with a Remington typewriter at her fingertips — points them to a door.

The cemetery administrator receives them: a small, thin, bald little man with a long white beard stained yellow from nicotine. He moves like a bureaucrat who is imitating a priest about to give absolution.

"Comrades," he says, and his shrill voice seems like it couldn't be coming from his little body: it is the voice of Tito Gobbi, reanimated after all these years in the least appropriate body. "Comrades, I wonder if you understand that this is a cemetery: a cemetery, a

graveyard, a burial ground, not a side branch of the carnival at Rio."
He taps his left index finger against his right palm. "Not merely a
cemetery, but one of the most elegant cemeteries in the world, in the
same class as Montparnasse and Père-Lachaise." He blinks as if he had
dirt in his eyes. "Magicians and clowns? To the circus with them!
That's where they belong."

"We make people laugh," Salma dares to say.

The administrator seems not to hear her. "We have received a
lot of complaints. Next time I see you here, I call the police." He
opens the door. At last he looks at Salma with wide, reddened eyes.
"People come here to cry, miss. People come here to show that they
have a sensitive and tragic side. Why do you want to deprive them of
that pleasure?"

5

It is in the cemetery in the town of Bauta that Salma breaks down and cries. During the funeral of "the Emilia who lived in the little old house."

Her performance was to have consisted of something very simple: lift up a big red cloak so that the clown Don Fuco could appear from under it. But Salma hasn't done what was expected of her. She has allowed herself to be overcome by tears and sobbing, and her arms haven't had the strength to lift the cloak, so the clown hasn't been able to move, remaining trapped between the folds of cloth. It has been odd, very odd indeed, to see this young woman in her sequined leotard and her giant cloak, crying disconsolately over the Estévez-Pazó family tomb.

The mourners have not halted their ceremony. They have even pretended not to see the outlandish character.

Later, the three of them are sitting silently in the entrance of the Masonic Lodge. It is a luminous, lifeless, stifling midday. The town is shining so brightly that the walls seem made of glass. Apart from the light and the barking of dogs, the only thing that seems to have any kind of life here is the smell of burning sugarcane that wafts in from the fields.

★

Salma explains that she has been obsessed for several days by a matter that has weighed on her. An issue that does not let her be as happy as she would like.

"And tell me if you two don't think it's terribly important: I can't remember my mother's face, and that's with me turning it over and over in my head; and, yes, I can see her hands all covered with spots, her fingernails infected with the fungus she could never get rid of, I see her swollen feet with their bunions, and her varicose veins that looked ready to explode any day, and I see her old patched-up house robes, and I can even see her hair if I close my eyes, her hair that I liked to feel between my fingers when I got home at dawn to eat the soup that made me happy again to be alive. But her face, what you'd really call her face, that has disappeared from my memory."

Don Fuco asks Salma to stop by the old Van Dyck photography studio on their way back and retrieve a photo of her mother. "Having exact memories is of capital importance," he says. He also invites Victorio to accompany her. Victorio is to wait for her on the corner by the fire station; they should absolutely not enter the girl's room together.

Salma promises that she will only need a second.

The "second" that Salma requested has become an hour. So Victorio knocks insistently on the entrance to the old Van Dyck photography studio.

Preceded by the fragrance of Kenzo cologne, a young man appears in the doorway. Tall, dark, elegant, with almond eyes and shaven head, he is dressed all in beige linen, with open shirt and baggy pants. Around his neck he wears a complete collection of Santería necklaces that stand out against his sculpted chest, as neat and distinguished as his clothing. Victorio notes that he has placed a folded handkerchief in the neck of his shirt — to collect his sweat, he guesses, the way bus conductors usually wear them. Nobody has to tell him, of course, that standing before him is El Negro Piedad, better known as Sacredshroud.

"Hello," he greets him, smiling, amiable, and again he smiles, feigns a smile, because the truth is that Victorio feels afraid.

The other doesn't reply; he smiles, too, but he doesn't reply. He opens the door a little wider to let him through. "Is this Triumpho?" he asks in an excellent voice, strong but sweet at the same time, without seeming to ask anyone in particular, without ceasing to observe Victorio with a protective smile. There is a childish gleam to his almond eyes.

"My name isn't Triumpho," Victorio explains with all the calm he feels he can muster, "my name is Victorio. I was born on the same day as the assault on the Moncada barracks, and my parents, committed Fidelistas, decided to give me this name, Victorio. My name is Victorio, at your service." He has attempted to dress up his words in irony. He resorts to what he imagines is his best expression of meekness. He exaggerates his embarrassment. He adds a pinch of self-pity. He tries to keep El Negro Piedad from noticing his fear.

"Committed Fidelistas!" El Negro exclaims, serious, as if he can't believe what he's hearing. He laughs again, and his laughter becomes even more forthright, fascinating, enchanting. "Come on in, come on in."

Salma is lying on one of the rickety old beds, motionless, curled up into a little ball.

"Victorio! If you only knew how much I . . . like your name! Your name is so . . . how can I put it? . . . so . . . victorious!" He jabs at Victorio with a finger that is as strong as a pistol. "It's a good name to get through life with, isn't it?"

Victorio dares to ask, "What happened to Salma?"

"Salma?" El Negro asks uncertainly. "Who is Salma?" He pauses to run his hand over his shaven head, which shows off the beauty of his mulatto and Chinese traits. The expression on his face is suddenly almost sad. "Oh, her? Isabel, her name isn't Salma," El Negro Piedad explains in a pitying tone, "her name is Isabel." Utterly serious, El Negro Piedad, better known as Sacredshroud, sits down on the other bed. "Isabel has told me that you are a philosopher," he declares without dropping the grieved look on his face, "and I've been dying to meet a philosopher."

"I'm nothing," Victorio corrects him, "nothing at all, a poor devil."

"You're not a philosopher? What a pity, I had such high hopes! So tell me, what are you doing here?"

"I came to see her," Victorio explains bombastically, with the expression of someone living through a tragedy.

Sacredshroud frowns at him. He caresses one of Victorio's hands and asks again, "What did you come here for?" He nods toward Salma, who is still curled up into a ball. "Isabelita told me that you're a fag, is that true?" El Negro finishes taking off his shirt, which he hangs ceremoniously and carefully on the back of a chair. A tattoo rings the muscle of his left arm like an armband. Victorio admires his perfect torso. "Even if she hadn't told me, boy, you look sad, like every fag who's over forty." He pauses to look at Victorio with a respectful expression. Now he is holding one hand over the other, both of them over his fly. Victorio can't decide whether this posture is votive or defensive. Then he pulls out an elegant little box of menthol cigarettes, picks one, and lights it with mannerisms that would seem appropriate to a prince. He half closes his eyes. He inhales the smoke as if the future of the world depended on it. He looks, Victorio thinks, as if he and infinity were alone here in the room.

Victorio lowers his eyes, shrugs his shoulders, tries and manages to make himself smaller, feels and manages to transmit this sensation. Salma moves for the first time. She raises her face, too, and looks at

Victorio. She has been beaten black and blue. Victorio cannot suppress the look of alarm on his face, his desire to come close to her.

El Negro Piedad squeezes his arm forcefully. "Leave her alone," he orders in his sweetest voice, "she got what she deserves." Salma looks at him without hatred, without reproach, with an enigmatic expression of mute dauntlessness. "I need your help, Victorio," pleads El Negro Piedad, "this girl is wild, skittish, she refuses to be led down the right path, the path that will take her out of poverty."

"What do you mean?" Victorio's naiveté is feigned, of course.

Sacredshroud stubs out his cigarette on the sole of his shoe. He stands up. My God, Victorio acknowledges in amazement, he has got the looks of a colossus. Sacredshroud uses his most persuasive voice: "If she keeps going on the path she's on, she'll end up like Chichi, her beloved little brother."

And now, for the first time, Salma loses her composure. She bolts upright, gesticulates, looks at Victorio with terrorized eyes. She raises her hands, perhaps in an attempt to keep the words from coming out of Victorio's mouth; he understands what Salma is trying to tell him, what she wants to keep him from asking. But curiosity turns out to be stronger than kindness, sensitivity, or terror; much more intense than any act of politeness or pity. "Her brother's fine," Victorio exclaims with all the candor he is capable of. "He's living in Rome, in an apartment near the Quirinal Palace."

Salma covers her face with her hands.

El Negro Piedad, better known as Sacredshroud, again looks very sad. He tries listlessly to laugh, he makes a movement with his body, a bit artificial, he tries to cover his ears as if he had heard the business about Chichi, Rome, and the Quirinal too many times. "Yes, of course," he stresses, "he hooked up with an Italian prince who looks like Marcello Mastroianni, et cetera, et cetera." He looks in every direction with an astonished expression; now he brings a hand to his forehead. He doesn't look like a nineteen-year-old man, but a thirty-year-old. Beauty, Victorio tells himself, is a dangerous disease. "Her brother is in prison," El Negro reveals, as if each word hurt him.

Quickly, Salma jumps to her feet, naked, on top of the bed. "Shut up!" she screams.

El Negro seems not to hear her. "He's in for armed robbery. He wounded some poor old woman with a knife — all but killed her — and came away with twenty-seven dollars and thirty cents."

Salma suddenly grows calm. She is standing on the rickety old bed, naked, motionless, bruised from the beating. Possessing a strange dignity, she says nothing.

El Negro Piedad, better known as Sacredshroud, comes up to her, kisses her nipples, bites them softly, embraces her. "I love you," he says in a convincing tone. "I love you and I want the best for you." He turns to Victorio. "Help me, Victorio. Make her see reason. We could make so much money — thirty thousand, forty thousand dollars — and then live the only kind of life that would make this miserable life worthwhile!"

Victorio thinks that in this destitute country where everybody has gone crazy, there is no more reason; madness is a virus that has possessed everyone's brains. "What do I have to do to help you?"

"Convince her to put on an elegant dress and put on enough makeup to cover the marks of her obstinacy. I'll come pick her up to take her to the Havana Café in the Hotel Cohiba at twelve o'clock sharp. Midnight, I'll be here." He looks at his watch. He picks his shirt up from the chair and puts it back on. He appears tranquil and satisfied. He opens the door of the old photography studio. A gust of hot, humid air blows in through the door.

Before he leaves, El Negro Piedad pulls out a key and turns toward them with a generous, almost imploring expression. "One important detail: I am going to lock the door now, from the outside, just so I can be sure you'll be here at midnight." He kisses the key and kisses the joined tips of his fingers. The childish gleam still glows in his almond eyes.

Worried, obviously frightened, Salma combs her hair, puts on her makeup, and picks out her best shoes, an ugly pair in burgundy satin, and her best clothes, a tailored dress in a glossy mauve fabric, nothing plain about it, with two straps and an exquisite, showy detail: a gilded fleur-de-lis over the right breast. She hides a photo of her mother in the skimpy front of her dress. "Let's skip this trap," she orders.

"How?"

"You'll see, easy. This isn't the first time. He's crazy," she says while adjusting her dress, on the verge of tears. "I'd die before I'd show up at the Havana Café, that nutcase is likely to kill us both. I wonder if you noticed he's a schizo — yeah, he is, it runs in the family."

"He didn't seem so dangerous to me, Salma, he just looked like a sad little boy."

"Because you don't know him. Because you let him charm you. I've seen him carrying a pistol stuffed in the back of his pants. You know what he wants me to do? Seduce an Estonian saddle maker, a Russian mafioso, a millionaire no doubt, an old geezer, a hundred years old at least, the most disgusting, degenerate old man I've seen in my life, trying to set up his horse harness business here, or a harem for his personal satisfaction. I've never seen such an ugly, slimy, wicked old man as him. I swear on my grave of my dead mother," she joins her index fingers to make a cross, — may she rest in peace, that if that old Lithuanian —"

"Not Estonian?" Victorio interrupts.

"Same thing, you, who cares? Disgusting ugly old men don't have homelands." She falls silent for a few moments, and then adds, "Well, nobody has a homeland, you; that's the truth, and I swear to you that if that old Estonian or Lithuanian or Latvian touches me one more time, I'm going to cut off that ridiculous piece of tripe that he so pompously and stupidly calls 'my virility.' I'll castrate him, by God Almighty up in heaven, I'll castrate him!"

Victorio has stopped paying attention to her venting and has helped her finish getting dressed. Salma looks at herself in the mirror. She raises her eyebrows, touches her pink-powdered cheeks, puckers her crimson lips into a fake kiss.

Then she leaves the mirror. She looks at her friend. Her voice suddenly sounds affected, with sarcasm in the background: "You let yourself get seduced by El Negro Piedad, you?" She doesn't let him answer. "I admit, he's good, he's real good, and if you saw him naked . . . No, my dear, for your health's sake, I won't go into details — a Cuban, a real Cuban, you! Ay, Virgencita del Perpetuo Socorro, what a well-endowed brute he is." She sighs and raises her eyes up to heaven, that is, up to the ceiling, in mock compassion. "You, more than anyone, should understand what I mean. But let me put it clearly: he doesn't like men or women, he just likes himself. His name should be Narcissus. El Negro Piedad is madly in love with himself," Salma declares; "he's the only man I've ever slept with who has made me doubt whether I'm a woman, and who has made me think I'm just a prolongation of himself: his leg, his arm, his chest, his dick, whatever! He's a miracle of self-love. He gives a heavenly screw, but I think he doesn't do it out of generosity, he does it for the honor of driving somebody else crazy. Ah, and he loves mirrors — on the ceiling, on the walls; he loves being able to see himself all over, all at once and in every posture. Besides, let me tell you, he only gratifies men for money, so . . ."

She has to stop to catch her breath, and Victorio snatches the moment to explain: "Don't be ridiculous, Salma. I hate to disappoint you, but your dear Piedad Sacredshroud, who is indeed a good-looking man, has left me colder than an iceberg. I'm sorry, dear, I really am,

very sorry, I know you would have liked a good passionate drama —
maybe some other time, but not now, not this time, at least not with
your Narcissus. And now, let's get going! If you really do have a way
to escape, the sooner the better," Victorio rudely orders.

Salma obeys him in silence, perhaps feeling frightened. "Come
over here," she directs. She pulls out a wooden ladder from under one
of the rickety old beds and leans it against a wall. She climbs up. Victorio now notices a wooden rectangle in the ceiling, which Salma effortlessly pushes open with her hand. She climbs higher and gestures
to her friend to follow. He also goes up the ladder.

They climb through the small rectangle and find themselves in a
forgotten photography lab, with cobwebs so large they look like
props. They don't see the rats: they sense them. Sometimes they feel
them moving, spying. The door is held shut with twisted wire. They
have little trouble opening it.

Now they are standing on a narrow, filthy cement staircase, with
no stone steps and no handrails. It smells of dust, of sparrow nests,
of dried flowers, of cockroaches, of vinegar, of damp earth, and of
course, of gas. Above one of the lintels, a pair of bats are sleeping.

The staircase takes them up to the flat rooftop of the old Van
Dyck photography studio. There, as you might imagine, are the shattered water tanks, the birdcages, the clothesless clotheslines, the broken furniture, a few television antennas rusted by the sea air and
knocked down by the wind, and lots of dead sparrows. They can see,
blackened by the rain, the small tower of the chapel of Our Lord of
Patience and Humility. A little farther off, the two towers of the train
station and the perpetual flame of the refinery. The color of the flagstones on the rooftop terrace has turned aqueduct green, thinks Victorio, and he recalls the reservoirs built by Don Francisco de Albear
y Lara. The drains are stuffed with piles of dead leaves, bird bones,
beer cans, bits of wood, and every other type of trash. The wind
blows in dirty and fetid.

Calle Apodaca. Its darkness can induce terror. They go down Calle Revillagigedo to Monte.

"This part of Havana has lost its former urban, cosmopolitan air, and now it has a sorry village atmosphere," Victorio observes.

"I've always seen it just like this," Salma replies.

Gloomy shadows, dirty houses, dusty sidewalks, broken streets. Groups of ten, twelve men, standing on the street corners, not doing anything except making noise, shouting, holding shouted conversations, unintelligible conversations in an unthinkable Spanish. The groups turn to watch Salma and Victorio walk by. Another characteristic of villages, where life becomes so needy that it aggravates people's curiosity, where the emptiness of your own life gives singular value to everyone else's most insignificant movements.

They stop in front of the magnificent entranceway to the palace of Don Miguel Aldama. They linger as they walk by the former Campo de Marte, now called the Parque de la Fraternidad, the Park of Brotherhood. Victorio has Salma look at the park.

"Just another park, you."

Victorio explains that, no, they are standing in front of one of the most beautiful parks in the city, built by the dictator Machado. "In the center of the park grows a ceiba tree that is supposedly nourished by soil from every republic in the Americas," he says professorially.

She claps her hands. "Then, if I hop over this little fence and stand on top of that soil, I can walk from Bolivia to Brazil, from Argentina to Mexico, from Paraguay to Chile."

"They say," Victorio continues, paying no attention to her puerile commentary, "that the dictator Machado buried an evil charm under that ceiba, a powerful piece of witchcraft that would keep the Island from ever being happy."

Salma laughs. "So tomorrow let's come back with picks and shovels, what do you think?"

They walk up Calle Reina. Salma's ignorance about Havana doesn't surprise Victorio. With a line of reasoning that belies the relative youth of his forty-six years, he tells himself that most young people are like her, they don't know anything, though the most remarkable detail is that they don't care, either. You might say that, for them, Havana has no history, as if they were wandering around a city that had just been created. For the youngest people here, Havana has no history, and this is perhaps a kind of defense mechanism; the oldest people here invent a different history — a false one, which is what every history, after all, must be — in which Havana ends up as a sort of Susa, Persepolis, or Sybaris, which they have had the good fortune to inhabit: this, you will comprehend, is by any reckoning another sort of defense mechanism; and so, between the Havana-that-does-not-exist and the paradise-lost-of-Havana, they find themselves in the peculiar reality of this dreaming fantasy, this subtropical delirium, under the sun, by the edge of a beautiful, a diabolically beautiful bay, open to the perilous waters of the Gulf of Mexico, swarming with sharks and lost souls.

6

The window (he couldn't have said which one) opens onto the night. Tonight displays the false luminosity of clouded, rainy nights when the moon is shining despite it all, round and lovely, surrounded by halos of humidity that are said to unhinge madmen: an aggressive moon, which manages to break through the heavy, motionless, reddish cloud cover. Small fishing boats are also glaring, upsetting the calmness of the sea.

Black is Don Fuco's telescope on its tripod by the window. Victorio bends over and moves it, observing: Aldebaran, Altair, Antares. He doesn't know if these are actually the stars he is naming: the names are sonorous, lovely, and he takes the liberty of rechristening those luminous points with the names he knows and others that he doesn't know.

He envies the fishers in their tranquil boats. The sea has always seemed to him more noble than the land. Victorio likes its way of seeming so resolutely unsure; he likes the way that it is dangerous and doesn't try to hide the fact, while the land, which is just as precarious, masks its threats with meadows and hills and valleys and roads and flowers and savannas and gentle rivers and silver moonbeams and pure-voiced mockingbirds that gladden the mountains and the plains. Land is deceitful. Besides, if you find yourself needing to overcome something as terrible as the sea, something so elusive, so difficult, in order to reach the mystery of faraway places, doesn't that constitute a powerful incentive, not to say the only incentive, for travel?

The lights on the boats look like fallen stars, and they, too, deserve to have names. He can't be certain: he thinks he can see the silhouettes of the fishers. He guesses at the patience of the fishing lines, guesses at the man who is in the process of eliminating his destructive nervousness. Sometimes, man is capable of adapting to the eternity of fish.

In the distance, above the horizon, a hot-air balloon is silhouetted against the low cloud cover. Victorio knows, he thinks he knows, that it is displaying several signs. It must be a promotional balloon, for tourism, he says to himself, though it makes no sense to fly a promotional balloon through the sky this late at night. Dawn is breaking. It looks reddish, immaterial, illusory, in a city like this one, which stops living as soon as dark begins to descend. In an attempt to be precise: the artifact out there doesn't remind him of a hot-air balloon, but of the shadow of a cloud that looks like a hot-air balloon.

The balloon approaches. The wind is carrying it swiftly in the direction of the ruined theater. What, he wonders, will the unbelieving people of Havana think when they see this immense hot-air balloon pass by with its red glowing basket? He tries to put himself in the place of those skeptical inhabitants, who stopped believing in miracles years ago. The telescope is useless. All he can see with it is an even cloudiness and the same old stars. With his naked eyes, however, he can contemplate the balloon in all its splendor. Red, green, yellow. A wicker basket, in which stands a man whom he recognizes at once. El Moro is waving good-bye from the basket. Victorio sees his dark naked torso, his spacious smile, his wide eyes; he smiles and responds to his good-bye.

★

In reality, of course, Victorio is lying down on the *recamier* and he hasn't seen any balloons floating by. Now he does think he can hear a sound, over there above the stage, around Giselle's tomb. He gets up. He doesn't turn on the lights, so as not to waken his companions. He lights the thick candle in Don Fuco's candlestick and heads out barefoot from the dressing room toward the stage. His footsteps are furtive. Fearful. Distrustful. Things aren't silent: nor could you say that the sounds that can be heard are suspicious. The howling must be from the wind; the sound of beating wings must come from all the bats. As for the applause, that could be rain. It has started raining, for certain. But no, it's not so certain after all, because the usual drips aren't falling on the boards. Victorio walks down into the orchestra seating. He gets as far as the frayed screen, where he sees the black armchair for taking journeys. He sits down in it. He doesn't take a journey. At least not in the sense you would when you sit in this armchair. He sees himself as a child, sitting on El Moro's lap, inside the airplane on the embankment that serves as a landing strip.

"Triumpho, Triumpho!"

Salma's cries fill the ruins of the theater with echoes and bats. She enters, excited. She jumps up onto the stage with surprising agility and runs over to the screen, oriented by the candlelight. Seeing Victorio, she spins around with her arms held wide. She stops and adopts Taglioni's pose from the rotogravure in the dressing room. She ends up sitting on her friend's lap. She kisses him repeatedly.

"Ay, Triumphito," she says ecstatically, "that door over there, the one that opens onto the dressing rooms, was thrown open enthusiastically; I can still hear it, and I know I'll always hear it: the hinges creaked, and there she was. Who was it? I wasn't sure, I didn't know who it was, you, I didn't guess right away. It was a woman, but if I say 'it was a woman,' that's like saying nothing. I know she opened the door to the dressing rooms, and she wore a patched-up house robe and her eyes were shining, I think the light that was lighting up her eyes came from the woman's own body, and of course you've guessed right, Triumphito, it was my mother, my very own mother: she had broken into the dressing room like it was the most natural thing in the world. I felt dizzy, you, and at the same time I had the strange sensation that I wasn't there; I saw her again, not like she was there in front of me, but like she used to be when she'd talk to me about my father, the trumpet player in New York, about how we'd go, her, my brother Chichi, and me, into the Apollo Theater up there in Harlem, to hear my father play with Dizzy Gillespie, with Chico O'Farrill, while Patti LaBelle and Sammy Davis Jr. were singing. Chichi and I were by my mother's side in the old Van Dyck photography studio; the place looked so pretty — not the horror you saw, dismal, dirty, sad, no, not at all — clean, fragrant, wide open, and I was so happy, I went outside naked and nobody shouted insults at me, can you believe it? Not a single insult, you. They threw flowers to me from the balconies on Apodaca and Corrales and Cienfuegos, they said the nicest things to me, that I was a prize among women and things like that, you. What happiness, fuck! What happiness to be reconciled with my neighborhood, with my neighbors, that my nakedness didn't offend them or embarrass me. I was sure that I was also lit up from inside, so sure, you, so sure, as sure as I am that I'm sitting here in front of you. I was convinced that the light went right through my skin, like my skin was made from some kind of rice paper. I left, I left again, I mean that I went out once more without leaving this old theater; haven't I ever told you that I love to bathe in the pouring rain? Well, there I was, under the pouring rain, in one of those intense, fleeting summer squalls when, for an hour or two, we have the conviction and the hope that the world is coming to an end. What a miracle, the world is dissolving in water, and there you are in the middle of it watching it being destroyed, turning into water and water and water, water falling on top of water. For me there's nothing like standing in a thunderstorm in June, July. My mother taught me, she, who never liked to do anything fun, she always went out to bathe in the thunderstorms, the only grown woman among all us kids and adolescents, dancing with us, singing,

> *San Isidro Labrador,*
> *ni quites el agua ni pongas el sol . . .*

> Saint Isidore the Farmer,
> don't take away the water
> and don't bring out the sun . . .

and she'd turn to face the lightning, so much lightning, and she'd jump to the sound of the thunder, so much thunder, and I'd imitate her, running, dancing, singing under the rain. I relived the glorious thunderstorms of my childhood with my mother again. And it was like I could taste the pineapple stinging my mouth; I was sitting down and looking out at the countryside at my grandmother's house — my grandmother lived in Bauta, in La Minina, you know? — at the point in the village where the houses are giving way to savanna, to corrals where they raise pigs, next to a little pond with more frogs than water and the dirty water that was there was completely covered over by *malangueta* lilies. I'd sit down in front of the fence, in the grass, to eat pineapple while I watched horses and cows grazing: the cozy feeling of lying under the yellow acacia and seeing how the wind makes the flower petals fall onto me. Ay, Victorio, you, tell me, haven't you ever woken up to the smell of coffee that your mother was filtering? I don't mean coffee from one of those Italian coffee makers, I mean pouring a jarful of boiled water through the coffee in a woolen filter. The intense smell would wake me up; I'd be half-asleep, watching my mother filtering the coffee, and I'd feel like the luckiest girl in the world, because my mother would also notice that her little girl had opened her eyes, she'd come over to me and tell me, 'The sun is out — if my baby girl has opened her eyes, the sun is out.' Oh, and another thing I loved to do, you: go upstairs at night onto the rooftop of my building, where the old Van Dyck photography studio had been, you've seen the rooftop; I'd lie down there on the terra-cotta flagstones — I knew that everybody else was absorbed in the nonsense they put on television, no one knew where I was, nobody was spying on me — and lying on the rooftop up there, exposed to the land breeze that was blowing toward the bay not far away, I'd devote myself to watching the stars. Knowing that those shining points were always there calmed me, made me feel safe, made me feel protected by some force larger than myself, larger than all of us put together, and whenever someone tried to burst my bubble — you know how people can never abide the happiness of others — by attempting to give me scientific explanations, telling me that in all probability some of those stars are already dead, and that all that's left is their light traveling through interminable space, instead of making me feel sad that would make me even happier — what am I saying! — much, much happier. I didn't explain to you: at the time, and even now, I imagined that stars were really little people from distant worlds, and the only testimony we had of them was their light, something like flashes of souls that had managed to cover millions of light-years, and on the other side of the universe, on the other edge, those little people could see us shining just as brightly, like stars, and would you believe it, you: I believed that the brightest stars corresponded to the happiest beings? So for them to tell me that what I was seeing was light from a person who was dead, that was the best way of proving to me that eternity was possible; and I logically concluded — you can't deny my logic — that if I was seeing the brilliance of someone who no longer belonged to the world of the living, then someone else would see my own brilliance when I had left this world. So, far from frightening me with their scientific opinions, they made me even

more certain of the twinkling that would be the proof of my immortality, do you follow me, Triumphito?"

She pauses briefly to stretch her arms in lazy happiness.

"The fact is," she then exclaims, talking like a madman, which
is the only way one can speak logically, "that I loved to enter a darkened room and have a man waiting for me on the bed. Listen, learn:
men who are waiting on the bed while a woman takes off her clothes
are worse than caged beasts. I know the sensation I stirred in them,
that tormenting feeling of being overwhelmed by the pleasure that
will soon arrive but hasn't arrived yet: it perturbs them; it kills them;
they don't realize, they never realize (what brutes!) that waiting for
pleasure is the only true pleasure, because the other side, satisfying
their pleasure, is always pretty disappointing, you; so the real pleasure
is the pleasure of waiting, don't you agree, Triumpho? At least that's
what we think, those of us who haven't really known the nature of
pleasure. And that man, waiting for you, naked, nice and naked, falls
onto you with a desperation that turns into joy. Ay, Mother of the
Word, how I loved to lie down on the grass and let a boy caress me!
Triumphito, how I loved to see their faces, surprised to find themselves with a girl who was ready to satisfy them! They'd kiss me
clumsily, caress me like they were touching fancy furniture or the
Virgin's mantle, they'd bite my little tits — sometimes they'd bite too
hard, they were new at it! But guess what, it didn't hurt me, I didn't
care. I loved to see their joy, see them half bewildered and half boastful. I'd say things to them, the things they wanted to hear; and let me
tell you, spreading my legs to the open air in front of those classmates
of mine was quite a defining experience. Most of them had never
before seen the wet opening that was throbbing for them, waiting for
them, and when they entered my body as if I weren't me, I'd observe
their expressions, halfway between pain and supreme pleasure —
none of these memories is important at all. I heard the hinges creak
on the door to the dressing rooms, I saw my mother walk in, full of

light, like a saint, and it was like all those little moments of happiness had come together into a single magnificent ball of lightning, and the most magnificent part of it: I saw my mother's face in all its details."

"For you, it fills you with happiness to find your memories; I'd like to be rid of mine."

"I don't understand you. Memories are just about the best things in life."

"My sweet Salma, listen: a moment ago a remembrance came that I am always running from; a jarring memory that keeps returning and returning, which is a characteristic of jarring memories.

"I saw myself as a child, in the hangars of Agricultural Fumigation. It was morning, nice and early; the sun was shining like it does in Chartrand's paintings, a timid kind of sun that ennobles landscapes, a sun that isn't yet setting them on fire, and the grass and the trees were still endeavoring to conserve some of the night cool; work hadn't started yet, El Moro was getting his Fokker ready to fly, 'the apple of my eyes,' as he called it; he and a mechanic were checking the fuel, the engines, all the mysterious things that have to be checked in planes that are about to take off. I always climbed up into the cockpit; I'd sit there and imagine that I was flying around worlds that I'm not sure now exist. I knew that I couldn't touch any of the controls, any of the buttons, but that didn't keep me from flying. El Moro climbed in, I remember, and sat me on his lap, and I remember that he smelled of starch and clean sheets and that his breath was as fresh as if he had been chewing on peppermint leaves. He hugged me against his chest and said, 'Today we're going to fly, Lieutenant. I'm going to show you my palace and the mule named Cicero, and I'm going to show you your palace, the one that belongs to you, because among the ruins we'll put out some white smoke, and the towers of your palace will come up through that smoke — you want to fly with me today?' I didn't answer, I didn't have to, he knew how much I wanted to fly, and I think he also secretly knew that I would have gone to the ends of the earth with him. I don't think the Algerian was too far from knowing the fascination he inspired in that boy. He knew it and he didn't know it; that's how these things always are: he didn't know that for me he was the symbol of all human beauty, and at the same time he did know it. He played on that, without intending to. He paid attention to me the way you would to a little boy, the way you would to a little girl. He wanted to be my friend, and without realizing it he made me fall for him like a secret lover. But there was Papá Robespierre to protect me from danger; my father stood next to the cockpit and shouted, 'Hey, Moro, you gotta go now, it's getting late,' and I passed from El Moro's hands to my father's, who set me down on the embankment that served as a landing strip. El Moro put on his helmet and started the engines. While my father and I were walking away toward the hangars, the plane glided down the strip, took off, did a few pirouettes in the sky — El Moro couldn't help playing those sorts of games. I saw the plane turning loops, as always; this time Papá Robespierre went pale and started shouting, I know that there were sirens wailing, the ambulance that was always sitting unused at the hangars took off, and a fire truck even went out on a salvation mission without knowing where or why it was going, and no matter how hard I close my eyes, Salma, no matter how hard I shake my head, as if I could shoo away memories like flies, I see the plane, or rather, I see the flames, the big flames that had forever overtaken the plane of El Moro.

"El Moro disappeared together with his plane, and all at once I learned a lot of things that life has later done nothing but confirm."

219

"My poor darling," says Salma, moved. She kisses him on the forehead. "That's over and done, you, what's past is past."

"The past is never past, my girl; that's a lie: time doesn't move forward, time is an ill-willed whirlwind that keeps spinning around in place."

"Look, don't get grandiose on me. Come, follow me, I'm going to show you something."

Salma takes Victorio by the arm. She leads him to the stage.

Where a large dining table is set for a sumptuous meal. The Bruges lace tablecloth is splendid. Candelabras with spiraling candles and trembling flames. Limoges china. Silver dinnerware. Diaphanous crystal glasses from Bohemia.

Don Fuco welcomes them. Don Fuco spreads his arms. In silence, Salma and Victorio stand behind the chairs that have been assigned to them, waiting for the old clown to raise his empty cup and tells them what he wants to toast. The clown merely laughs. His forthright laughter seems to be sufficient. Ceremoniously, without a single word, they all lift up their empty glasses. They sit down. They begin to laugh. No one pours white wine, or red wine, or even water into the Bohemia glasses. No one carries in any platters of food. They sit there at a sumptuously set table on which there is no food nor drink. They see the bottoms of their soup bowls, where plump, rosy nymphs, pursued by lusty satyrs, run cheerfully among absurd trees. They can't stop laughing. Sometimes they seem to hear applause. In the middle of laughing, Salma manages to say that the applause is really the beating of all the doves' and bats' wings. Between guffaws, Victorio explains, "No, no, don't you realize? It's the rain." More calmly, Don Fuco asserts, "Don't doubt it: it is applause, old applause imprisoned between these walls."

Part Four

1

Applause, old applause imprisoned between these walls. At times they hear the motifs of an aria. An extraordinary voice resounds between the devastated walls. Melodies from *The Magic Flute, Aïda,* or *Cecilia Valdés.* The despairing voice of La Lupe turns into the joyous grandeur of Celia Cruz. Lecuona's piano, Bola de Nieve's loud baritone. Edith Piaf, Elena Bourke, Sarah Vaughan. Now and then, lights, beams of light fall in different directions, and there is no telling where they have come from.

Naked, his body painted white, the clown walks across a tightrope that one imagines is strung from one corner to the other of the orchestra pit. To keep his balance, he raises a many-colored umbrella in his right hand, while in his left he manipulates the marionette that reproduces himself, naked and gleaming white. He sings. His lovely tenorino voice intones an odd melody, which Victorio does not recognize. He leaps, and his resplendent figure seems to remain fixed in the darkness of the ruinous theater.

Victorio thinks he can hear the applause. He pays no attention. It is, clearly, old applause imprisoned between the walls. And the tightrope. What tightrope? Where is the tightrope?

2

Giselle's tomb. Labyrinthine hallways. False openings. Half-hidden doors. Holes hollowed out by Don Fuco the clown.

Victorio emerges into the Havana afternoon. He actually feels that he has done the opposite: that he has left behind the Havana afternoon and gained access to the ersatz afternoon of some variety theater. A cloud-covered afternoon. No rain falls. The heat is therefore magnified as if in a cauldron. Everything, even life itself, seems to be on hold, waiting for the storm. Beset by the humid, sweltering heat, and by the flies that this suffocating weather brings out, old women carry their stools or boxes out to the sidewalk and sit there fanning themselves with copies of *Granma* that no one has read, seeking some stray breeze from the north, some breeze mistakenly blowing their way; you can see the befuddlement and annoyance on the old women's faces: no one ever gets used to this humid heat, to the wall of dirty water that is this heat, nor can the passing years make a habit of this inferno. Truth be told, you could die of old age at a hundred and ten, still hoping that the window blinds might rustle from a puff of cool wind, like the ones that God sends to regions better regarded, better loved by Him.

Victorio has decided that the theater is the place for him. Said just like that, in all solemnity, as if you could hear the drums rolling when he pronounces this categorical sentence: "The theater is the place for me." True, like everyone who decides to respond to a calling, such as priests, seamen, ascetics, nurses, artists, and suicides, Victorio feels that he should first tie up a few of the loose ends that he has left out there, where life develops (if it really does develop) in perfect and habitual boredom.

He has gone walking around Havana. He has done the rounds of his favorite palaces: the lovely white mansion dating from the turn of the century, classical, conventional, yet with daringly modernist elements on the balconies and windows; the Casa de la Araucaria, with a robust *Araucaria excelsa* pine tree in the garden, built by the Italianist scholar Aurelio Boza Masvidal; the marvelous house with which Juan Pedro Baró hoped to prove his love for Catalina Lasa, the first art deco house in Havana, with a garden designed by Forestier (whose name was never more aptly employed) and built with marble from Carrara, ornaments by Lalique, sand from the Nile.

He makes the rounds of these palaces in a way he has never known before. He doesn't feel exactly anxious. He covets no ownership. These exceptional Havana palaces do not awaken his envy or his self-pity. His admiration remains intact, but he no longer suffers from seeing them as the spaces that he desires but cannot attain. As if now the palaces were somehow his.

He returns to Calle Galiano, to the corner where the building in which he was so unlucky once stood. The building has been demolished. Now they've begun collecting the rubble. A security cordon blocks it off. Several cranes pick up the stones and let them fall, with a tremendous racket and columns of smoke, into the dump trucks.

Victorio stops to watch, pretending to be just another person. He makes his way through the crowd of spectators who are standing behind the barricades. Emotionless, he looks at the steps from the old staircase. The window frames. The shattered panes. The remains of skylights and arches. An armless Saint Barbara. Pieces of tables and rocking chairs. Several washbasins. The headless Venus from the staircase landing. An iron bedframe. Stoves and clocks. Bathtubs covered with dirt. In a few spots wildflowers are already springing up.

Victorio can see Mema Turné sitting on a primitive pine chair, wearing her black Quaker-Marxist dress with ample neck and long sleeves. The dress makes her sweat desperately. On her sleeve she wears a red armband that says PUBLIC ORDER. On her bald head, a straw hat tied to her chin with a kerchief, red as well. Victorio hates once more her thin mustache and her suction-cup eyes. Her outrageous baritone martin voice repeats, monotonous and authoritarian, "Keep it moving, keep it moving, no one's allowed to stand here." In spite of Mema's intimidating tone, the spectators do stop in front of the protective barricades as if they don't hear her. Victorio can't resist the temptation: he picks up a smallish rock and tosses it at the old woman. He manages to hit her in the leg. The old woman jumps to her feet, flicks out her spotted tongue, and yells, "Go ahead, *gusanos,* worms! Attack, cowards! The full weight of History will fall on you, the people united will never be defeated." The spectators applaud.

Victorio wanders down Calle Reina and Avenida Carlos III. He passes (without a glance) the School of Letters and Art. He turns down Zapata. He rounds the Colón Cemetery. He sits in the lovely park where the Bureau of Investigations stood before the revolution. He rests his elbows on the bridge across the Almendares, "this river with its musical name," and thinks of Dulce María Loynaz, of Juana Borrero, and of Julián del Casal.

The neighborhood of Santa Felisa, the neighborhood of his childhood, is completely transformed, though it would be impossible to explain how. Everything is exactly the same, strangely identical, stuck in a time that has nothing to do with the time of reality. Nevertheless nothing looks the same; the neighborhood has been scandalously transformed. Victorio has experienced this sensation many times in Havana: the landscape has been modified precisely because it so obstinately remains unchanged. The passage of time has aged walls, columns, roofs, streets, trees, people, leaving them singularly motionless, like objects in the Museum of Useless Things. There, sitting inside the everlasting door to the corridor down which three families live, is old Ricarda. Still perched on her stool, just as Victorio remembers her, she keeps her feet soaking in a pewter basin of hot water, as is her custom, to counteract her aching rheumatism and the chilblains in her heels. As is her custom, she is asleep. It's all unchanged: the same old Ricarda, the same stool, the same basin, the same water, the same feet, the same problems. As if ten years hadn't passed. In any case, it cannot be the same Ricarda, nor the same basin, nor, of course, the same water.

The door to the humble apartment that once belonged to Victorio's family stands unlocked. The man who returns after a ten-year absence stops to caress the old boards that have lost successive coats of paint and now display the color of worn, worm-eaten, perhaps waterlogged wood. Sun, hurricanes, rainstorms, blasts of wind are, he imagines, among the fiercest manifestations of weather and time. The whirlwinds of time.

Victorio dares enter the little dining-living room, over which a churchlike silence spreads. Inside, the paradox of this neighborhood persists: everything is identical and different. The floor, like a chessboard, black and white tiles. The wicker rocking chairs, in need of varnish, faded tatters of cushions. The dining table covered with the same cracked glass. The tall blue vase with the bouquet of crepe paper flowers, which La Pucha, Hortensia, his mother, spent her free hours arranging, is now covered with dust and fly droppings. The same painting of the Sacred Heart of Jesus, the only religious symbol that Papá Robespierre was unable to banish when he set about burning saints and virgins to the accompaniment of La Pucha's wailing. Right next to the Sacred Heart, another photo, also religious in its own way, of a young and hope-inspiring Fidel Castro, giving the famous speech at which a dove settled on his shoulder. Elephants, Buddhas, damsels with parasols, troubadours with lutes, Chinese girls, dogs, doves, Spanish beauties with ornamental combs and mantillas, ghastly knickknacks, fakes porcelain statuettes bought for next to nothing in La Quincallera, in Sears, in El Ten Cents, in Los Precios Fijos. The bookshelf with the complete works of Lenin. Mao's little red book. The photograph of Papá Robespierre in Red Square, Moscow, overcoat, fur hat, winter, below zero, back in '75, '76, Victorio can't remember, some time when they must have awarded him a trip to go along with his being inducted into the Order of the National Vanguard. A trip whose main objective was to contemplate Lenin's mummy. The illuminated photograph of La Pucha, Hortensia, his mother, surprised while walking along Calle Monte, reddish dress, hair pulled back with a white flower, her smile as timid as ever. The photographs of Victoria, his sister, and Victorio — in La Concha, next to a gigantic beer bottle, on the Marianao beach — have been removed: their outlines on the wall persist.

Victorio reflects insistently: everything is in the same place as ever, but nothing is the same. He still doesn't know, cannot explain to himself, where the dissension lies between present and past, since each wall, each piece of furniture obstinately persists in fixing, in making permanent, a reality that cannot be the same, yet is. Reality takes revenge and transforms itself into itself.

The doorway to the bedroom, the only bedroom in the minimal house in Santa Felisa, is covered by the same curtain as ever, the one from his childhood, with geometric motifs, red triangles, blues rhomboids, green circles, black squares. He hears coughing. Papá Robespierre, it couldn't be anyone else, clearing his throat. With unaccustomed calm, Victorio walks forward. He tries to make no noise, not for his own sake but for the old man's. No, this time he isn't possessed by the fear that his father always inspired in him. Facing up to the man whom he always feared more than anyone else in this life holds no importance for him at this point. He even finds it funny to think that he was once terrified of him. He draws the curtain aside. In his wheelchair, Papá Robespierre holds his head low and a book on his lap. The door to the little patio is open. Victorio sees the invalid against the backlight, in a shadow that washes out details.

"Papá," he says.

The old man doesn't move.

"Papá," he repeats, afraid that the old man's deafness has gotten worse.

With a great effort, the elderly man then raises his head.

"I'm Victorio."

Papá Robespierre rests his chin against his chest, as if keeping his head up cost him too much effort.

Victorio enters the room. He is surprised by the bad smell, the rank stench, of accumulated sweat, of dirty clothing, of urine, of an unwashed body. Victorio notices that the photograph of the German Walter Ulbricht is missing. He sits down on the unmade bed. In the distance he can hear a salsa band. Papá Robespierre has become an old man, so old that Victorio can scarcely recognize his father almighty in him. His eyes are sunken, small, colorless; his pupils are blurry, as if they had been replaced with two chunks of glass. His son gets the impression that his eyes are not looking in any particular direction. He is wearing the beret with the Cuban flag. Even so, his hair sticks out like greasy white fuzz. His yellowish beard, grown long, which at one time gave him the look of a biblical patriarch (Job before the wager between Yahweh and Satan), now turns him into the image of a homeless man (Job after the wager). This image is fostered by his shirt, which was once a glorious olive green, and now looks yellowed, frayed, and dirty. He is wearing the medals he earned on all those cane harvests, on all those army mobilizations, on all those work battalions; these, too, have lost the gilded sheen they had in former years when Victorio thought they were made of gold.

Papá Robespierre's hands tremble. Water runs persistently from his nose, which he constantly has to wipe with the back of his trembling hand. With great difficulty he raises his head toward the ceiling. For an instant. Again he lets it fall heavily. The salsa band stops. The silence grows long and heavy, like a great dead animal. The distant cheer of the salsa band can make the room's squalor more dismal. Still trembling, the old man's hands attempt to grasp the arms of the wheelchair. The book slips from his useless legs and hits the ground. He also tries to wipe the water dripping from his nose. Victorio helps him.

From nearby kitchens comes a strong smell of recently filtered coffee. An argument can be heard, fierce words without any background: somebody is refusing to visit somebody or other. The band again goes on the attack:

> *El cuarto de Tula le cogió candela,*
> *se quedó dormida y no apagó la vela . . .*
>
> Tula's bedroom is all on fire,
> she fell asleep and left the candle burning . . .

Papá Robespierre looks at Victorio through reddened eyes. The bedroom in the minimal house in Santa Felisa grows even darker, as if the afternoon had given way to night. One of the veins that stand out on his father's temples is making his forehead swell and throb. His nose continues dripping.

231

The neighbors end their argument. Another neighbor, perhaps the same one, sings along with some hit singer, one of those singers who don't belong to any country and who sing ballads that have no nationality, about loves of overwhelming intensity, about desperate meetings and departures. This doesn't mean that the salsa band has stopped playing: both commotions, the singer and the band, mesh in an odd way.

Papá Robespierre coughs again. The cough makes a bellows-like sound in the cavern of his chest. He looks at his wrist as if he wants to see what time it is, except he has no watch. The old man again rests his chin against his chest, and seems to have fallen asleep.

A fly begins to bother him. Victorio shoos it.

In some nearby house you can hear a clock chiming the hour, an antiquated sound, one you wouldn't expect to hear in the year 2000. Whenever he hears a clock's chimes, Victorio experiences an inexplicable discomfort, as if he were the victim of some confusion or some fraud. On the other hand, the chimes serve to remind him how much he enjoyed, as a child, listening to the sounds in his neighbors' houses, the auditory promiscuity that allowed him to reconstruct, after his own fashion, other people's lives.

Papá Robespierre is sweating. Victorio takes a towel that is hanging from a nail and dries the sweat that is running down his forehead, down his neck. The old man lifts an arm. On the wall above the bed, La Pucha, Hortensia, his mother, had hung a Madonna and child. It is a mestiza Madonna, made with rough clay and vivid colors. Covered in dust. Empty eyes that have come unpainted. Like Papá Robespierre's eyes, the Madonna's eyes do not look in any particular direction. Victorio turns on the lamp with the porcelain base, some kind of running nymph, Lladró-style, that had seemed so elegant to him as a child, and that he now discovers in all its pretentious vulgarity.

★

No, it isn't raining. It isn't even cloudy. The afternoon is gorgeous, clear and cool. And this proves to Victorio that, sometimes, life. That sometimes, life, what?

He wanders off again along sidewalks that shimmer like desert sands. The trees provide no shade. A carnival atmosphere on the broken streets.

He heads all the way down Calle 51, passes the old Quinta San José mansion where Lydia Cabrera lived, the Bilacciao peanut factory. He stops to rest at the Puentes Grandes bridge, where again he inevitably invokes Juana Borrero and Julián del Casal, who would arrive at her house here in the tram that once ran from Avenida Carlos III. When he reaches the wooded park that surrounds the July 26 Clinical Surgical Hospital, he recalls Salomé, the dazzling ephebus who liked to like to stroll around naked at night among the trees that screen off the railway line, and who turned up dead one day, his head split open and a wild stick shoved up his ass; to date, his killers have not been found.

Victorio skirts the sports complex and the Fuente Luminosa, the fountain that Cuban jokers have christened with the nickname "Paulina's bidet." Again he walks slowly, for a long time. Walk, stroll, ramble: these are the three synonyms on which at some point his fate seems to have settled. He leaves behind the Plaza de la Revolución and the National Library, where he spent the hours of a magical adolescence in the music room.

He reaches the bus station. Now the rain has started falling. A fine, patient drizzle, inappropriate for a city that isn't characterized by its refinement or patience. The night begins to take on a pleasantly sultry atmosphere. The city is strangely empty. Unlike the city, however, the bus station is full to the brim. Especially on the second floor, where those who are on the waiting list persist in waiting. Women, men, old people, children, lying on the floor, resting against suitcases, boxes, trunks, with the dejected expressions of those who know for certain that they have a night of waiting ahead of them, that is, an endless and pointless night. The place swarms with people hawking peanuts, candles, coffee, costume jewelry, cold pizzas, miraculous prayers, croquettes and bread, leather shoes, dog collars, pencils and notebooks, devilishly ugly plastic saints, coconut candy, towels, pillows, hair clips, and burners for kitchen stoves. A woman in her forties, dressed in black, makeup applied without the benefit of a mirror, has a portable radio tuned in to the mellifluous music of Radio Encyclopedia (Paul Mauriac and his orchestra? Richard Clayderman? Barry White?). An incredibly ugly, grimy, dandruffy old man, stinking of sweat, with dreadfully bad breath, sexless, of course, and nicknamed Coridón, is selling little Olympic flags, stamps from some conference, cassettes of Latin American national anthems, movie posters, and mimeographed poems by an Uruguayan semi-poet, a leftist and therefore necessarily pretentious.

Victorio heads for the restroom. He is dying to pee. That is the only reason that has caused him to pull into the horror that is the bus station. Whenever he enters this waiting room, where it seems that nothing will ever happen, he is overcome by a terrifying sadness. Lucky for him, he thinks, he doesn't have any relatives to visit in the interior of the Island. A famished little old man is nodding and dozing as he sits on a stool by a table, on which there is a plate of twenty-centavo coins and a caged, and therefore restless, parrot that flutters desperately. There is no one in the urinals. Another piece of good fortune. To be able to urinate calmly, without being stared at obliquely by the hopeless-queens-of-the-urinals. What a pleasure, emptying a full bladder! What a pleasure, listening to your urine hit the porcelain of the urinal! What a delight, shaking yourself, getting rid of the last drops of urine, pulling up your underwear, fixing your dick like someone who has just accomplished an arduous, meticulous, hygienic task!

Someone crosses behind Victorio and stops two urinals down. Almost instinctively, Victorio delays the action of closing his pants. Now he is the one with the grim gaze, the oblique stare, the hopeless-queen-of-the-urinal. It's worth it to lower your eyelids, twist your eyes. An opulently vigorous prick, stout, blood-red, abundant, noble, breaks through two equally opulent fingers. Translucent, the salutary and beneficent stream of urine gives testimony to a faultless pair of kidneys. Victorio casts a quick glance at the man's face, half hidden by shadows and by the visor of a Florida Marlins baseball cap. He doesn't actually care, he couldn't care who the owner of this marvel might be; he doesn't know what he looks like, nor does he need to know. He looks at nothing but the prick. There are some pricks that aren't mere pricks, they are the aleph, the yin-yang, the alpha and omega, the stars on whose energy whole astral systems are centered.

The man finishes his piss and shakes his virile pride self-confidently. He gives it a good shake — not just self-confidently but meticulously, affectionately, very carefully, so that not a single drop of urine will stain his underwear. Then he leaves it hanging there, abandoning it to its own life. He shakes it again, unnecessarily, more tenderly. Victorio notes the triumphant way in which that handsome piece of flesh begins to turn into a divine mast, leaning slightly to the left. Long and opulent, rosy and clean, the glans tops off a marvelous stalk, rutted by a hydrography of deep-flowing veins.

Such an image cannot suffice: that is what the man must think, for he has introduced his right hand, with ostentatious, theatrical gestures, inside his pants, and has taken out a pair of luxuriant balls, as if he were setting out two loaves of bread. Corona of dark and hispid hair, thick and sinewy member, succulent balls. Victorio takes a bold step forward, stops at the urinal that stands next to the stranger. The stranger, in turn, does not touch his masculinity; perhaps he is trying to show that it is capable of shaking and moving on its own. Indeed, it does move up and down. And this kind of movement seems to be its way of sending an invitation. Victorio brings his hand over, slowly and quickly; he takes up this weapon with gentle violence. The stranger's prick has a soft hardness. It is very solid, very hard: at the same time, and at heart, it has a seductive blandness, a harsh frailty. Victorio notes that it is seething, he feels it pulsate in his hands like an animal that is both confident and fierce. He feels how the blood courses through the vast rivers of those veins. He moves it back and forth. Its skin is a delicate sheath. Its glans hides and peeks out, hides and peeks out disquietingly.

One of the stranger's hands goes to Victorio's head and presses it down. The other hand presses on the back of his head. Victorio kneels obediently. He tries to fill his mouth with saliva, for he knows full well (anybody would know full well) how much males like it when their manhoods enter the warmness of the wet mouths of other kneeling men. But when he is just about to let this splendor enter his mouth, the stranger takes a step back. Victorio hears, for the first time, his tender, somewhat sad voice, warning, "No, Victorio, before I can gratify you, you have to tell me where Salma is."

Without even standing up, Victorio lifts his eyes. He meets the perfect, smiling face of Sacredshroud.

He walks up Rancho Boyeros. Turning onto Calle Bruzón, he disappears among the broken sidewalks, overflowing sewers, frightful little houses, until he thinks he is out of danger on Avenida de Ayestarán. He is marching at a quick pace, running without running, of course, so as not to call attention to himself; excited, sweating, his heart in his throat, constantly looking back. He goes up Ayestarán and reaches Avenida Carlos III. At the first bus stop, miraculously, a bus is taking on passengers. He doesn't know how, but he is able to get on. He shamefully tells the conductor, "Pardon me, I don't have any money to pay for the bus."

The conductor, a tall black man with a thick mustache and long sideburns, in a uniform worn out from too much laundering, looks at him mistrustfully. He apparently perceives the truthfulness of the shame that Victorio feels, and replies with a generous smile that belies his fierce expression, "No problem, neighbor, go ahead on in."

On the bus, Victorio recovers his serenity. It is filled with exhausted people. The heat might be infernal, but Victorio experiences the happiness of having freed himself from a great danger. He doesn't mind the elbows shoving him, the terrible smell of sweat, the disturbing, awkward silence of everyone traveling on the bus, all holding on to the metal pipes as if they were grasping their last remote hopes for life. He doesn't mind that a van is passing the bus, blaring through loudspeakers a deafening voice:

> On every block, a Committee.
> In every neighborhood, Revolution . . .

A woman who is nearing fifty, squat and fat, sweating profusely and carrying an ancient General Electric fan in her free hand, maintains her balance with difficulty and looks at Victorio with eyes in which complicity mingles with hatred, self-pity, sadness, fury, tenderness, resignation, and, in a single phrase, she sums up what perhaps everyone there is thinking: "Damn, it isn't easy."

"No, it isn't easy." Here's a phrase, Victorio reasons, that is recited in Cuba with the same frequency that people like to swear, "Hell, it's hot!" Two phrases that, for that matter, are often teamed together: It isn't easy, buddy, this kinda heat isn't easy.

"It isn't easy." A phrase that can be pronounced at any time, under any circumstances. It isn't easy, if you decide to go to the movies, to church, to a party, to court, to the drugstore, to the corner store, to a Santería ceremony, to the hospital, to the Almendares park, to a bar, to a photography studio, to the farmers' market, to stroll down the street, along the beach, under the fierce blows of the sun, and try to soothe your burning skin. It isn't easy — my God, it isn't easy — if you decide to wait endlessly for something: a bus (a camel), a warning, electricity, a rainstorm, a letter, a boat, a piece of news, a friend, a clap of thunder, nostalgia, a bribe, a caress, an airplane, spring (which has never existed), winter (likewise), an advantage, a memory, a lover, a smile, a low blow, a carrier pigeon, envy, secrets, slander, a dart, a denunciation, death.

"It isn't easy." If you are waiting for something but you don't know for sure what it is.

"It isn't easy." Waiting for waiting's sake, that is, waiting without expectations, that is, hoping without hope, not a drop of it, nothing to expect, nothing to hope for.

He doesn't go straight to the theater. He is afraid of being fol-lowed. So he walks down toward the sea. For a while he makes long detours; he sits in a park. It is a park that was improvised on the site where a famous bookstore once stood. He knows it's dangerous. He is too tired. Despite the late hour, a group of small children is play-ing here. One of the little boys is a traitor and is about to be shot by firing squad. The other kids line him up against the wall of the build-ing next door and fire at him with their wooden rifles, bam bam bam! The boy falls down while the others jump with glee.

Victorio doesn't know how long he has waited in the park. The kids have left. The silence that falls is so exact that he can see it coming, touch it, cold as a dead man's skin. This is the time for lustful, desperate couples, for drinkers of rum, for police.

There is something shoddy, cardboardlike, about the way the street looks. The worm-eaten walls that passing years have undone, the salt deposited by too many tides and sea breezes, the rusty foundations exposed to view, the moldy beams, the respectable tombstones (*pulvis es et in pulverem reverteris*), are all as graceful and as shameless as the painted walls used on the commercial, profit-seeking, horrendous stage. Equally artificial, the light consists of only what the moon can give: artificial; a reflection of some other light. A legitimate metaphor, Victorio thinks, would be "the mirror of the moon illuminates the street like the footlights of a run-down theater."

The heat lulls and is capable of causing confusion. The heat in this part of the world is the best hallucinogen. Even his skin, the cotton of his shirt, gleam when they come in contact with the scanty light, the one-act-comedy light of the moon.

Victorio sweats, and breathes in the odor emanating from his underarms. He constantly tries to dry the palms of his hands on his pants, and only manages to get them damp more quickly. He bends over, picks up a rock, and throws it far away, toward the overgrown lot where, years ago, a building was to have been constructed. He throws the rock with the affected movements of a major league pitcher. That's what memories are, he says or thinks, rocks that we throw as far away as we can. Life must be to turn each memory into a powerful home run. Fine, a rage for phrases: we human beings are ridiculous, so what can you do?

Violins are playing. Sometimes just one; sometimes a violin ensemble. What are they performing? Victorio doesn't know, he can't identify it. He likewise hears voices singing. The street is empty. It's the dead of night. Not even the usual police are about. The violins and the singing reinforce the loneliness of the street, while the loneliness of the street exaggerates the sound of violins and singing.

An eclectic building, never before seen, becomes visible before Victorio's eyes, as if this were one of Don Fuco's magic acts: white-gray-blue-yellowish, ornate, crammed full of perilous balconies and pointless windows. Dirty. Ornate. Havana. Very Havana, this dirty, ornate building. There is an air of Paris, of Barcelona, of Cádiz about it: in other words, of Havana. Tall columns and covered walkways, there to protect the hapless passerby from the harshness and excesses of the heartless sun and heat and mist. The facade displays several doors; some of them — most of them — are not original. What is original and what isn't in this city? Four, five closed doors. Only the sixth is open, and it leads to a staircase. Like any other staircase in Havana, this one is narrow, dark, steep, perfect for a film about murder and mystery. Damp and stifling, smelling of the various odors associated with food, secretions, gases from the street, humidity, sleep, grease, urine, time. Despite the darkness, Victorio can see the peeling paint on the walls, the humid stains, the dirty old marble steps that were once white. Between the smooth-worn handrail of precious wood and the staircase steps, there stretches a sumptuous border of tiles from Seville that look like they were just unpacked.

Dirty, downtrodden, unpainted, worn out, exhausted, Havana tries to rise back up. Her head held high, very high; her gaze firm, unwavering; discouraged and unwavering. It doesn't matter if her body is tumbling down. Havana is like an old empress, bereft of wealth and bereft of empire, who still clutches on to her majesty and the value of her long-gone memories, her long-gone power.

His feet rapidly grow used to calculating the distance that they need to rise from one marble step to the next. His hands are only good for making sure he doesn't lose his balance. One hand, his left, caresses the wall; the other, his right, holds on to the handrail. His sense of smell tells him that he is coming closer and closer to a community of women and men. His ears can hear the violin and singing voices more clearly every second.

He reaches the first landing: he has left the street behind and the darkness here is total. The second flight of stairs begins to smell of herbs and flowers. A cologne, Sietepotencias, mixed with herbs and flowers. Victorio is sweating more and more. It's the heat. Climbing the stairs, too. The staircase seems almost vertical. From the dark, into the dark. On every floor, the doors and windows look locked shut. Is nobody here? Same with the last floor, where, unlike on the others, a cool gallery opens onto a central patio in which royal palms are growing. Victorio thinks: he is standing, for the first time, on a level with the spreading plumage of royal palms.

At the end of the corridor that opens up to the right there is a spiral staircase. Made of the finest wood, with gorgeous, daring, unbelievable details carved by master carpenters who have not managed to outlive their own refinements. The staircase must be over a hundred years old. And here it is, intact, as if time held no authority over it. At a certain point, the staircase opens up toward a row of balconies, which are also made of finely carved and excessively ornate wood.

There is a large, well-lighted room. Fifteen or twenty women are singing, all dressed in white, with white mantillas, white lace, white silk, white turbans, white handkerchiefs, white shoes, white stockings, sitting on little wicker rocking chairs. Wearing perfume. Fanning themselves with white fans. The perfume is stirred up, becoming stronger or weaker with each movement of the fans. The room is full. A little farther off, a group of men. All wearing impeccable cotton twill, linen, or wool suits, white as white. Suits from many years ago that have been conserved with perseverance inside wardrobes in which lavender plants have been hanging. Their shirts are also white and retain the body that starch once gave them. Everyone is smoking.

Not just the men; the women, too: the oldest women are savoring enormous Havana cigars that give off a bluish smoke whose quality seems unreal. They smoke and relish it. They smoke as if nothing else mattered in the world. They observe the cigar between their fingers in the same way you might observe the relics of a saint. They turn it over. They look at it as if it held some extraordinary secret. Then they bring it to their lips with expert slowness. They savor the smoke. Their heads uplifted. Their eyes closed. How delicious! Only a real Cuban, Victorio thinks, could savor a cigar so voluptuously.

In the center of a room stands a table laden with sweets. And beyond it, a magnificent altar, decked in lily-white lace tablecloths, tablecloths done in Richelieu embroidery, hemmed in buttonhole stitching, tablecloths with festooned trim. The altar is covered with burning candles and white flowers — amaryllis, mariposas, gardenias, asters, jasmines — as well as plates of sweets, ex-votos, little bells, sepia-toned photographs in frames that must have once been gilded. In the center, tall, full-sized, immaculate, escorted by black cherubs and two palm leaves: Obbatalá, the Virgin of Mercy, Her dress long, Her hands held tight, and Her benevolent face — which looks as if it could not have been carved from wood — serene. At Her pious, magnanimous feet are the fiddlers.

Victorio makes it up the last few steps of the spiral staircase. Everyone turns to look. The women rise from their rocking chairs, which continue rocking. The fiddlers stop playing. Victorio feels all their stares stabbing into his skin like darts. The fiddlers are the first to react: they return to their instruments, and again the melodies for Obbatalá are heard while the singing resumes, and the rest of those present light candles and kneel. Only one black nonagenarian with blue eyes and long, limp white hair draped over his shoulders, wearing a guayabera, twill pants, and two-toned shoes, supporting himself with a cane that isn't a cane but a wild stick, comes up to Victorio and gestures to him with a trembling hand that he should follow. The old man stops before the altar. He takes Victorio's right hand and raises it. A young woman, scarcely more than a girl, whose head is covered by a mantilla and whose cheeks are as white as her mantilla and her dress, whose arms are covered with bracelets, brings a pewter basin into which water, powdered eggshell, perfume, and flower petals have been poured. She dips a branch of jasmine into the perfumed water. They sweep the wet branch over Victorio's now naked torso. He enjoys having the girl moisten his torso. He smiles at the Virgin of Mercy, he flirts with Her: "Hey, beautiful, bless you, Obbatalá, mother of us all."

It's the dead of night. To the sound of violins and more violins, the women are singing,

> Blessed is he that comes
> in the name of the Lord . . .

3

The days grow shorter and shorter, the harshness of the daylight dwindles. The sea breeze begins to threaten, sweetly yet vigorously, and to stir the unseen, blurry gray sea. Winter is beginning, that is, the euphemism that in Havana has always been known as "winter." For a few days at least, you can breathe. Horizon and coastline let you look at them directly, without dazzling you too much, and every day there are fewer children who head down in the afternoon, after school, to romp on the Malecón.

He tries to sleep on the floor, next to the relics, on a pallet of blankets, in the dressing room of Anna Pavlova, the Great One. Beside him, Salma and Don Fuco give themselves over to serenity and the luster of their own exhaustion. Salma is wearing a gauze dress spangled with tiny stars and colored beadwork. There must be something cheery in her dream, because a smile steals across the tranquil expression on her distant face. Don Fuco is dozing in the usual white robe and the ancient, ridiculous Shylock cap, and you can tell he is sleeping because he isn't moving, simply because of that, since there is no other difference between the sleeping clown and the waking clown.

Victorio, on the other hand, is restless: he has slept, and awakened, and fallen asleep again, and awakened again. Over his forty-something years, he has rarely been granted the good fortune of a beneficial sleep. During these last nights of the year 2000, his sleep crisis has grown markedly worse. He goes from the shock of wakefulness to the shock of nightmares, and from nightmares once more to the wicked glimmerings of wakefulness, without always knowing for certain on which side of sleep he finds himself.

He gets up. He envies Salma and Don Fuco, who, he is certain, are dreaming of the astral plane. Victorio rises from the floor and from the rags and netting that compose his bed in the dressing room of Anna Pavlova, the Great One. He is half naked, half awake. He leaves sleep behind.

He goes to the window. The only mystery of night is that it holds no mysteries. The sea is even darker than the night; it is a prolonged nonexistence, out beyond the wall. A wall named Malecón, much as it might have been called Jetty, Breakwater, Seawall. A wall that has often been given symbolic connotations, such as the Havana native trapped on the Island, the Havana native facing the sea, the man watching the horizon, the man looking nostalgically into the distance, waiting for revelations and messages. What is sure as can be about this wall is that all it's good for is enjoying the cool, putting up with impossibly hot nights, and for joining bodies; that is, for putting up better with the heat of the climate and heat of your body. Right now, for example, there's a couple kissing desperately, and more desperately still, touching each other as if they each wanted to be sure of the other's existence. A policeman — a real presence if ever there was one — strolls down the wide sidewalk and, at a certain point, when he is closest to the couple, it is as if he too has become part of the libidinous duo: a relationship is suddenly created between the police and the pair, for a matter of just a few seconds, true; yet there's no doubt that, if not their bodies, at least their three energy fields are mingling shamelessly, with the promiscuity that is no myth, no mere symbol in this city where the first, last, the only thing that matters is to mate, to bang, to shack, to screw, to fuck and fuck. In appearance, the policeman continues on his beat, at his martial pace, in his neat uniform and severe boots, while the couple keeps kissing, and everything around the couple, including the wall, the sea, the policeman, and the night, seems to depend upon their union.

Distant rays of lightning brighten the horizon and the night. Is this all? Is this the world? Is it really morning now in Australia?

He can't turn on the lights — his two companions would wake up. He limits himself to lighting the big candle that Don Fuco uses, and it turns out that the candle gives off little light. Its insecure and feeble flame serves only to keep him from falling into the nearest hole, and perhaps to help him plan his next step. If there is no light, there is no theater, thinks Victorio as he faces the impassible darkness of what he imagines must be the orchestra seating. He can't tell where the tomb of Giselle is. The piano, however, that much he can find, because the piano is a white, lovely patch in the midst of shadows.

He hears thunder. Above the stage, the staccato of a few raindrops, hitting the roof like stones, which in a few seconds turn into a full-blown rainstorm. The flashes of lightning slip in through the cracks in the roof. Victorio knows that in this part of the world known as the Greater and Lesser Antilles, storms can be truly intense and insistent, and can make men lose their senses. He is ignorant of the scientific truth that hides behind this pronouncement, because he is unaware of the fact that, in general, the reality of these lands mocks all truths, whether legal, scientific, religious, or profane. The Antilles are islands, thinks Victorio, where the gods decided to die, and the devils are trying to live forever.

Victorio is walking through the theater and waiting for something and not knowing what. He feels that the theater is moving like

247

a boat adrift. He has always had this perception, since his childhood, when they should have closed all the doors and windows, sealed them up with stone and mortar, due to the intensity of the storms.

As in his contemptible little room on Calle Galiano, now, too, he is waiting for something. A miracle? A catastrophe?

The rain makes the silence of the theater more powerful or more solemn. This is a moment when the theater does not belong to Havana, or to Cuba, or to anything; it is a place or a hallucination outside of time and space.

The rainstorm is bursting energetically, torrentially, definitively. It is the closest thing to the Deluge ever conceived by the deceased gods and the brutally surviving devils of the cursed island.

Sitting in the orchestra, Victorio remains quiet, calm, motion-less, as if he were waiting for something. Miracle or disaster, it's all the same. And isn't it true that any locked door becomes an un-known, screaming be opened? That, at least, is what Victorio thinks, or says; and he laughs at himself, because he is well aware that a locked door proposes something much more simple and immediate: nothing other than to keep you from entering, from looking, from being tempted. Such as, for example, the dressing room doors. The locked doors to the dressing room of Lorenzo the Magnificent and the dressing room of the Guignol. He is moved more strongly than ever by his curiosity to enter the only place in the ruined theater that Don Fuco has taken the precaution of forbidding to them.

For the first time, in a fit of disrespect or daring or debatable in-dependence, he takes the bunch of keys that the clown always leaves hanging by the handless pendulum clock. He steps lightly across the floor, he walks on air, and his footsteps therefore cannot be heard. He makes no footsteps, nothing could give him away: his curiosity has transformed him into a shadow. He must try several keys in the lock before he discovers which is the obscure and insignificant little key that can set in motion the uncomplicated gearworks of the grim-looking padlock.

The door, it turns out, is stiff. Victorio has to push hard against it to make it open. The dressing room is small and empty. The only thing in it is a player piano or organ with a large golden crank.

Victorio shuts the door and approaches the instrument. It is made of glossy, polished wood: it looks like crystal. Inscribed in Gothic letters, it says "Lorenzo Nadal." Victorio checks to see that the door is shut tight, and he turns the crank, starting up the mechanical works of the player piano.

Nobody would be able to see Victorio right now. He deduces that this is the key difference between bad music and good music. It's that real music makes you invisible. The listener escapes and reappears elsewhere. All your senses switch functions. All that is hermetically sealed becomes diaphanous. He thinks he has finally recognized that life is everlasting and fleeting. He listens to the music, and tells himself, "This apparent paradox is usually called happiness, joy, gratification, satisfaction, delight, contentment, fruition, pleasure."

This next door is simple to open. Stepping across the threshold is nevertheless not a simple matter. What name should he give to this instinct, which begs him to lock the door again and go lie down on the pallet to try and sleep? There is no doubt about it, curiosity proves stronger. He makes an effort, takes a step, a second, a third, and here he is, inside the dressing room.

The candlelight is so diffuse, its active radius is very limited, but that doesn't keep Victorio from noticing the many marionettes, the unsuspectedly enormous number of marionettes that hang from the tangle of cords stretching from one end of the room to the other. How many are there? Two thousand, three thousand? Marionettes of every size, material, color, dress, and expression. Black, Chinese, white marionettes. Clothed marionettes and naked marionettes. Contented and annoyed marionettes. Marionettes that are laughing, marionettes that are crying. The unbelievable profusion of marionettes does not impede him as he makes way through to the back of the room, where he finds, against the wall, a small theater of boxes and boards, nothing too fancy, a simple framework sitting on a table covered with a black cloth. The box is painted, gracefully decorated with the intent of imitating the eclectic splendor of the proscenium of the Paris Opera. The curtain has been concocted from a lovely red cloth. A real shell, a seashell, serves as the shell-like prompter's box.

Right next to the puppet theater there is another table, not covered by cloth, with several cases where more marionettes are resting. Victorio approaches and sets the large candle in its candlestick on the table. By the bashful light of the candle he tries to see the marionettes resting there in their cases, as if in their beds or their sarcophagi. He looks closely at them. He can't tell whether what he is seeing is real. He also intuits that if it isn't real, it isn't false, either. There is a small cardboard airplane that looks burnt. A shirtless, dark marionette that recalls El Moro. The next marionette looks like a dead woman and the dead woman is similar to Salma's mother. The next marionette would represent Salma herself. Any closer resemblance between the marionette and the person would have to be impossible; no one could understand how this might be a coincidence. Farther off, far away, sitting in the basket of a hot-air balloon the size of a ball, Victorio thinks he has found Victorio, he thinks he finds himself in the form of a puppet covered with strings, solemn and badly dressed, looking famished, like a bum.

Pinned to a small bulletin board are pieces of paper with notes that are not clear, scrawled hurriedly in careless calligraphy. Victorio feels that he can decipher such phrases as "collapsed building," "rooftop terraces," "hunger," "sacred shroud," "church," "cemetery," "death."

He turns to the puppet theater. Opens the curtain. On the miniature stage there are no props, just two suspended marionettes: a ballerina and a policeman. And a pistol has been placed in the policeman's left hand, while the ballerina's pearly white or eternally white tutu has been theatrically stained with red paint, simulating blood.

"Pandora's great sin was curiosity," booms a voice behind him.

Victorio notices that there is much more light now in the Guignol's dressing room. He turns around. Don Fuco is not carrying any light in his hands, just his white robe and his ancient and ridiculous Shylock cap.

"Curiosity, the great sin," the clown exclaims, amused, swishing the luminous whiteness of his robe.

"Please forgive me," Victorio tries to excuse himself, caught red-handed, ashamed, not knowing what to do.

The clown makes a dainty gesture with his hands, raising them as if trying to stop something that is collapsing on him, and exclaims in his finest tenorino voice, "No, my friend, no, don't blush: Pandora was a mortal, after all, a human being; luckily for her, she didn't participate in the divine essence. You've been more than discreet. Logically, you should have entered the dressing room long since. By my calculations, you should have opened this door more than a month ago."

Victorio recovers from his shame and, emboldened, picks up the marionette that to all appearances represents himself. "What does this mean?" he asks.

The clown lifts his hands to the spot on his chest where his heart supposedly lies. "Please don't commit the vulgar error of thinking that someone tried to make a puppet that looks like you." He opens his eyes in a sad gesture. "These Punchinellos are older than me, and that is saying a lot. They are more than two hundred years old — no, my friend, please don't stare at me with that look of incredulity. The puppets you see here were made in the sixteen hundreds by Giovanni Briocci. There are others here by Hoffman, and from the collection of Carl Engel, and I have a number from the Salzburg school, and others from the Osaka school, and if they look like us . . ." He moves his hands as if he were conducting an imaginary orchestra, then stands motionless for several seconds. "But, no, my friend, they do not look like us: marionettes are superior. As Heinrich von Kleist asserted, a puppet would never do anything in an affected manner, because affectation appears when the soul (*vis motrix*) inhabits any other point than the center of gravity of a movement. Puppets have the advantage of being weightless, my friend. They know nothing of inertia, and inertia is the enemy of dance. Puppets are different from dancers because the force that raises them into the sky is greater than that which ties them to the earth. In 1801, Kleist said that puppets need the ground as much as elves do, and he concluded with a marvelous assertion: only a god might, in this regard, measure up against mere matter, and this is the point where the two ends of the ring that we call the world join together."

The clown strides forward with his adolescent gait, crosses the dressing the room, and pulls back a curtain that Victorio has not noticed. It is a curtain or tapestry in gold and sepia tones, depicting a hot-air balloon that rises toward the cupolas of palaces high in the clouds. The curtain or tapestry hides a small door that opens onto a darkened room. The clown crosses the threshold and the room lights up. A long table is covered with black cloths. The only furniture in the room. The black pieces of cloth take on different forms all along the table, so it is obvious that the cloths and the table are all hiding something.

"Now you are inside my sanctum sanctorum, my *locus solus,* my Valhalla, and here you'll see something wonderful," the clown exclaims in a magician's voice, and he raises the first piece of cloth. Victorio can see a bell jar that contains a dense fog. The clown winds a key several times, and to the tune of Chopin's *Revolutionary* Etude, executed in the tones and insipid sounds of a music box, the fog rises. There, inside the bell jar is a man in a white shirt, riding a sorrel colt; something suddenly stops the horseman, whose shirt stains red; the terrified sorrel rears its forehooves; the horseman falls onto the grass. Don Fuco winds the bell jar mechanism several times; several times they watch the man in the white shirt, who rides a colt and who is shot dead (by a bullet?) onto the grass.

The second bell jar is uncovered, its mechanism is wound, and a poor parody of a Chinese or perhaps a Japanese melody is heard. A young man, sitting at a table set for supper, laughs; the young man laughs and, laughing, spits up blood; the tablecloth is covered with blood, blood covers the young man's clothes, the young man collapses onto the table.

In the third bell jar the chords of Beethoven's *Appassionata* Sonata ring out, and a man with an umbrella appears, sitting on a wicker rocking chair and rocking sadly, sorrowfully. And so, in each bell jar a scene takes place to the beat of a different piece of music. The dolls are disturbingly precise. They look like tiny people. They have the color, the spirit, the vulnerability, the grief, the desperation of human beings. As soon as the clockwork mechanism stops and the artificial music ceases in each bell jar, fog obscures the jar's interior.

"Everything is here," declares the clown, self-satisfied, and his look of complacency and his firm gestures show how certain he is.

253

"Everything is here," the clown repeats. "The whole island can sink tomorrow; what can never disappear are the ruins of this theater."

"How did you get . . . ?" Victorio tries to ask, looking at the marionette that represents him and experiencing deep feelings of confusion. "I mean, all this, the place where we're standing, the theater, everything in it."

The clown performs a dance step and spreads his hands, as if the geography to which he was referring were too remote. The clown goes to a wardrobe and takes out a harlequin's outfit, red, yellow, and black, and makes Victorio put it on. He takes out a wig of bright green hair and places it on Victorio's head. "Come on, put on these clothes, your country looks down on you with pride."

Victorio kisses the key to the palace that he wears around his neck, and gets dressed. In an old chest, Don Fuco now discovers a laurel crown, which isn't really made of laurel leaves but of tin. With theatrical gestures he places the crown on the green wig.

Walking backward, as one should do for kings, the clown Don Fuco steps back from the harlequin. He admires his finished work. He smiles with satisfaction. Don Fuco does not leave: he vanishes into the shadows.

Two knocks are heard at the stage, next to Giselle's tomb. For several seconds there is no other signal. It is raining. Hard. Rain is falling on the peaked roof above the stage. It sounds like an ovation. Victorio draws near the false tomb. He sees, he thinks he sees, that someone is pushing against the prop cover of the tomb. Jostling it gently, carefully, but firmly; if they had done it a little more decisively, the cover would have given way easily. Whoever is on the other side, you can tell that either they don't understand the mechanism of the entrance, or else they prefer to act with restraint. They don't want to make any noise, that much is obvious, and they allow another long period of calm to stretch out in the Pequeño Liceo of Havana. No new sound disturbs this primitive silence. Victorio even comes to thinks that he has been a victim of fear, of the delirium that fear induces: say what you will, fear remains the most potent way to transform reality. Victorio walks very carefully, barefoot, in his harlequin outfit, his wig and laurel crown, which isn't made of laurel leaves but of tin. He slips in among the old orchestra seating. He has left the candlestick on the marionette table. He makes do with the scanty light that filters in through the cracks in the roof, along with the rain. The rain is so intense that the bats have ceased their clumsy gliding across the space above him.

Two, three, four concise knocks. The only consequence is that they awaken Salma. Victorio sees her appear in the gauze and spangles of her dress, from the left side of the stage; he sees her come down into the orchestra seating, close to him. "What's going on?" she asks without asking, her eyes confused by a dream from which she has perhaps not yet shaken free.

He raises an index finger to his lips in a sign of silence.

The disorder of Salma's sleepy eyes rapidly turns to fright: besides being potent, the influences of fear are also swift. She needs no explanations: Salma understands. Victorio then sees her close her eyes, as if this momentary loss of sight might sharpen her sense of hearing. More knocking is heard at Giselle's tomb. There is nothing restrained about these new knocks. Salma and Victorio run to the end of the pit. They hide behind the tattered screen with countryside scenes of palm trees, brooks, and huts. Salma's hands squeeze Victorio's. He feels the chill of her sweating hands against his. For a few minutes all they hear is the knocking of the thunderstorm against the roof. They would have preferred a rapidly unfolding outcome of noise and aggression; the truth is different: a century passes before they hear more noise, breaking glass, and see a policeman appear, a policeman soaked with rain, rising from Giselle's tomb. Hesitantly and without hesitating, the officer steps toward the stage. A circle of water forms around him. He walks forward cautiously. He carries a flashlight in his hand, which he switches on to see where he is going. The policeman looks far too sure of himself for his self-confidence to be real. To all appearances he lacks the serene gait that the uniform gives police. There is even something in his figure that Victorio seems to remember, and which he cannot at first decipher. Salma cries out, in a mute, whispered scream, "It's El Negro Piedad!"

Indeed, as he walks stealthily and never stops looking in every direction, there are moments when the flashes of lightning that enter through the cracks in the roof reveal the proud profile of Sacredshroud. Strange at it seems, during those dangerous seconds Victorio finds him handsomer than ever.

What happens at this precise instant seems like a dream, another dream, even though this time it is a matter of the ordinary stuff of which reality is composed. In the center of the stage, a candelabra laden with thick candle stubs rises, calmly and rapidly. The echoing rain dies down and a flute is heard playing the melancholy melody of "The Swan," piece number thirteen of *The Carnival of the Animals* by Saint-Saëns. The shock of it not only immobilizes Salma and Victorio: even the policeman, El Negro Piedad, better known as Sacredshroud, stands paralyzed, his arms hanging limp. White feather headdress, classic tarlatan tutu, and pointed dancing slippers: performing a perfect *pas de bourrée,* Don Fuco enters the stage. A timid look on his face, he moves both arms like wounded wings. Any turn of phrase that might be used to describe this scene enters inevitably onto the plane of paradox. Extremely laughable; extremely moving. An old clown parodies a ballerina; an extraordinary ballerina figures the death throes of a swan. For a while, Salma and Victorio forget about El Negro, forget about where they are; they feel the excitement of witnessing an act whose essence vanishes like smoke. A yearning to laugh out loud; a yearning to cry. They have to suppress both laughter and tears. Comic, tragic, ridiculous, distinguished, poignant, hilarious. Any pair of contradictory words would do.

El Negro Piedad, better known as Sacredshroud, seems to recover from the shock. As might have been expected, he escapes the enchantment long before Salma and Victorio do. While Salma and Victorio are moving from surprise to admiration, the pimp, or the policeman (you can no longer tell), is coming out of his surprise merely to fall into the coarse realization that here, in a ruined theater, under the light of a handful of candles, a terribly ugly old man, decked out in a tutu, is dancing grotesquely to the tune of some weird music. All three observe the same thing and all three observe different scenes.

Neither Victorio nor Salma hears the shot. They let themselves be dazzled by a flash that could be another bolt of lightning. They think they see a multitude of bats escaping in terror from the ruins. The Old Man-Ballerina-Clown-Swan stops still in the center of the stage. He tries to raise his hand to his head. He takes two more steps, two wavering steps. He falls headlong. Near the proscenium. Don Fuco's feather headdress is rapidly turning red. The music stops. All that can be heard is the fluttering of the bats and a sound like stone falling against stone.

In one agile bound, El Negro Piedad is on his knees next to the clown's inert body. He lifts Don Fuco uncaringly. He looks into the dead man's eyes and uncaringly lets him fall. Victorio notes El Negro's almost sad expression. Melancholy makes the face of Sacredshroud more beautiful.

Salma appears backstage. Victorio doesn't know when the young woman found the time to leave his side and travel around the orchestra pit until she reached the stage. The fact is, she's there, in her gauze dress and colored beadwork. In her hands she is carrying the bronze bust of José Martí.

Still kneeling, El Negro Piedad now looks at the blood, at his own bloodied hands. He is about to stand up, but Salma brings the bronze head of the poet down upon his head. For a moment the eyes of Sacredshroud appear captivated. You might swear that he is smiling just before he falls forward and lies outstretched on top of the ballerina, on top of Don Fuco, both of them lit by the flickering flashes of the storm.

4

The old clown's body is wrapped in a black velveteen cape. He is wearing the pointed dance slippers, the tarlatan tutu, and the feather headdress. Dressed in that getup, his dead body would be hard for them to take and carry through the streets without calling attention to themselves. They haven't noticed that their precautions are pointless, given that Salma is dressed in a spangled gauze dress and Victorio is sporting a green wig, a harlequin outfit, and a laurel crown that is really made of tin. With some trepidation they go outside, into the driving rain, into the early Havana morning of soaked and badly lit streets, of facades that look like rubble. Salma realizes that she is still carrying the bust of José Martí, and she sets it down carefully, like an abandoned baby, at the door of an office building that has been closed because it is danger of collapsing. Fortunately, Don Fuco's body weighs little, and it is raining furiously. They have no problem moving the corpse a couple of blocks. But the streets are empty only of pedestrians, not of police officers wearing black raincoats. As soon as they see the police car and the first pair of watchmen, they duck into the first staircase they find. The building is four stories tall. Rainwater is oozing through the walls. If Victorio's calculations are correct, if his knowledge of Havana is not mistaken, at the top of the staircase there should be an access door to the rooftop terrace. With Salma's help, he hoists Don Fuco over his shoulder. They begin climbing. Salma holds Don Fuco's feet, to help Victorio. After the fourth floor, indeed, a door opens onto the early morning rain. The storm remains the same, omnipresent and aggressive. They rest against the water tanks.

Worn out. Panting. Soaking wet. The weight of the dead body makes Victorio lose his vision momentarily. Salma looks at him with a frightened question in her eyes, and she wipes the sweat mixed with rain from his forehead. Victorio guesses what Salma would like to ask him. He tries to laugh. He doesn't have the strength to talk. At this odd hour of the morning, this unknown hour, this storm-swept predawn hour, silence is complete silence, and silence becomes the supreme authority. Victorio manages to keep his smile, his only defense against Salma's doubts. What else can he do? He would have liked to tell her about his dream, about the hot-air balloons, and, above all, about the Guignol. He would be happy if he could give her any kind of encouragement. First, he thinks, he should find his own courage.

After resting, without exchanging a word, they continue their march. Victorio shoulders the body of Anna Pavlova, the Great One, which is the body of Don Fuco. As everyone knows, crossing from one rooftop to another in Havana has never been very difficult. The paths through Havana have always been many, and one of the safest is the one that can be traced across the roofs and terraces. They trek across the highest part, across the rainy skyline of Havana. Neither the sleeping people of Havana nor the waking police notice that a young woman decked out in tulle and a forty-something man in a green wig, a harlequin outfit, and a laurel crown made not of laurels but of tin, are carrying the dead body of an elderly man in a tarlatan tutu.

Epilogue

For a long time, beneath the storm, moving between storage rooms, dovecotes, water tanks, rabbit hutches, clotheslines, moving between so many antennas for so many televisions, moving between the falling rain, Salma and Victorio carried the corpse of the clown. They rarely stopped to rest. Time was growing short. Dawn must have been near, though the early morning sky remained so dirty and so soaked with rain that believing in day was like believing in the dogmas of faith. But a moment came when Victorio couldn't go on, and he came to a halt as if by order: a sharp pain jabbed at his back, an ache that ran all down his dorsal spine. Salma saw her own pain and fatigue in the mirror of her friend's faintness. She helped him lower the dead old man. Darkened with blood, the feather headdress further accentuated the pallor of the clown's face, whose makeup had been dissolved by the rain. They sat him down and leaned him against the dark and badly built wall of a wooden shack, which they guessed was an improvised carpentry shop. From the damp wood rose a pleasant aroma of wet pine, cedar, and mahogany. The rain did not let up. They couldn't be sure whether the whistle they heard was from a ship or a train. That must have been a flock of seagulls flying tediously through the storm. When day began to break and the first glimmerings of dawn mingled with the perpetual flame of the oil refinery, Salma looked at Victorio in surprise. She thought she was seeing him for the first time. In that ridiculous red, yellow, and black harlequin outfit, that green wig and tin crown, he was the perfect image of a clown. She couldn't repress her guffaws.

"Not that you're so elegant," he exclaimed in another explosion of laughter.

Then they saw the city that was emerging from the shadows, like another shadow, or like a relic. "Do you think they need us?" she asked, still laughing, pointing to the ruinous buildings and battered rooftops in the distance.

Victorio felt as if he were being freed from his own weight, from the cursed law of gravity. Salma watched him stand up, ridiculous and handsome in his outfit, and saw his sudden joy. "Now it's our turn," he replied, convinced.

And indeed, at their feet, still sleeping in the rain, Havana appeared to be the only city in the world ready to shelter them. It also seemed the sole survivor of four long centuries of failures, plagues, and collapses.

Havana–Palma de Mallorca–Havana,
1999–2002

The Stage That Was Havana

Clowns perform impromptu high-wire acts above the ruins of Havana. Brightly colored hot-air balloons pass effortlessly from reality into dreams and back again. A bronze bust of Cuban poet and independence hero José Martí is wielded as a deadly weapon. Abilio Estévez's second novel, *Distant Palaces,* is packed with striking, magical images. Unlike the exotic "magic realism" that has become a commonplace of Latin American literature, these images are imbued with the magic of art and artifice — that is, the magic of the theater, where the alchemy of the imagination can transform a cardboard reality into unreal yet truer perceptions of beauty. Estévez began his literary career as a playwright, turning to prose only in his forties with his first novel, *Thine Is the Kingdom* (1997). He is recognized today as one of the premier prose stylists in the Spanish language, but his apprenticeship in drama is worth bearing in mind. Theater is one key to his prose. The twin aspects that define theater — the shabby reality of the props that make up the world, and the beauty into which they are transformed by the herculean efforts of performers — form the two poles around which his writing revolves.

This isn't magic realism, and it certainly isn't social realism. But it is one way to face up to life and make it worth living in Havana today.

The spirit of the theater pervades *Distant Palaces.* I am not just referring to the ruins of the "Pequeño Liceo of Havana," the fictional private theater that serves as the setting for much of the novel, nor to the street performances that become the novel's key theme. Its characters are creatures of the theater, in more ways than one. They have the iconic intensity of characters in a play. The main character of the novel has been afflicted since birth with the theatrically inappropriate name of Victorio — not a common name in Spanish but one that, for a Cuban, immediately calls to mind a kind of revolutionary fervor that has now become a bit of an embarrassment, particularly for this semi-closeted gay man whose very existence contradicts the manly pretenses of the revolutionary era. "What, did your parents hate you?" his new friend, the young prostitute who goes by the name Salma, asks him. She rebaptizes him on the spot with the even more ridiculous name *Triunfo* (or Triumpho, as I have half-translated it), referring to the Triumph of the Cuban Revolution in January 1959. Salma, for her part, has named herself after a Mexican film star, and until she learns to become a performer in her own right, she papers over her dreary reality with the ersatz magic of Hollywood dreams. Don Fuco, the old clown who welcomes this odd couple into the ruins of his theater, uses a name lifted from a character in the stage comedy by Galician playwright Alfonso Castelao, *Old Men Shouldn't Fall in Love*. Don Fuco trains Victorio and Salma — or better, *initiates* them — in all the arts that he uses in his street performances: magic, dance, music, theater. "The only value to be desired is that of artifice," he tells Victorio, and when he serves a glass of plain water in a crystal glass, it tastes like cool, rich juice. The true substance of life lies in performance.

The novel itself is a theatrical piece of writing. Estévez's prose often takes on an insistent musical rhythm that demands to be read out loud. (I can only hope that I have captured some of these rhythms in the translation.) Victorio, Salma, and other characters in the novel spontaneously quote poetry and song, citing verses ranging from Cuban poet Gastón Baquero to contemporary singer Carlos Varela (Salma's favorite): these scenes reflect Cuban reality, for few people in the world are as ready to break out in song as the people of Havana, but they also serve as theatrical leavening while reiterating the novel's theme of the enduring power of art. Simple names become elaborate motifs, repeated like the refrains of an opera. Victorio's mother is never simply his mother, but always "La Pucha, Hortensia, his mother." The triple repetition reveals something about the woman (and about Victorio): the down-to-earth nickname "La Pucha" stands for the woman as she was known to her working-class neighbors; her religiously conservative character is revealed by her more pretentious yet old-fashioned given name, "Hortensia"; "his mother" is Victorio's inadequate synthesis of the woman's twin aspects. The phrase, then, is revealing, but it is repeated as much for the musical quality of the repetition itself as for the revelations it brings.

Estévez set his first novel, *Thine Is the Kingdom,* in the waning days of the Batista dictatorship, during the weeks and days leading up to the "Triumph of the Revolution" on January 1, 1959. Virtually all of the plot takes place in the working-class Havana suburb of Marianao where Estévez himself was born and raised, among a crowded polyphonic cast of the score of vivid characters who make up the micro-neighborhood with the overtly symbolic name of The Island. (The Island has a brief cameo in *Distant Palaces,* when Victorio walks past "the place where the ninety-year-old Doña Juana caused a devastating fire on the thirty-first of December in 1958.") Estévez sets his second novel in a different waning era: the year 2000, the last days of the twentieth century, when Havana itself — after forty-one years of revolution and isolation — has become so worn and faded that the metaphor of the shabby stage seems all too appropriate. Scarcely more than half the length of the earlier novel, *Distant Palaces* has a smaller cast of characters, but it encompasses a far broader setting: all of Havana, which in essence becomes the book's protagonist.

The novel opens with Victorio living in a miserable one-room apartment carved from a building that once was an opulent palace. As if this reduced life were not bad enough, he gets the news that the building is about to be demolished before it can collapse of its own

weight, a depressingly common occurrence in the older sections of
Havana nowadays. Because of the ravages of time and neglect, the
people of Havana are being deprived of the timeless art represented
by these old palaces — art that had outlived the craftsmen who carved
their elegantly curving spiral staircases "in the days when people
had the patience to work." Newly homeless, Victorio undertakes an
Ulyssean journey around the poorest, least picturesque, and touristic
neighborhoods of Havana, in a seemingly vain search for the palace,
the site where he can savor the pleasure of living, that should be his
by birthright. All palaces, in a Havana that abounds in aging palaces,
now seem far too distant.

In a tense counterpoint with the squalor of everyday life, however, the world of art remains a vivid reality. *Distant Palaces,* just like
Estévez's first novel, swirls with references to Cuban and world art,
music, and literature. Being men and women of Havana, after all, the
characters of the novel ceaselessly drop names and cite works. Salma
deliberately misquotes José Martí's saying, "trenches of ideas are more
powerful than trenches made of stone," in the confidence that Victorio (or any other Cuban) will understand her reference, but also in
the knowledge that she is keeping true to Martí's legacy by adapting
his words to her current circumstances. Nineteenth-century Cuban
poets (Julián del Casal and Juana Borrero, Plácido and El Cucalambé), Cuban singers and songwriters (from Sindo Garay and
"Freddy" to Carlos Varela), composers of Italian opera, French ballet
dancers, painters from Watteau to Monet: all coexist in this world
where nameless politicians are endured, while art endures.

In this tour of Havana, the seemingly most fantastic stories and
events are, in fact, the most real. At one point, Don Fuco tells Victorio the story of a black Cuban violinist who married a German
princess and played to packed houses throughout Europe: this is
based on the real life story of Claudio José Domingo Brindis de Salas
(1852–1911), widely considered the greatest Cuban violinist of his

time, though Don Fuco fuses his life's tale with that of the purely fictional — I think! — Russian princess Marina Volkhovskoy. At another point, Victorio enters an apparently abandoned apartment
building and follows the sounds of violins and singing until he
reaches a room filled with men and women, all dressed in white, performing ceremonies around an altar for "Obbatalá, the Virgin of
Mercy." This scene, too, is based on a Cuban reality. Obbatalá is one
of the principal *orishas,* the deities of the Afro-Cuban religion of
Yoruba or Santería; the daughter of Olofi and Olodumare, she symbolizes purity, justice, and balance, and in honor of her purity, her
followers often vow to dress entirely in white, and their ceremonies
in her honor are performed just as they are described here. Obbatalá
is equated with the Catholic saint *la virgen de la Merced,* an apparition
of the Virgin Mary whose official title in English is Our Lady of
Ransom, though I have chosen to translate her name more literally
from Spanish as the Virgin of Mercy.

The antics of the old clown, Don Fuco, who rescues Victorio
from homelessness, may also seem to belong to the realm of the fantastic, but in the touristic Havana of 2001, such street theater was
a commonplace: gangs of clowns, on stilts, singing, playing drums
and instruments, would make their sudden apparitions among the
throngs of tourists in Old Havana, not overtly asking for tourists'
change but not averse to receiving it, either. Don Fuco's performances are fantastic only because he does not direct them at the
tourist trade. Instead, he targets the people of Havana themselves. He
and his little troupe put on their guerrilla theater precisely in the sites
least likely to be frequented by tourists: hospitals, funerals, cemeteries, gay hangouts, and, above all, the poor neighborhoods that are off
the beaten tourist track, far from the Old Havana-Malecón-Heming-
way Marina axis that defines the tourist's Havana. High on Don
Fuco's list of targets are the poor working-class neighborhoods that
ring the Cuban capital: La Jata, Diezmero, El Cotorro, El Husillo,

and of course the many crowded neighborhoods of Marianao, the place where, as we have discovered, Victorio (like Estévez himself) grew up.

During his odyssey through Havana, Victorio returns to his old family house, and there he faces the central paradox of the city: that the places that have remained the most unchanged over time, the ones that have not been rearranged or refurbished or repainted in decades, are those in which the destructive passage of time is most evident. "Each wall, each piece of furniture obstinately persists in fixing, in making permanent, a reality that cannot be the same, yet is. Reality takes revenge and transforms itself into itself." Havana-as-museum is a dead place, and a place of death, whether it remains fixed in place because of tourist demands for exotic displays, or because of the inability of its own citizens to change. Don Fuco's theater of life provides a necessary answer to this living death. Between the collapsing palaces of Old Havana on the one hand, and the mushrooming nonentities of foreign-financed tourist hotels on the other, there has to be a space for Havana and its people to live, to change, and to grow on their own terms. In the end, Victorio and Salma decide that the people of Havana need their laughter; and despite it all, they agree to endure.

David Frye